CW00517291

Anonymous

Famous Boys; and how they Became Great Men

Anatiposi

Anonymous

Famous Boys; and how they Became Great Men

Reprint of the original, first published in 1875.

1st Edition 2024 | ISBN: 978-3-38283-206-3

Anatiposi Verlag is an imprint of Outlook Verlagsgesellschaft mbH.

Verlag (Publisher): Outlook Verlag GmbH, Zeilweg 44, 60439 Frankfurt, Deutschland
Vertretungsberechtigt (Authorized to represent): E. Roepke, Zeilweg 44, 60439 Frankfurt, Deutschland
Druck (Print): Books on Demand GmbH, In de Tarpen 42, 22848 Norderstedt, Deutschland

FAMOUS BOYS;

AND

How they became Great Men.

DEDICATED TO

YOUTHS AND YOUNG MEN,

AS A

STIMULUS TO EARNEST LIVING.

"TRUTH IS STRANGE, STRANGER THAN FICTION."

LONDON:
WARD, LOCK, AND TYLER,
WARWICK HOUSE, PATERNOSTER ROW.

CONTENTS.

LIST OF ILLUSTRATIONS.

PREFACE.

LORD STANLEY said at Accrington, "I believe that one of the most important volumes that could possibly be written—and when it is written it ought to find a place in every hamlet, almost in every cottage—would be a biographical record of a few selected instances of those eminent and illustrious persons who, in various occupations and departments of life, have raised themselves from the ranks." The reason is obvious. Biography serves the excellent purpose of informing the irresolute and desponding how the true man has not repined but worked. If his social position has been low—the first round on the ladder—the greater need to work in order to ascend. Has his education been neglected? does he find himself, when he wakes up to his real position in life, ignorant of the mere rudiments of knowledge?—*nil desperandum,* others have been like him, and by dint of diligence and patience greater difficulties have been overcome; he will also gird himself right manfully for the fight. Biography has no truer lesson to teach than this: that as sure as any object is pursued with diligence, with industry, with unfaltering perseverance, whether it is mental improvement, the attainment of honourable independence, or progress in any good and useful work, the end desired is certain to be attained. There is no law so infallible, there is no end so sure, as that industry is certain to meet with its just reward.

Every youth, doubtless, in his first start in life, proposes to himself an object intending to make life practical and real. In such an epoch of personal history, good intentions and earnest resolves are embraced; a strict line of conduct is marked out, and, as it is supposed, an undeviating life entered upon. But there come the blandishments and seductions of ease and pleasure, and the numberless excitements which drive away purposes and resolutions to dare nobly and act truly. Subsequently, it may be, a review of the past may show the pathway of life strewn with good intentions, with the wrecks and waifs of purposes uncompleted and promises unfulfilled. At such a time there is no refuge in the belief that circumstances have been adverse. Circumstances and opportunities are not needed to make great men; great men make opportunities. The strong, resolute man, the courageous determined youth, are not swayed by obstacles or unforeseen difficulties; these hindrances, which turn away the timid and less courageous, only serve to make them more energetic and resolute. How many youths are there who will pass through life with the keenest mental capabilities, but, lacking purpose and determination, will achieve nothing—dying as though they had not lived! More than every other thing *action* is the one thing needed. A purpose once formed, and then death or victory. It is in these respects that the lives of Famous Boys, and the biography of great men, serve for examples and encouragement to those vacillating between desire and execution—the intention and the fulfilment of a noble purpose.

FAMOUS BOYS;

AND

How they became Great Men.

HORACE GREELEY:

THE MODERN FRANKLIN; EDITOR AND PROPRIETOR OF THE "NEW YORK TRIBUNE."

"FAMOUS BOYS; and how they became great men!" of all subjects, that is one of the most interesting. "How they became great?" That is *their* secret, well worth knowing and understanding; and, if we mistake not, so interesting in the relation, as to put fiction in the shade, and give another proof, if proof were needed, that "truth is stranger than fiction." The antecedents of some of the greatest men were so humble, so lowly, as not only furnishing matter for astonishment, but incentives to any youth with a spark of determination and perseverance in his breast, that he also will make an effort to rise above slothful dispositions, adverse circumstances, and any and everything which may tend to keep him poor, ignorant, and unknown. It is not necessary, either, that we should go into any past age for examples; there are men now living, famous men, whose lives will be read ages hence by generations unborn, with as much interest and delight as we now read the lives of Franklin, of Milton, or Bunyan. Let us cite one instance.

We are standing in the printing-office of the "New York Tribune," opposite one of the miraculous printing machines that is adding its quota to the *hundred thousand* newspapers printed in New York every morning. We are impressed with the marvellous exactness and rapidity of the machine; we listen to accounts of the number of hands employed in producing one newspaper; the list of editors, reporters, readers, messengers, compositors, and machine-men; the admirable arrangements for telegraphing news in the briefest time from the most distant places; the plans for anticipating information by the English steamer, so that the news is frequently circulated through the Union before the steamer arrives at the wharf: impressed with all this, we vent our astonishment in one word—*wonderful!* But true as this undoubtedly is, it is not more wonderful—not *so* wonderful—as the life of the man who owns the machine, and who is the life and vitality of the whole concern—the world-famed Horace Greeley. It is his glory and honour that his position has been won from poverty and obscurity, and that it is maintained in the strictest honour and integrity. His boyhood, as the boyhood of all worthy and great men, must be marked with some peculiarity; but, if we mistake not, it is a peculiarity that any boy may stamp his early days with—*the spirit and purpose of industry.*

Horace was born in the year 1811, under difficulties, it is said, "as he was black as a coal." Twenty minutes elapsed after his birth, before it was quite certain whether he was to live or not; at the end of that time, he lay a smiling infant in his mother's arms. His mother, who of course was Horace's first instructor, was tall, muscular, well-formed, and had the strength of a man without any other masculine quality; she was very active in her habits, had a perpetual flow of spirits, an exhaustless store of songs, and possessed a boundless good-will to every human being. She hoed in the garden, laboured in the field, and, while doing more than the work of an ordinary man, would joke and sing all day long; and then in the evening she would pass the hours in reading, or reciting stories to those about her. Horace, in after years, has borne testimony to the effect of these evenings. "These stories," he has said, "served to awaken in me a *thirst* for knowledge, and a lively *interest* in learning, and in the incidents of history." The first result was an expressed desire to go to school in his third year, where he made such good use of his time, that he soon learned to read. This reading capability was a marvellous power in his hands, which, in his fourth year, he turned to good account. In that year he commenced the habit of book reading, or, more properly, book devouring; which habit never left him during all his youthful years. In his fifth and sixth years it was his custom to lie on his face under a tree reading; hour after hour would thus be passed, completely absorbed in his book; and if no one stumbled over him or roused him, he would read on unmindful of dinner-time or sunset. This absorbing passionate delight in books was the reason of determining him to become a printer; this conclusion was arrived at while he was yet a child; his reason was quite conclusive: "They made *books*." A gentleman who knew him relates that, "one day Horace and I went to a blacksmith's shop; Horace watched the process of horse-shoeing with much interest. The blacksmith, observing how intently he looked on, said, 'You'd better come with me and learn the trade.' 'No,' said Horace, in his prompt decided way, 'I'm going to be a printer.'" He was then only six years old, and is described as very small for his age; no wonder that the choice of a trade by so diminutive a piece of humanity should mightily amuse the bystanders. The blacksmith in after years, when Horace was a printer, and a printer of some note, used to tell the story with great glee.

Horace learned to love books to so great an extent, that from his sixth to his ninth year it almost amounted to a passion. The stock of books belonging to his father was very small, and not very interesting to a boy of his years; consisting of a Bible, a "Confession of Faith," and about twenty old volumes, chiefly on religious subjects. But there was an oasis even in this desert. A weekly newspaper came from the neighbouring village of Amherst, which had, no doubt, with the exception of his mother's tales, more to do with the opening of Horace's mind and the formation of his opinions than any other thing. His eagerness to possess the coveted sheet is well remembered. An hour before the post-rider was expected, Horace would walk down the road to meet him, bent on having the first *read*; and when he had got possession of the precious paper, he would hurry with it to some secluded place, lie down on the grass, and greedily devour its contents; and this when only in his ninth year! We are assured that at this period there was not one readable book within seven miles of his father's house which he had not read. He was, in fact, never without a book. As soon, says his sister, as he was dressed in the morning, he flew to his book; every moment of the day which was not employed at school, or any of the duties set him to perform on the farm, was spent with his book. He was usually so absorbed, that when he was wanted, it was like rousing a deep sleeper from a heavy slumber. When he went to the cellar and the wood-pile his book was in his hand; he read when he went to the garden, or on visits to his neighbours. For his evening studies, he kept in a secure place an ample supply of pine-knots; as soon as it was dark he would light one of these cheap and brilliant illuminators, put it on the back log in the spacious fire-place, make a pile of his school and reading books on the floor, lie down on the hearth with his head to the fire, his feet coiled away out of the reach of stumblers, reading the whole of the long winter evening, silent and motionless—dead to all the world around him, alive only to the world to which his book had transported him.

While Horace was thus acquiring knowledge, a cloud was gathering round his home. It is said the way to thrive in New Hampshire was to work very hard, keep the store (or shop) bill small, stick to the farm, and be no man's security. Of these four things Horace's father did only one—he worked hard. He was a good workman, methodical, skilful, and persevering. But he speculated, and lost money by his speculations. He was "bound," as they say in the country, for another man, and had to pay the money which that other man failed to pay. He had a free and generous nature, lived well, liberally treated the men whom he employed, and in various ways swelled the account at the store. The sad result was an execution from the sheriff, and a sale of Greeley's home. At this juncture Horace was not ten years old; to his honour it is recorded, that thirty years afterwards he discharged some of the debts then unpaid. His father, after this break-up and destruction of his prospects, removed to Westhaven, and obtained a scanty livelihood for his family as a day labourer. Here, as at Amhurst, Horace roamed far and wide in pursuit of books; he read all the ordinary round of common histories, romances, and novels, and everything that came in his way.

About his eleventh year, Horace thought it time to do something towards being that which he had always resolved to be—a printer. His father rather damped his courage by telling him that no one would take an apprentice so young; but he was not thus to be diverted from his purpose. To solve his doubts, he one morning trudged to Whitehall, a town about nine miles distant, to make inquiries. The only printer in the place told him he was too young; there was nothing for it, therefore, but to trudge home again.

The part of the town of Westhaven in which Horace and his parents resided was celebrated for the drinking habits of the inhabitants. It is a singular fact, and much to the honour of Greeley, although both his parents were accustomed to a liberal use of intoxicating drinks, neither he nor his brother could be induced to partake of them, or to use tobacco. One day, on the occasion of a neighbour dining with the family, a bottle of rum was produced. Horace, either disgusted at the taste or smell, said earnestly:

"Father, what will you give me if I do not drink a drop of drink until I am twenty-one?" His father, who took the question as a joke, answered, "I'll give you a dollar." "It's a bargain," said Horace. And it *was* a bargain. Many attempts were then and subsequently made to induce him to change his resolution; but from that day to the present time Horace has never taken any intoxicating drinks as beverages.

Time wore on when, in his thirteenth year, Horace saw an advertisement in the "Northern Spectator," for an apprentice on the paper. He sought his father at once, who replied to his importunities: "I haven't time to go and see about it, Horace; but if you have a mind to walk over to Poultney, and see what you can do, why, you may." We may be sure that Horace *had* a mind.

It was a fine spring morning, in the year 1826, when one of the owners of the "Northern Spectator" might have been seen in his garden planting potatoes. He heard the gate open behind him, and without turning or looking round was conscious of the presence of a boy. Mr. Bliss, however, continued his planting, and quickly forgot that he was not alone. In a few minutes he heard a voice close behind him—a strange, high-pitched, and whining voice—it said: "Are you the man that carries on the printing-office?" On looking round, he saw standing before him a boy apparently about fifteen, of a light, tall, and slender form, dressed in the plain farmer's cloth of the time—cut, as a matter of course, with a total disregard to appearance or fit. His trowsers were very short, and he was without stockings; he had on an old felt hat that seemed much like an inverted quart measure; his hair was white, and was tinged with orange at the ends. The excellent man had much difficulty to restrain himself from laughing outright at the odd figure before him; he answered, however, "Yes, I'm the man." Horace—for it was he—next asked: "Don't you want a boy to learn the trade?" "Well," said Mr. Bliss, "we have been thinking of it. Do *you* want to learn to print?" "I've had some notion of it," was the reply. The newspaper proprietor was both astonished and puzzled—astonished that such a fellow, as the boy *looked* to be, should ever have thought of learning the art of printing; and puzzled how to convey to him an idea of the absurdity of the notion. With an expression in his countenance, such as that which a tender-hearted draper might be disposed to assume if a hod-man should apply for a place in the lace department of his establishment, he said: "Well, my boy—but, you know, it takes considerable learning to be a printer. Have you been to school much?" "No," said Horace, "I hav'n't had much chance at school. I've read some." "What have you read?" "Well, I've read some history, and some travels, and a little of most everything."

Fortunately for Horace, Mr. Amos Bliss had been

for three years a school inspector, and had acquired by practice considerable facility as an examiner. He could not, therefore, resist the temptation to try his hand upon this queer subject. He first commenced with a few easy questions, but immediately advanced to the hard ones, with which he had been accustomed to puzzle candidates for the office of schoolmaster. Horace was a match for him. He answered every question promptly, clearly, and modestly. In Mr. Bliss's own account of the interview, he said: "On entering into conversation and a partial examination of the qualifications of my new applicant, it required but little to discover that he had a mind possessed of no common order, and an acquired intelligence far beyond his years. He had had but little opportunity at the common school, but he said 'he had read some,' and what he had read he well understood and remembered. In addition to the ripe intelligence manifested in one so young, and whose instruction had been so limited, there was a single-mindedness, a truthfulness and common sense in what he said, that at once commanded my regard."

The result was, that Mr. Bliss consented to take Horace, and allowed him to go into the office at once. At the close of the day, one of the apprentices said: "You're not going to hire that tow-head, Mr. Bliss, are you?" "I am," was the reply; "and if you boys are expecting to get any fun out of him, you'd better get it quick, or you'll be too late. There is something *in* that tow-head, as you will find out before you're a week older."

The arrangements were soon settled with Horace's father, when he arrived at the object of his ambition by having a place assigned him in the office, "copy" and a composing-stick placed in his hand, and a few words of instruction given him by the foreman. This was all the assistance given, and indeed all the assistance needed: he seemed to comprehend intuitively the mystery of the craft. In perfect silence, without looking to the right hand or to the left, heedless of the sayings and doings of the other apprentices, though they were bent on mischief, and tried to attract and distract his attention, Horace worked on, hour after hour, all that day; and when he left the office at night, could set type better and faster than many an apprentice who had had a month's practice. The next day he worked with the same intensity. The boys in the office were puzzled. They thought it absolutely incumbent on them to perform an initiating rite of some kind; but the new boy gave them no handle, excuse, or opportunity. He committed no "greenness," he spoke to no one, looked at no one, and seemed utterly oblivious to everything, save only his copy and type. Towards the close of the third day, however, the oldest apprentice took one of the large black balls with which printers used to *dab* the ink upon the type, and, remarking that in his opinion Horace's hair was of too light a hue for so black an art, applied the well-inked ball to his head. All the men in the office stood still to observe the effect. They were astonished. Horace neither spoke nor moved, but went on with his work as though nothing had happened. That was all the fun got out of him. In a few days all were excellent friends.

During Horace's stay in East Poultney there were a number of intelligent men residing there — the editor of the paper, the village doctor, a county judge, a clergyman or two, some two or three persons of political eminence, a few well-informed mechanics, and others. The gentlemen had formed themselves into a society, under the name of "The Lyceum," which had become so famous as to attract to its meetings persons who lived nine and ten miles away: as a matter of course, Horace became a member, and, young as he was, became, according to one of his early admirers, "a real giant at the debating society." His strength lay in his memory. Everything he had read he remembered, because he had read attentively; his mind was stored with the most minute details of important events. In the society he was never treated as a boy; his opinions were received with as much deference as those of the sheriff. This is the more wonderful, when his appearance is remembered: he never made the slightest preparation for the meetings. In the summer he only wore two garments, a shirt and a pair of trowsers; the shirt sleeves were rolled up above his elbows, and the trowsers were so short that his legs seemed thrust through them. He was often jeered and laughed at by the boys for his homely dress. Once, when a very interesting question was to be debated at the society, one of the members, noted for the elegance of his dress, and his unpaid tailors' bills, advised Horace to get a new "rig out" for the occasion, he having undertaken to lead one of the sides in the debate. "No," said Horace; "I guess I'd better wear my old clothes than run in debt for new ones." But the reader may ask, why run in debt at all? He had forty dollars a year; this surely ought to have kept him in good and substantial clothing. And so it would have done if he had not sent every dollar that he could save by the most rigid economy to his father, who was at the time struggling with the difficulties of a new farm in the wilderness. This pious custom, which will ever redound to his honour, Greeley continued during all the years of his apprenticeship, and for years afterwards; in fact, so long as his father's land, buildings, and stock were unpaid for.

During the four years that Horace lived at East Poultney, he boarded, a commom custom in America, in the tavern. How he conducted himself, and what he was thought of there, we learn from an anecdote related by a distinguished New York physician, who chanced to dine at the Poultney Tavern. "Did I ever tell you how and where I first saw my friend Horace Greeley? Well, thus it happened. It was one of the proudest and happiest days of my life. I was a country boy then, a farmer's son; we lived a few miles from East Poultney. On the day in question I was sent there to sell a load of potatoes. This was the first time I had been intrusted with so important a piece of business. After I had sold the potatoes, I put up the horses at the tavern and went in to dinner. There were a good many people at dinner, the sheriff of the county and an ex-member of Congress among them. I felt considerably abashed at the first; but I had scarce begun to eat when my eyes fell upon an object so singular, that I could do little else than stare at it all the while it remained in the room. It was a tall, pale, white-haired, 'gawky' boy, seated at the further end of the table. He was in his shirt sleeves, and was eating with a rapidity and awkwardness that I never saw equalled before or since. He neither looked up or around, or appeared to pay the least attention to the conversation. My first thought was, 'This is a pretty sort of tavern, to let such a fellow as that sit at the table with all these gentlemen; he ought to dine with the ostler.' I thought it strange that no one seemed to notice him. And so I sat, eating little myself. At length the conversation at the table became quite animated, turning upon some measure of an early Congress; and a question arose how certain members had voted on its final passage. There was a difference of opinion, and the sheriff, a very finely dressed personage, to my boundless astonishment referred the matter to the unaccountable boy, saying, 'Ain't that right, Greeley?' 'No,' said the unaccountable, without looking up; 'you're wrong.' 'There!' said the ex-member; 'I told you so.' 'And you're wrong too,' said the still devouring mystery. Then he laid down his knife and fork, and gave a history of the measure, explained the state of parties at the time, stated the vote in dispute, named the leading advocates and opponents of the bill, and, in short, gave a complete exposition of the whole matter. A moment after, and he had left the dining-room. I saw him no more, until years after I met him in the streets of New York."

The printing-office at East Poultney closing, was the signal for Horace to start upon his wanderings. He had arrived at his twentieth year when he appeared equipped for the road, his jacket on, and his bundle and stick in his hand. His landlord, desiring to give him some token of remembrance, addressed one of the boarders thus: "Now, there is that brown over-coat of yours. Horace is poor, and his father is poor; you are owing me a little, as much as the old coat is worth; and what I say is, let us give the poor fellow the over-coat, and call our account settled." This feeling proposition was at once acceded to, the landlady giving him also a pocket Bible. Thus, with their united good wishes, he started upon his long journey home.

By a lift in the canal boat, and walking the rest of

the way, he arrived, tired enough, at the end of his six hundred miles' journey. After resting a little while, he obtained employment at Jamestown, which was twenty miles away from home; but, as he could obtain no wages, he walked back again. The next place he tried was Lodi, fifty miles away, but found at the end of his work no wages: he returned at the end of six weeks, as poor as when he first started. In a few days he made another start—this time to Erie, thirty miles away, in the same rustic style—slouched hat, red cotton handkerchief, &c. After being taken for a runaway apprentice, he was employed by Judge Sterritt on the "Erie Gazette." He stayed here seven months. The judge tried several times to induce him to "dress up a bit;" but his unvarying reply was, "You see, my father is on a poor place, and I want to help him all I can." All his personal expenses, during the seven months, were *six dollars*; the rest, with the exception of fifteen dollars, kept as a reserve, he proudly handed over to his father.

His engagement at Erie coming to an end, he determined to try his fortune, as others had done before him, in New York. After a journey, marked with difficulty and deprivation, he arrived there on the 18th of August, 1831. He was not troubled with much property. He had ten dollars in cash, the clothes on his back, the few things in his bundle, and his stick; altogether, cash and clothes, on the morning of his entrance into the great city he was worth ten dollars and seventy-five cents! He was a perfect stranger: there was not one human being that he could call upon for sympathy or advice; and, to make matters worse, he had all the appearance, with his timid and bashful air, of an overgrown boy. It certainly was not a very cheering prospect. After taking breakfast at the boarding-house where he resolved to stay, he found his way to the office of the "Journal of Commerce;" and was surveyed by the late David Hale, one of the proprietors, who replied to his application for work: "that, in his opinion, he was a runaway apprentice, and that he had better return to his master." All that day was spent as fruitlessly; and the next day, Saturday, with the like results. On the Sunday, Horace went to church twice; and, as if in reward for his devotion, he heard in the afternoon, from a shoemaker, a friend of his landlord, that printers were wanted at West's, 85, Chatham Street. Next morning he was on the steps of the office by half-past five.

Had Thomas McElrath, Esq. (who kept the bookstore under the office), passed thus early, and if he had noticed Horace sitting on the steps, his red bundle on his knees, his pale face supported on his hands, his air and attitude one of dejection and anxiety, he would have deemed it very improbable that one day that sorry figure would be his partner, and that he would be proud of the connection!

Horace thought it very long before any one came to work on that morning; at last one of the workmen arrived, with whom he fell into conversation, and was glad to find that he also was a Vermonter. "I saw," said the workman subsequently, "that he was an honest, good young man, and determined to help him if I could." When the foreman arrived, Horace's new friend tried to interest himself in his behalf. The work upon which a man was wanted, was a polyglot Testament—the most difficult and tedious work upon which a compositor can be employed. Several men had already given the work up, after a short trial. The foreman, with his experience of compositors, no more believed that the figure before him could set up a page of the Testament than that he could fly. However, to soften the disappointment, he said, "Set up a case, and let him try!" When Mr. West, the master, came into the office, he inquired with considerable irritation from the foreman, if he had hired "that fool?" adding, "For God's sake, pay him off to-night." Horace meanwhile worked on with his usual diligence and in perfect silence. In the evening he presented "the proof" of his day's work to the foreman, who was perfectly astonished to find that Horace had set up more of the Testament, and with fewer errors, than any compositor since the commencement of the work. Of course, sending him away was now out of the question; he was an established man. But still the work was difficult. In order to earn tolerable wages, therefore, he was in the office before six in the morning, and did not leave before nine in the evening. The men and boys in the office soon found an endless source of amusement in his dress and appearance. His attempt to change his appearance did not much mend matters. One evening, when the winter had set in, Horace, instead of returning immediately after tea, was away for two hours. Between eight and nine, as the men were assembled round the "imposing stone," a tall gentleman entered, dressed in a complete suit of faded black, and a shabby, over-brushed hat. The whole figure was that of one who had seen better days. Presently the gentleman advanced into the strong light of the office, spreading out his hands and looking down at his dress, said: "Well, boys, and how do you like me now?" "Why, its Greeley," screamed one of the men. It *was* Greeley, converted into a decayed gentleman, by a Jew for five dollars. Cheer upon cheer rose from the men, in which the *venerable gentleman* joined heartily. The suit, as such suits generally are, was a decided failure—in fact, it was a dead take-in.

After this, Horace worked at several offices for about fourteen months, when it happened that the idea of a newspaper for "one cent" got into the head of a Dr. Sheppard; but, not finding a printer that would undertake it on his own account, he made an overture to a friend of Horace's, Mr. Francis

Story, foreman of the "Spirit of the Times," to fit up an office specially to print it. Story offered Greeley, for whom he had a warm friendship, a share in the speculation. The capital of the two printers was not very burdensome, being only one hundred and fifty dollars. On the morning of January 1st, 1833, the "Morning Post" and a fearful snow-storm came upon the town together. On the third day of the third week the "Morning Post" had ceased to exist. The printers lost by the paper about sixty or seventy dollars. By dint of industry, however, they soon made up the loss, and were in a good way of business as general printers. Unfortunately, in the seventh month of the partnership, Story, while out on a pleasure excursion, was upset in a boat and drowned. Greeley, on this distressing event, acted with the strictest integrity. He sent Story's mother half the outstanding accounts as they came in, and received in the vacant place a brother-in-law of his deceased partner.

After a time another partner was added to the firm: the three members being Horace Greeley, Jonas Winchester, and E. Sibbett. Their united capital amounting to three thousand dollars, and possessing, in addition, as they thought, considerable editorial ability, a second newspaper was started, under the title of the "New Yorker." On the 22nd of March, 1834, the first number appeared, and sold to the extent of *one hundred copies!* In September it reached a circulation of 2500; the second volume began with 4500. For seven years the paper gradually increased its circulation until it reached 9500, and yet it did not pay! It would have paid, and paid well, *had the subscribers paid.* At the end of the seventh year of the paper, Horace passed through all the apprehended horrors of bankruptcy. He subsequently wrote, of this period: "Through most of that time I was really very poor, and four years of it bankrupt, though always paying my notes and keeping my word, but living as poorly as possible." One afternoon he went into the house of a female friend, and, handing her a copy of the paper, said: "There, Mrs. S., that is the last number of the 'New Yorker,' you will ever see. I can secure my friends against loss if I stop now, and I will not risk their money by holding on any longer." He was, however, over-persuaded to battle with his difficulties one year more. In order to eke out the needed expenses, he took the entire editorial charge of the "Jeffersonian," a weekly paper; in addition to which he supplied the "Daily Whig" with its leading article! But even this was not enough: during the political excitement of 1840, he started another paper, the "Log Cabin," to appear weekly. An edition of 20,000 was struck off and sold the first day; eight thousand more were printed and sold next morning, and altogether of the first paper 48,000 were sold. In a few days the number of subscribers reached 90,000! Finally, it and the "New Yorker" gave way for the present "Tribune," which Horace started when he was scarcely solvent. Any other man might have found more difficulties to do this; Greeley was known to be an honest man, and therefore fearlessly trusted. The "Tribune," started with six hundred subscribers. Five thousand copies were with difficulty given away. The expenses of the first week were five hundred and twenty-five dollars, the receipts ninety-two! This sorry prospect soon brightened, looking lightsome and cheerful. The paper was made interesting by printing extracts from Carlyle, Cousin, and Moore. Dickens's "Barnaby Rudge" was printed entire in subsequent editions. Good reports of meetings and lectures were secured. Greeley himself reported a trial of interest at Utica, sending from four to nine columns per day to the "Tribune." And then, to fill up his spare time—as if such a man ever had any spare time—he delivered generally two lectures in the week. The lectures were thus quaintly announced: "Horace Greeley will lecture before the New York Lyceum at the Tabernacle this evening. Subject, Human Life. The lecture will commence at half-past seven precisely. If those who care to hear it will sit near the desk, they will favour the lecturer's weak and husky voice."

On the 5th of February, 1845, our hero experienced the common fortune of New York newspaper owners—the total destruction by fire of the "Tribune" office. The property was worth 18,000 dollars, and was only insured for 10,000. In this sad emergency temporary offices were taken, type borrowed from other newspaper proprietors (some of these were political opponents;) and, wonderful as it may seem, the very day after the fire, the "Tribune" duly came out! This instance alone is a miracle of energy and perseverance.

In 1848 Greeley became a member of Congress, beating his opponent, Gen. Taylor, at the election by 3177 votes. The "Tribune" had meanwhile attained to the most healthy condition. The circulation was always on the increase; the advertising matter so large as to necessitate three, four, and five supplements each week; the price was increased to a shilling a week, and that without loss of subscribers. The annual profits are computed at £6000.

"The *thing* called Crystal Palace!" as Carlyle named it, attracted two thousand Americans to Hyde Park: amongst them was Horace Greeley. "We mean," he said, "to attend the world's fair at London, with very little interest in the show generally, or the people whom it will collect, but with special reference to a subject which seems to us of great and general importance—namely, the improvements recently made, or now being made, in the modes of dressing flax and hemp, and preparing them to be spun or woven by steam or water-power." He was not much impressed with the procession at the opening; he thought a parade of the New York firemen would beat it. He could not see what the *master of the buck hounds*, the *groom of the stole*, the *mistress of the robes*, and "such uncouth fossils," had to do with an exhibition of industry. Having been appointed a member of the jury on hardware, he devoted a month, from ten to three each day, to the duties. At the banquet he was nominated by Lord Ashburnham to propose the health of Mr. Paxton. The sights in London did not impress him very much; the Epsom races he declined to attend, for three reasons: he had much to do at home; he did not care a button which of thirty colts ran the fastest, and he preferred that his delight and that of swindlers, robbers, and gamblers, should not "exactly coincide." While in London he spoke on slavery in Exeter Hall; and gave important evidence to the Parliamentary Committee on the "Taxes on Knowledge." After being seven weeks in London he started for Paris, then to Lyons, Turin, Genoa, Pisa, Florence, Padua, Bologna, Venice, Milan and Rome, and back to London. A rapid tour through the North of England, Scotland, and Ireland, completed his travels in the United Kingdom; after a good passage in the "Baltic" steamship, he arrived at New York at six o'clock in the morning, and, determining to be ahead of all his contemporaries, he rushed to the "Tribune" office, and set up with his own hands the chief news brought by the boat. Only a short time elapsed before the news-boys were shouting, "Yival of the Baltic; extra Tribune." Then, and not till then, might Horace be seen on his way home.

In this, the briefest sketch of this eminent man, in which we have seen him rise from the most obscure position, to literally take his place amongst princes, there are furnished incentives and encouragements to the most desponding. Here is a young man, whose *forte* is simply industry: whose maxim and practice have been the employment of every moment to some good and useful purpose. That, surely, is a quality which may be imitated. We do not find in Horace any special or striking marks of genius: probably most towns and villages could furnish a better specimen; but, how few can compare with him in *purpose* and *determination*? We shall best imitate him, by setting before us some task of usefulness, and, like him, bending our whole strength, and concentrating our whole energy, to its fulfilment.

JAMES GORDON BENNETT:

FORMERLY FARMER'S BOY IN THE HIGHLANDS OF SCOTLAND, AND NOW THE "WALTER" OF AMERICA, EDITOR AND PROPRIETOR OF THE "NEW YORK HERALD," THE LEADING AMERICAN NEWSPAPER.

No doubt every good man and every great man has done things which he has afterwards regretted; and no doubt the life of James Gordon Bennett contains circumstances which his friends would desire it did not contain. But then, this remark is applicable to the life of every man, be his position what it may. Our business is to profit by the experience of others to render the actions of their lives subservient to our good; and to preserve so much of their example as may be valuable to posterity. The subject of our present sketch is the proprietor, editor, and presiding genius of the "New York Herald," the most-widely circulated newspaper in America; a paper occupying the position in that continent that the "Times" does in England.

James Gordon Bennett was born at New Mill, Keith, in the romantic county of Banff, Scotland, in the year 1800. The family consisted of his father, mother, and three other children: Margaret, Annie, and Cosmo. The occupations of the district were chiefly pastoral, besides stocking-knitting and flax-dressing; at some one of these it is understood the senior members of the family found employment. Bennett was early sent to school in the neighbourhood, and remained there fourteen or fifteen years, when he went to Aberdeen, and resided there two or three years attending a seminary, being intended, like his brother Cosmo, for the ministry. As a boy he possessed good natural abilities, was of a poetic turn of mind, enthusiastic, fond of solitary rambles, punctilious on points of honour with his school-mates, and full of confidence in his own powers. He early contracted good habits, pursuing his studies with zeal, and had an ambition in everything to excel. He is said to have been of a generous, noble disposition. In reference to his student life at Aberdeen, he thus writes:

"At the seminary which I attended when a youth, situated on the banks of the Dee, on the bosom of a range of dark heath-clad hills, our teachers mixed in all our sports, took part in all our play, and would go down with us to the river, undress like the boys, plunge into the clear water, and swim away like ducks among the whole group. In music, dancing, playing, and swimming, our teachers mingled with us just like brothers on a footing of perfect equality. It was only during the hours of study that the difference of pupil and preceptor was visible." "Oh, those happy, happy days, when I studied Virgil in the morning, played at ball in the afternoon, and swam through the warm translucent pools just as the sun receded from the eye beneath the high, dark mountains of another land."

Bennett began to put on the armour of manliness very soon after he left the parental abode. In other words, he was inclined to think for himself, and, with a degree of self-reliance extraordinary in a youth, to act upon his thinking. The history of the world had taught him the necessity of maintaining an independent spirit, and it happened that the show of independence in his case was evolved by his daring to entertain sentiments opposed to the peculiar religious tenets of his ancestors, and in which he himself had been educated. He had been reared in the inculcation and practice of certain religious externals, but he could not be misled by what he conceived to be the formality and the error of either one sect or another. He believed he detected the prevailing faults of most of them, and was disposed at all hazards to break from allegiance to any particular form in which he had been brought up. He has said that he used to sit by the river-side, and regret that the world was not blessed with one universal belief in matters of religion—with one sect only.

At Aberdeen he pursued the usual routine of college life, besides reading every book that came in his reach. He belonged also to a literary club, which used to meet in the grammar school, in the same room where Byron once conned the lessons of his youth.

Bennett was a boy when he broke loose from the discipline and restraints of school, and owned no master but himself. The thought of being educated to sacrifice his personal independence at the dictation of any Church was insupportable to him. He seemed to himself to be destined to grapple with the world in a foot to foot and hand to hand contest, and he prepared himself by every means for the coming struggle. Excited by the histories which he had read, the scenes of Scotland's progress had a great charm for him, and on every vacation he travelled to behold the identical spots consecrated by the valour of the men of the past. He left Keith in 1815, never to return to it except as a visitor. From that time to the period of his embarkation for America, he appears to have divided his time between study and travelling. The life of "Benjamin Franklin, written by himself," and published in Scotland in 1817, seems to have encouraged the disposition in him to seek his own fortune; and the influence of the career of Napoleon probably was not slight upon his naturally ambitious and aspiring spirit.

Bennett visited Glasgow for the first time in 1817, and has left on record a graphic account of the impressions made by all he saw and heard whilst there,

He says: "I did not then know much of Walter Scott, for he was comparatively unknown. His novels were just coming into notice. All Scotland was getting mad, and even then I panted, at that early age, for the like fame and distinction which were forming into a halo of glory around the great Unknown. Educated in the best and highest principles of morality, of virtue, of literature, my past life looks like a romance. Before I was twenty I had wept tears of joy over every consecrated spot in my own native land."

As far as can be ascertained, the enthusiastic lad even at this period had signified his intention of being no longer a charge to his parents. His education had been sufficient to enable him to fly to it as a resource in any emergency; and though he was too much tempted to cultivate the acquaintance of the muses to grapple with the safer rules of human destiny, yet he was prepared to undergo every peril and privation to become a free man, subject to no control except that of his own taste and conscience. There was one circumstance, however, that was favourable to the future usefulness of the boy. He did not spurn the valuable lessons of history, or the mental and moral experience of philosophers. Besides, he was zealous to acquaint himself with the wisdom of the best writers of every nation, and thus he laid the foundation for following up their investigations as he himself grew older, in a contest with the reality of practical life. Uncertain as to the end to which this determination would lead him, he seems to have entertained dreams of visiting America, as a field that promised to realize something of the ardent anticipations of youth. At the time, the emigration from Scotland to the British North American provinces and the United States amounted to a passion with the people. Sometimes two thousand persons would embark in a single week. The fever had its effect on young Bennett, and he was prepared to change the uncertain and doubtful prospects before him in Scotland for the opportunities which might arise in a land more marked by enterprise and more favourable to talent and industry.

"My leaving Scotland," Mr. Bennett has said, "was an act of impulse—little judgment. I resided at Aberdeen. I had a few literary associates imbued with the same tastes, and passionately attached to the same pursuits. I met one of them one day in the street; he said:

"'I am going to America, Bennett.'

"'To America! When? when?'

"'I am going to Halifax on the 6th of April.'

"I mused, I thought, I spoke.

"'William, my dear fellow, I'll go with you. I want to see the place where Franklin was born. Have you read his life?'

"On the 6th of April, 1819, I prepared for embarkation. The vessel was to sail in the evening.

All the morning, up to the noon of that day, I spent on the banks of the Dee, where it meets with the ocean."

Such was the rapidity with which the visit to America was decided upon, thus soon was the youthful adventurer at sea, with his thoughts alternately turned to the east and to the west. He had no money beyond a small sum, which he calculated would defray his expenses for a few days till employment could be obtained. At length he found himself at Halifax, where he commenced the labours of his new life by teaching. In this occupation, to which necessity rather than choice called him, he persevered for a time; but his experiences were not of the most agreeable kind. Among incidents of this kind of life one may be mentioned, that will serve to illustrate the character of the young pedagogue. He had been engaged three months in instructing a very dull boy in the art of book-keeping. When the term expired Bennett, who needed the sum of ten dollars due for tuition, sent his bill to the mother of the lad for payment. In due course she called on Bennett, and with tears in her eyes expressed her sorrow and regret that her boy had not availed himself of the opportunities of learning which she, in her poverty, had desired to afford him. She spoke of the payment as a sad loss to her, and one which must give her no little uneasiness, but did not do so until she had settled the bill and taken a receipt. As she took her leave of the schoolmaster, he slipped the money he had received into her hand again, and with a few words of good cheer, bade her farewell. His necessities at this time would have been much alleviated by retaining the money, which he had thus voluntarily relinquished; but he contrasted his strength and ability to earn with that of the poor widow, and did not long feel his loss, poor and friendless as he was—a stranger in a strange land.

As far as is ascertainable, Bennett's entire residence at Halifax was marked by a severe struggle for existence, and it is not to be wondered at that he should have remained there but a short time. In the summer, or autumn, of 1819, he was in the territory of Maine, and thence he embarked in a schooner for Boston, his emotions on first visiting which place were scarcely ever after effaced from his recollection. Mr. Bennett's experience at Boston, at first, was as severe as can be well imagined. He knew no one there, and, being soon entirely without money or employment, knew not what course to pursue. He made several desperate struggles to find employment suited to his capacity; but his youth, and the fact of his being a stranger, operated unfavourably with him. One day, he was walking on what is called the Common, despairing almost of all hope, and complaining alike of the callousness of the world and the severity of Providence. He had had no food for two days, and knew no means by which he could procure any, without becoming a mendicant. In this dilemma, as he paced the ground, and debated with himself on the mysterious ways of Providence, and was propounding to himself the now really serious question: "How shall I feed myself?" he saw upon the ground something that seemed to look him directly in the face. He started back, paused, and, having recovered from his surprise, picked up a York shilling. This gave him courage. It appeared to be a special gift at the moment, at once rebuking his complaints and encouraging him to persevere. He treated it as a good omen; for, having obtained something to eat, he at once went to work in earnest for employment. He soon found a Mr. Wells, a countryman of his, to whom he made known his history. This gentleman had been a pupil of the celebrated Joseph Priestly, and he listened to the story of the young adventurer with much interest, and finally invited him to take a clerkship, or salesman's place, in his establishment. From this post he was transferred to be proof-reader in the printing office of Wells and Lilly, then a leading firm in the book trade of the United States. Here he had facilities for adding to his stock of knowledge, in addition to the counsels of one of the best scholars known to the book trade of the country. While Bennett was with the firm he appears to have pursued his studies with his usual ardour, and to have used his time with more discretion than is ordinarily displayed by young men of his age. There is no evidence that he had any taste for the pleasures, as they are called, which destroy the best hours, and too frequently the best energies, of young men. He was, at least, now ready to try his temper and spirits in a conflict with the world, as it stood before him, and hemmed him in on all sides.

About this time, Mr. Bennett composed a considerable amount of poetry; but he was never much distinguished in this class of composition. At the time referred to, the majority of the then existing newspapers, in the different cities of the American Union, were wretched specimens of journalism, and those of Boston and New York did not form any exception to the common rule. Mr. Bennett, however, studied these journals, such as they were, as well as the conductors of them. He gathered, from their conduct and representations of public opinion, the true temper of the men he aspired ultimately to rival and excel, as well as the condition of society. His experience, so far, in the literature of the country, had enabled him to forsee that there would open, eventually, a field for his active, and industrious, and enterprising habits. He found his way to New York as early as 1822, where, having toiled a little experimentally upon the press, he was fortunate enough to meet with a Mr. S. Wilmington, the proprietor of the "Charleston (South Carolina) Courier." He accepted a situation on that journal, where he was employed chiefly, in 1823, in making translations of the news from the Spanish papers received by way of Havannah; in addition to this, he wrote generally for the "Courier;" and from Mr. Wilmington's enterprise in boarding vessels far off at sea, in order to obtain the earliest news, took his first lesson in that system of journalism which he subsequently was instrumental in raising to comparative perfection, first, by suggesting possibilities to others with whom he was associated, and secondly, at a late day, by executing, according to his own views, and entirely without regard to cost, an elaborate but completely organized system of news expresses.

When Mr. Bennett arrived in New York from Charleston, he was uncertain as to the best course to be pursued to obtain a livelihood. He attempted, however, a renewal of his old profession of a schoolmaster, and in October issued an address to the citizens of New York, in furtherance of the intention. He was again unsuccessful in this undertaking; and subsequently we find him delivering lectures on political economy in the old Dutch Church, Anne Street, New York.

In 1825, Bennett made his first attempt to become the proprietor of a public journal. At the commencement of the year, a John Tryon published a newspaper called the "New York Courier." Mr. Bennett wrote for it for some time, at a small salary, such as would have been spurned as unsatisfactory wages by any merchant's carman or porter. After a time, Tryon found that the people were not ready to support his new enterprise, and appeals to the advertising community did not save him from loss. Bennett purchased the establishment; but ultimately it was again transferred into the hands of its original proprietor. Bennett was very successful as a writer and reporter at this period, and was employed at different times, as occasion prompted, on different journals. He was chiefly employed, however, upon the columns of the "National Advocate;" he also contributed to the "Mercantile Advertiser," "Washington Inquirer," "New York Courier and Enquirer," "New York Globe," "New York Mirror," "Philadelphia Pennsylvanian," and other newspapers, to say nothing of his contributions and literary ventures of another class. It is not our purpose, however, to follow him through the varying success that attended his literary speculations, to express any opinion upon his mode of conducting them, or the particular views he advocated. The great fact of his life was the establishment of the "New York Herald," in May, 1835. Penny newspapers had then only recently been attempted. The thing was quite new to the public, whose appreciation of the change was at one time doubtful; the old prejudice operating—that if a thing was cheap, it must of necessity be deficient in quality. Bennett, however, took the initiative. He published the "Herald" daily at two cents., or one penny. At first it was conducted with necessary caution as regards expense, but in a style, at least, to command attention. Opinions now vary as to Bennett's mode of management of the "Herald," according to the clashing interests or prejudices of parties for or against him. One thing is certain, that by indomitable energy, tact, and perseverance, he has reared a colossal establishment of material and intellectual power. The "Herald" is read in every portion of the globe where its correspondents reside, and its circulation is larger than that of any other American newspaper. Bennett is now a rich man; his life has its uses, as exhibiting to our youth what may be accomplished under the most adverse and trying circumstances, by perseverance, energy, and self reliance.

GEORGE STEPHENSON AND HIS SON ROBERT, THE RAILWAY KINGS.

THE COW-BOY, AFTERWARDS THE GREAT ENGINEER.

SAM SLICK described very accurately the use of American railways. "What is it," he said, "what is it that 'fetters' the heels of a young country, and hangs like a 'poke' around its neck? that retards the cultivation of its soil, and the improvement of its fisheries?—the high price of labour, I guess. Well, what's a railroad? The substitution of mechanical for human and animal labour, on a scale as grand as our great country. Labour is dear in America, and cheap in Europe. A railroad, therefore, is comparatively no manner of use to them, to what it is to us; it does wonders there, but it works miracles here. There it makes the old man younger, but here it makes a child a giant. To us it is river, bridge, road, and canal, all in one. It saves what we hain't got to spare, men, horses, carts, vessels, barges, and, what's all in all—time."

George Stephenson and his son Robert have been mainly instrumental in bringing about the present splendid system of railways, both in this country and in America; therefore, their names and services will not be unremembered while the English language is spoken, or commerce has an existence. Strange as it assuredly is, the most imaginative fancy cannot conceive a more unpromising "start in life" than that experienced by George. He and his son have achieved a reputation and attained a success, when taken into account with their commencement, that is unequalled in the most marvellous biographical annals, and stands out as a star and beacon for all future wayfarers, and poor but resolute workmen. The eminence George attained was the result of his own individual efforts; birth, station, education, or any accidental condition had nothing to do with his destiny.

The home in which George was born is situated about eight miles from Newcastle-on-Tyne, in the colliery village called Wylam. It was, like the other cottages in the village, unplastered, had a clay floor, and was open to the rafters. "Old Bob," the father of George, had a deserved reputation for industry and carefulness; he was much respected amongst his humble neighbours. He was fond of birds, he loved children, and could tell a good story. Mabel Stephenson is described as a "rale canny body"—held in high repute by the wives of the village. "Old Bob" worked at the Wylam colliery; for his services as fireman at the pumping engine he received twelve shillings per week, upon which he had to keep the eight members of his family. Paying for the schooling of any of the children out of that pittance was of course out of the

Robertson, who taught him figures, but whose knowledge could not have been very profound, as the pupil soon outstripped the master. George worked out the sums in his bye-hours, improving every minute of his spare time by the engine-fire, solving the arithmetical problems set him upon his slate by his master, so that he soon became well advanced in arithmetic.

When George had attained his twentieth year, his wages were from thirty-five to forty shillings per week. In order to increase these earnings, he learned to make and mend the shoes of his fellow workmen. When he had soled the shoes of his sweetheart, Fanny Henderson, he was so delighted with the "capital job he had made of them," that he carried them about with him on the Sunday to exhibit them to his friends. His first guinea was saved from shoemaking; this was followed by other savings, until sufficient was obtained to furnish a humble house and to marry Fanny, who was taken to her new home on a borrowed horse, sitting behind her husband. His industry was increased, if that was possible, after his marriage. Subsequent to this event, an alarm of fire caused his well-intentioned neighbours to flood his house with water, so that his clock was spoiled. As he could not afford to take it to the clockmaker to have it cleaned, he took it to pieces himself, put it together again, and thus became clock-curer for the neighbourhood. On the site of the cottage then occupied by George, there has since been erected the Stephenson Memorial Schools. The late Mr. Robert Stephenson took deep interest in the erection of the building, which it was proposed to dedicate to the memory of his father, but which is now dedicated to the memory of father and son. After working about three years as breaksman at Willington, George removed to Killingworth, about seven miles north of Newcastle. It was at this place that he acquired the reputation of being an inventor, and where his mechanical ability had an opportunity of becoming fully developed. But it was here also that he lost his excellent wife—his dearly-loved Fanny, who left him with one child—the world-famed Robert. While mourning his loss, George had a situation offered him to superintend an engine near Montrose. This invitation he accepted, and, leaving Robert in charge of a neighbour, set out with his kit upon his back, and accomplished his long journey on foot. During his absence, his father, old Robert Stephenson, met with an accident while making some repairs to an engine; he had been severely scorched, by which his eyesight was destroyed. George's first act, on his return, was to pay out of the £28—his year's savings—£15, the amount of his father's debts. He soon after removed his parents to a comfortable cottage near his own.

He was anxious at this time to send his son to school. He had, in his own instance, found out the value of education, and resolved that Robert should have the advantages of which he had been denied.

In a speech which he delivered long afterwards, he tells us how this was effected. "In the earlier period of my career," he said, "when Robert was a little boy, I saw how deficient I was in education; and I made up my mind that he should not labour under the same defect, but that I would put him to school, and give him a liberal training. I was, however, a a poor man; and how do you think I managed? I betook myself to mending my neighbours' clocks and watches at night, after my daily labour was done; and thus I procured the means of educating my son."

The incident which obtained George the fame of being an engine-doctor, arose from an atmospheric engine at the Killingworth High Pit being unable to clear the water from the works. George saw the defect of the engine, and undertook to send the workmen to the bottom in a week. This promise he fulfilled, and received as a reward for his services £10.

This led to his becoming the engineer to the Killingworth Colliery. One of his improvements in the coal mines reduced the number of horses required, from one hundred to fifteen. He kept up his fame by all sorts of contrivances in the cottages of the colliers. One of his inventions was a "fley craw," to protect his garden-crops from the ravages of birds. To the delight of the women, he managed to make the smoke-jacks rock their cradles. To the clock of the watchman he attached an alarum, and invented a lamp which would burn under water. By dint of this industry he was enabled to put together £100, to give his son Robert an education as he proposed.

While at Killingworth, George went to see the engines which were working on the tramway at Wylam. After seeing one at work, he said "he could make a better one go upon legs." One of the lessees of Killingworth Colliery—Lord Ravensworth—hearing George's remark, authorized him to try his hand at fashioning a locomotive. He immediately set to work, and completed his engine in about ten months. It was tried on the 25th of July, 1814, and drew eight carriages—about thirty tons—at about four miles an hour. Subsequently, George invented the steam blast, which more than doubled the power of the engine. An accident having occurred in one of the pits, drew his attention to devising means to prevent explosions, which resulted in the construction of the Geordy Safety Lamp, which was prior to Sir Humphrey Davey's invention.

In 1822, George obtained his first railway engineering appointment. It was a line made for the Hetton Coal Company, about eight miles in length. It was opened in the November of 1822, on which occasion five engines, constructed by George, drew separately seventeen waggons, weighing sixty-four tons, at the rate of four miles an hour.

When the Stockton and Darlington Railway was projected, George offered his services to the director, Mr. Pease, the celebrated Quaker of Darlington.

He was appointed to the responsible position of engineer to the company, at a salary of £300 per annum. The work was all laid out by himself. Many country people remember him in his top boots and breeches, and can tell how pleasantly he chatted with them as he took his chance dinners of bread and milk at the farmhouses or road-side cottages. One day, when the works were near completion, George dined with his son Robert and his assistant, John Dixon, at Stockton. After dinner he addressed them thus: "Now, lads, I will tell you that I think you will live to see the day, though I may not live so long, when railways will come to supersede almost all other methods of conveyance in this country; when mail-coaches will go by railway, and railroads will become the great highway for the king and all his subjects. The time is coming when it will be cheaper for a working man to travel on a railway than to walk on foot. I know there are great and almost insurmountable obstacles that will have to be encountered. But what I have said will come to pass, as sure as I live. I only wish I may live to see the day, though that I can scarcely hope for, as I know how slow human progress is, and with what difficulty I have been able to get the locomotive adopted, notwithstanding my more than ten years' successful experiment at Killingworth." How this prophecy has come to pass every man and woman in the United Kingdom is witness.

In September, 1825, the line was opened, and was found to work excellently, the traffic in goods and passengers being beyond expectation. The next important work which George undertook was the surveying of the Manchester and Liverpool Railway. This was a work of considerable difficulty, owing to the opposition of the owners of the land. Lord Derby's tenants, and Lord Sefton's keepers, with the Duke of Bridgewater's retainers, not only opposed the survey, but threatened to duck George in a pond if he proceeded. Despite these obstacles, the survey was made. When the bill for the railway was introduced into the House of Commons, a committee examined George, subjecting him to a severe cross-examination upon his plans. The canal proprietors and land owners having secured a great array of legal talent to oppose the laying down of the line, George, in afterwards relating his experience, said: "I had to place myself in that most unpleasant of all positions—the witness-box of a parliamentary committee. I was not long in it before I began to wish for a hole to creep out at. I could not find words to satisfy either the committee or myself. I was subjected to the cross-examination of eight or ten barristers, purposely, as far as possible, to bewilder me. One member of the committee asked if I was a foreigner; and another hinted that I was mad. But I put up with every rebuff, and went on with my plans, determined not to be put down." After examining

George for three days, it was deemed advisable to withdraw the bill; but the directors, with great spirit, ordered a fresh survey. This time the bill passed the Commons, and was only opposed in the House of Lords by the Earls Derby and Wilton. No one at the present day is more convenienced than the Earl of Derby by the railway system: the Manchester and Liverpool rail conveys his family carriage almost to his own door. But, at the time when railways were first broached, it was the fashion not only to oppose them, but to ridicule and laugh them down. One of the leading reviews of the day said: "What can be more perfectly absurd and ridiculous than the prospect held out of locomotives travelling twice as fast as stage-coaches? We should as soon expect the people of Woolwich to suffer themselves to be fired off upon one of Congreve's ricochet rockets, as trust themselves to a machine going at such a rate. We will back Old Father Thames against the Woolwich railway for any sum." One of the counsel before the parliamentary committee said: "Who but Mr. Stephenson would have thought of carrying a railway over Chat Moss?—it was ignorance inconceivable—it was perfect madness." Mr. Giles, an eminent engineer, said the rail across the Moss would cost £270,000; Stephenson completed it for £28,000.

George received the appointment of chief engineer to the works, at a salary of £1000 per annum. His great difficulty was Chat Moss; but this was ultimately completed, to the astonishment of the most eminent engineers. During the progress of the work, the directors offered a prize of £500 for the best locomotive: ten miles an hour was all the speed desired. George and his son Robert set about the construction of their famous "Rocket" engine. On the day of trial four engines entered for the contest. The "Rocket" was first ready, and drew after it thirteen tons weight in waggons, and attained a speed of twenty-nine miles an hour. The other engines were failures, so that the Stephensons were awarded the prize.

From this period may be dated the commencement of the formation of those huge railway works which thread and cross the United Kingdom, in the construction of which George and his son have been immediately connected.

In 1835 George and his son were consulted by Leopold, King of the Belgians, relative to the formation of railways in his kingdom. For the services rendered, the king bestowed upon George the honour of an appointment of Knight of the Order of Leopold. This honour was subsequently bestowed upon Robert. When in Belgium the engineers invited George to a magnificent banquet at Brussels. The day following he had an interview with King Leopold. No sooner had he returned from Belgium than he received a request to go to Spain, to report upon the projected Royal North of Spain Railway. After thus spending the prime of his life in works that will prove a blessing to future generations, he retired to Tapton House, with the intention of enjoying his love of nature, first implanted in him by his father during their bird-nesting excursions. But he was not idle by any means. The same spirit that enabled him to rival all competitors in railway plans, induced him to desire to excel his neighbours in the growth of fruit and flowers. His grapes took the first prize at an exhibition open to all England. "Young men would call upon him for advice or assistance in commencing a professional career. When he noted their industry, prudence, and good sense, he was always ready. But, hating foppery above all things, he would reprove any tendency to this weakness which he observed in the applicants. One day a youth, desirous of becoming an engineer, called upon him, flourishing a gold-headed cane. Mr. Stephenson said: 'Put by that stick, my man, and then I will speak to you.' To another extensively-decorated young man, he said: 'You will, I hope, excuse me; I am a plain-spoken person, and am sorry to see a nice-looking and rather clever young man like you disfigured with that fine-patterned waistcoat, and all these chains and fang-dangs. If I, sir, had bothered my head with such things when at your age, I would not have been where I am now.'"

During his retirement, George Stephenson was often the guest of Sir Robert Peel, who, more than once, offered him the honour of knighthood, which he steadily refused. On one occasion, being applied to for the ornamental initials of his name, to be introduced in a work to be dedicated to him, he said: "I have to state that I have no flourishes to my name, either before or after; and that I think it will be as well if you merely say 'George Stephenson.' It is true that I am a Belgian knight, but I do not wish to have any use made of it. I have had the honour of knighthood of my own country offered me several times, but would not have it. I have been invited to become a Fellow of the Royal Society, and also of the Civil Engineers' Society, but objected to the empty addition to my name. I am a member of the Geological Society, and have consented to become president of, I believe, a highly-respectable mechanics' institution at Birmingham."

After attending a meeting at Birmingham, and reading a paper, "On the Fallacies of the Rotary Engine," a sudden effusion of blood deprived the country of one of its greatest benefactors. He died on the 12th of August, 1848, in the 67th year of his age, leaving his son Robert to carry out many noble monuments to perpetuate for all time the genius and perseverance of the Stephensons. Robert's services are thus recorded in the "English Cyclopædia" of Mr. Charles Knight:—

"Robert Stephenson was born at Willington, on December 16, 1803. His father, who had felt the want of early education, resolved that his son should not suffer from the same cause, and accordingly, though at that time he could ill afford it, sent him to school at Long Benton, and in 1814, placed him with Mr. Bruce at Newcastle. Robert soon displayed a decided inclination for mechanics and science, and, becoming a member of the Newcastle Literary and Philosophical Institution, was enabled to take advantage of its library; so that, as the Saturday afternoons were spent with his father, the volume which he invariably took home with him formed the subject of mutual instruction to father and son. Robert's assiduity attracted the attention of the Rev. William Turner, one of the secretaries to the institution, who readily assisted him in his studies, and was also of much service to his father, with whom he soon after became acquainted. Under Mr. Bruce, Robert acquired the rudiments of a sound practical education, and, under his father's direction, was always ready to turn his acquirements to account. There still exists, in the wall over the door of the cottage at Killingworth, a sun-dial of their joint production, of which the father was always proud. In 1818, Robert was taken from school and apprenticed to Mr. Nicholas Wood, as a coal-viewer, acting as under viewer, and making himself thoroughly acquainted with the machinery and processes of coal mining. In 1820, however, his father, being now somewhat richer, he was sent to Edinburgh University for a single session, where he attended the lectures of Dr. Hope, on chemistry; those of Sir John Leslie, on natural philosophy; and those of Professor Jamieson, on geology and mineralogy. He returned home in the summer of 1821, having gained a mathematical prize, and acquired the most important knowledge of how best to proceed in his self-education. In 1822 he was apprenticed to his father, who had then commenced his locomotive manufactory at Newcastle; but after two years' strict attention to the business, finding his health failing, he accepted, in 1824, a commission to examine the gold and silver mines of South America, whence he was recalled by his father when the Liverpool and Manchester Railway was in progress, and he reached home in December, 1827. He took an active part in the discussion as to the use of locomotives on the line, and, in conjunction with Mr. Joseph Locke, wrote an able pamphlet on the subject. He also greatly assisted his father in the construction of the successful engine, which we believe was entered in his name, though he himself ascribes the merit entirely to his father and Mr. Henry Booth, on whose suggestions the multitubular boiler was adopted.

"Robert Stephenson's next employment was the execution of a branch from the Liverpool and Manchester Railway, near Warrington, now forming a portion of the Grand Junction Railway, between Birmingham and Liverpool. Before this branch was completed, he undertook the survey, and afterwards the construction, of the Leicester and Swannington Railway, and, on the completion of that work, he commenced the survey of the line of the London and Birmingham Railway, of which he was ultimately appointed engineer, and removed to London. Under his direction the first sod was cut at Chalk Farm, on June 1, 1834, and the line was opened on September 15, 1838. Fully aware of the vital importance of obtaining good means of rapid transit, he still continued to devote much of his time to improvements in the locomotive engine, which were from time to time carried out under his direction at the manufactory in Newcastle, which for some years was exclusively devoted to engines of that class, and still supplies larger numbers than any other factory in the kingdom, independent of many marine and stationary engines. His engagements on different lines of railway have since been very numerous; but he is more remarkable for the magnificent conceptions and the vastness of some of his successfully-executed projects, such as the High Level Bridge over the Tyne at Newcastle, the viaduct (supposed to be the largest in the world) over the Tweed Valley at Berwick, and the Britannia Tubular Bridge over the Menai Strait—a form of bridge of which there had been previously no example, and to which, considering its length and the enormous weight it would have to sustain, the objections and difficulties seemed almost insuperable. With the assistance, however, of Professor Hodgkinson, Mr. Edwin Clark, and Mr. Fairbairn in experiments on the best forms of the various portions of the structure, the difficulties were triumphantly overcome, and in less than four years the bridge was opened to the public on March 18, 1850.

"Mr. Stephenson has also been employed in the construction of many foreign railways. He was consulted, with his father, as to the Belgian lines; also for a line in Norway, between Christiana and Lake Miösen, for which he received the grand cross of the order of St. Olaf, from the King of Sweden; and also for one between Florence and Leghorn, about sixty miles in length. He visited Switzerland for the purpose of giving his opinions as to the best system of railway communication. He designed, and is now constructing, the Victoria Tubular Bridge over the St. Lawrence, near Montreal, on the model of that over the Menai Strait, in connection with the Grand Trunk Railway of Canada, for uniting Canada West with the western states of the United States of America.* He has recently completed the railway

* The following account of this extraordinary bridge, completed since it was written, will be read with interest:—

"The present autumn will witness the completion of, perhaps, the greatest engineering work of our time—of that great bridge across the river St. Lawrence, of which the Britannia Bridge over the Menai Straits proves to have been but the precursor. The Grand Trunk Railway connects dependencies of the British Crown in North America, passing through the richest parts of both Upper and Lower Canada for a distance of 1200 miles. To the Grand Trunk Railway a direct and uninterrupted communication between the north and south

between Alexandria and Cairo, a distance of 140 miles, and has, during its construction, several times visited Egypt. On the line there are two tubular bridges—one over the Damietta branch of the Nile, and the other over the large canal near Besket-al-Saba. The peculiarity of the structure is, that the trains run on the outside—upon the top of the tube—instead of inside, as in the case of the Britannia Bridge. He is now constructing an immense bridge across the Nile, at Kaffre Azzayat, to replace the present steam ferry, which is found to interfere too much with the rapid transit of passengers.

"In addition to his railway labours, Mr. Stephenson has taken a general interest in public affairs and in scientific investigations. In 1847, he was returned as member of parliament, in the Conservative interest, for Whitby, in Yorkshire, for which place he con-

shores of the St. Lawrence was of vital consequence. Inasmuch as a bridge across the St. Lawrence was the key to the whole province, so, in possession of that key, the Grand Trunk Railway would command the whole external intercourse of Canada; whilst, without it, it must remain a mere provincial line. The difficulties of crossing the St. Lawrence were far from inconsiderable. Its width, even at the most available point, is very formidable; its current is very rapid; its depth not insignificant. Besides this, the navigation of the river, not merely by steamboats and other vessels, but by enormous timber rafts, had to be provided for; so that unusual elevation and unusual width between the piers were both required. There was another obstacle, more formidable—far more formidable—than all. In the winter season the river presents a field of ice from 3 to 5 feet thick. Could any bridge be devised to withstand such formidable difficulties? If possible, how was such a bridge to be constructed? The Britannia Bridge across

tinues to sit. He has also acted with great liberality to the Newcastle Literary and Philosophical Society, paying off a debt, in 1855, amounting to £3100, in gratitude, as he expressed it, for the benefits he derived in early life from that establishment, and to enable it to be as practically useful to other young men. He has most liberally placed at the disposal of Mr. Piazzi Smythe his yacht and crew, to facilitate the interesting investigations undertaken by that gentleman at the Island of Teneriffe, and very valuable results have been obtained. He has been an honorary but active member of the London Sanitary and Sewerage Commissions; he is a Fellow of the Royal Society, a member of the Institution of Civil Engineers since 1830, of which institution he was member of council during the years 1845 to 1847, vice-president during those from 1845 to 1855, and

the Menai Straits was opened in 1849, and it was not, therefore, unnatural that in 1852 the directors should look to Mr. Robert Stephenson as the engineer most competent to advise them. Mr. Stephenson determined to go out to Canada. He accordingly repaired there at the end of the summer of 1853, and after examining into the facts, made a public declaration of his opinion, that a bridge across the St. Lawrence was prcticable. On the 2nd of May following, Mr. Stephenson addressed to the Grand Trunk railway directors a report, in which he considered the whole question in three branches: first, as to the description of bridge best calculated to prove efficient and permanent; second, as to the proper site; and thirdly, as to the necessity for such a structure. Upon the first point he did not hesitate at once to recommend the adoption of a tubular bridge, as the description of bridge best fitted for a permanent, safe, and substantial structure in such a situation; on the second point, he was not a little influenced by conside-

president during the years 1856 and 1857. He has received a great gold medal of honour from the French Exposition d'Industrie of 1855, and is said to have declined an offer of knighthood in Great Britain. He is also the author of a work 'On the Locomotive Steam Engine,' and another 'On the Atmospheric Railway System,' published in 4to, by Weale.

"After the last tube of the Britannia Bridge had been floated to between the piers, and had been raised and deposited in the place, which, we may hope, it is destined to occupy for centuries to come, there was, as usual, a friendly dinner party, and those present congratulated Robert Stephenson on the complete success of his magnificent conception, and expressed the cordiality with which they participated in the triumph of so remarkable a work of science, which had met almost insuperable difficulties, and had

rations affecting the flow of the river and 'those almost irresistible forces' consequent upon the breaking up of the ice in spring. In considering the question whether a bridge could be constructed to withstand the pressure of the ice, it appeared to Mr. Stephenson to be of primary importance to ascertain really and precisely what that pressure was. This was a question of calculation; though, in the absence of any data, the difficulty was how to calculate. The result of that calculation in figures it would be unnecessary, even if it were possible, to state; but, whatever were the figures, they enabled Mr. Stephenson at once to realise one all-important fact. He arrived at the conclusion that 'the almost irresistible force' of this mass of ice would crush or sweep away any ordinary bridge, and that all the suggestions previously made for encountering the difficulty were only likely to result in disaster if carried into effect. Mr. Stephenson decided at last on the adoption of stone piers to carry the tubes at wide intervals,

created a new application of a system of constructive combination never hitherto imagined. In reply, he thanked his friends for their sympathy and the expressions of friendly regard, but he added, that even the triumph of that day did not recompense him for the days and nights of anxious toil and thought, the cares and anxieties which had attended the work, and the old friendships compromised; and he assured those present, that were another problem of the like magnitude and consequence to be proposed to him, not all the splendours of success, no honour or reward in expectation, would induce him to undertake it."

Since the above notice was penned, this worthy son of a great father has gone to the house appointed for all living. A newspaper telegram thus recorded his death:—"By the general public the loss is regarded

each pier having, on the side opposed to the course of the stream, large cut-waters of solid stone-work, inclined against the current, up which the ice would creep, and break itself to pieces by its own weight and pressure. He arranged that these wedge-shaped cut-waters should present angles to the ice sufficient to separate and fracture it as it rose upon the piers, but at the same time so obtuse as not to be liable themselves to fracture. These piers, therefore, were devised to answer the double purpose of piers and ice-breakers. They exihibit every indication of massiveness and power to resist pressure, as well as of stability to support the superstructure. Experience, indeed, has proved the piers suited for all the purposes for which they were designed. During the four years the structure has been in progress, it has fulfilled all the conditions its originator anticipated; and it has withstood, in the most satisfactory manner, the most violent pressures which have followed the breakup of the ice. Whilst the piers of this bridge are thus peculiar in their design, in order to meet the peculiar circumstances

as national, and by his friends, and all who had interviews with him, as a private and public bereavement. When he sailed for Norway in his yacht, soon after the close of the session, he was in indifferent health, and during his stay there he was attacked with a complaint of the liver. He returned to England, and on the voyage the yacht encountered severe weather, causing him to suffer from sea sickness. For the first time an attack of jaundice ensued, and on landing at Lowestoft it was necessary to carry him to the railway carriage. Upon his arrival in London it was found that he was in danger, dropsy having set in, and he was too weak to permit its being relieved. Congestion of the liver also took place, but the former disease was the immediate cause of his death. He died comparatively free from pain. During his illness he was unceasingly attended by the most eminent men in London. Mr. Stephenson was in his fifty-

of the country and climate of Canada, the superstructure, which creates in America so much surprise, is an elongated repetition only of the design for the Britannia Bridge. The Victoria Bridge is indeed remarkable for its extreme length, but its several tubes are not so long as those of the Britannia Bridge, and are only otherwise distinguishable inasmuch as that they are the longest tubes yet constructed without the adaption of the cellular principle. It deserves notice, however, that these tubes, in all their details, were designed, plate by plate and rivet by rivet, in the office of Mr. Stephenson, and were calculated for every strength and strain, and prepared and arranged in all their details, under the sole superintendence and supervision of his relative, Mr. George Robert Stephenson. Canada owes this bridge to one mind—the mind of Robert Stephenson. Had that eminent engineer expressed the smallest doubt or apprehension, the directors of the Grand

seventh year. He leaves no family, and his wife died some years since. As a proof of Mr. Stephenson's benevolence, it may be mentioned that he dispensed annually in charity several thousands of pounds in the most unostentatious manner."

The editor of the "Manchester Examiner and Times," in a leading article, earnest, eloquent, and truthful, sums up the characters and worth of these two noble men, who could add dignity to honours, but to whose names no title could add any eminence.

"Yesterday, the mortal remains of Robert Stephenson were consigned to their last resting place, in Westminster Abbey. The scene, we are told, and can well believe, was peculiarly impressive. There was an absence of all funereal pomp; nothing of the vulgar grandeur in which, on great occasions, we are accustomed to trick out the august solemnity of death.

Trunk railway would have shrunk from involving their company in an expenditure of a million and a half of money to carry a bridge accross the St. Lawrence. Until Mr. Stephenson had satisfied the Grand Trunk company, they would not entertain the idea of constructing such a bridge; and, unquestionably, Mr. Stephenson would never have satisfied the company unless he had thoroughly satisfied himself. It was the reliance of the company on Mr. Stephenson's experience and professional reputation that induced them to commence the bridge; and having pledged that experience and reputation, Mr. Stephenson, who would have been responsible for failure, is entitled to the full meed of honour and of fame which must hereafter attach to the successful execution of so great a work. He has indelibly inscribed his name on the structure which resists the ice of the St. Lawrence."

Yet the silent crowds which congregated along the route, the vast assemblage of distinguished men of all ranks and classes, which filled the venerable building, told with sufficient emphasis that a great man had been called away, and paid a fitting homage to the memory of one of England's most illustrious sons.

"This mournful event is one which has not failed to awaken corresponding emotions throughout the empire. All who take an intelligent interest in the welfare of their country, all who look with pride upon the industrial achievements of the present age, all with whom patriotism is a passion too noble to be absorbed in the glitter of military triumphs, all who see, or trust they see, in the successful subordination of nature to the wants of man a powerful auxiliary to the attainment of a better time for the whole human race, will mourn over the departure of one who stood foremost in the army of workers, and whose admirable genius had raised him to the highest rank among the architects of modern society. The lives of the two Stephensons, father and son, constitute a national epic. Had it been possible for them to have lived and performed half their mechanical marvels at some period prior to the dawn of authentic history, the wonder of their contemporaries would have transformed them into demi-gods. Their names would have been handed down as Hercules and Mercury, as Thor and Odin. Their favour would have been invoked whenever men were about to attempt any arduous enterprise, and in the depths of the forests, or the solitude of the rocks and mountains, species of rude worship would have commemorated the benefits they had bestowed upon mankind. Civilization and the printing press have rescued us from the possibility of such extravagancies. We have chronicled every incident of their lives. We know that the elder Stephenson was eighteen years old before he learned to write his own name, that he was a 'big raw-boned fellow,' earning eighteen shillings a week, acting as breaksman to a ballast engine, filling up his spare time by shoe-making and clock mending, and in due time the husband of Fanny Henderson, who, and no loose div'nity of Valhalla, was the mother of the great man just departed. In 1815 the father took out his patent for the first locomotive steam engine; in 1859 the son heard of the approaching completion of his own great work, the Victoria Bridge across the St. Lawrence, destined to connect the railway systems of North America. Fixing our attention on these two points, we are prepared to grasp the prodigious improvements with which their names will ever be identified. Politically, the period has been mainly occupied by the manufacture and the breaking up of the Treaty of Vienna, with which diplomatists were busy when the principle of steam locomotion was patented, and which has received its final *coup de grace* in the great battles of the present year. We need not point to the contrast between the fleeting triumphs of statecraft and the enduring achievements of industry, or show to which of these two classes of events mankind are likely to be most indebted for any permanent increase of freedom and happiness. That very public opinion before which the most powerful monarchs are constrained to bend, and weighed with which the bloodiest victories of the battle-field are light as chaff; that public opinion which flashes its impulses quick as lightning from capital to capital, and will eventually become the governing power of Europe, owes its aggrandisement, and almost its existence, to the inventions of such men as Stephenson. The railway, the steam vessel, and the telegraph are material instruments of civilization; the body in which the world's intellectual and moral impulses become incarnate; the brain and limbs by which the aggregate soul of humanity carries out its mighty will, and completes its ever-growing task.

"It is fit that the remains of Stephenson should lie in Westminster Abbey. The precincts of that venerable pile may be regarded as the nursery, the cradle, of our national greatness. It is a sacred spot, to which the thoughts of Englishmen throughout the world turn with a sentiment of idolatrous reverence. It is the shrine of a secular worship, surely the purest and noblest of its kind that the world has yet seen. Beneath its ancient roof repose the ashes of some of our greatest men—monarchs, warriors, legislators, and poets. Doubtless we are much indebted to them. We accept the legacy of gratitude without cavil. We will not detract from their merits by comparing them with a standard unfitted to their times. They served their generation according to the light that was in them, and England, such as the present age found it, was the offspring of their labours. Stephenson is as great a hero as any of them—the hero of the nineteenth century—the hero of railways, tunnels, and tubular bridges; of industry, manufactures, commerce, as well as indirectly of politics, morals, nationality, health, business, and pleasure. Thousands who have visited the 'Great Eastern' at Holyhead passed over his gigantic handiwork at Menai Straits, and the hundreds of millions of travellers by railway every year in Great Britain are, in some sense, his debtors. He has left enduring monuments of his genius all over the world, and the lesson which moralists have sought to inculcate of the greatness and the vanity of man, can hardly be impressed more forcibly upon the mind than when we turn from them to contemplate the narrow resting-place where his mortal remains were yesterday deposited."

LORD BROUGHAM:

THE BOY PHILOSOPHER AND MODERN DEMOSTHENES.

LORD BROUGHAM is one of the greatest men the world has ever seen: great in mental power, in intellectual achievement, in work done, and in age attained. Journeying back to the time of his birth, we have to pass through England's greatest social and political changes; the history of which cannot be written without a record of his name, and distinguished mention of his services.

He was born in St. Andrew Square, Edinburgh, on the 19th September, 1779, and when only seven years old entered the High School in a class of 164 boys.

Lord Cockburn, who was at the same school, relates the following anedote of him:—"Brougham was not in the class with me. Before getting to the rector's class he had been under Luke Fraser, who, in his two immediately preceding courses of four years' each, had the good fortune to have Francis Jeffrey and Walter Scott as his pupils. Brougham made his first explosion while at Fraser's class. He dared to differ from Fraser, a hot but good-natured old fellow, on some bit of Latinity. The master, like other men, in power, maintained his own infallibility, punished the rebel, and flattered himself that the affair was over. But Brougham re-appeared next day, loaded with books, returned to the charge before the whole class, and compelled honest Luke to acknowledge he had been in the wrong. This made Brougham famous throughout the school. I remember, as well as if it had been yesterday, having had him pointed out to me as 'The fellow who had beat the master.' It was then that I first saw him."

He entered the university when only in his fifteenth year; and, strange to say, when little more than sixteen he sent a letter to the Royal Society, in which he described a series of experiments in optics, and gave an exposition of the principles which govern that science. Shortly after, he sent them another paper on "Certain Principles in Geometry." The Society printed both papers in the "Philosophical Transactions" of 1796 and 1798. These early productions elicited replies and refutations from Professor Prevôst, of Geneva, and others. This resulted in a Latin correspondence with the most eminent philosophers of that period, in which young Brougham displayed great spirit and ability. While he was at the university he was pre-eminently conspicuous for his attainments in all the branches of study to which his attention was directed, and particularly in mathematics and natural philosophy, as well as in law, in metaphysics, and in political science.

After leaving the university he made a tour through Holland and Prussia, and on his return was duly called to the Scottish bar. It was at this time that he gave indication of his future success in oratory—frequenting the Speculative Society of Edinburgh, where he came in contact with many men, who subsequently attained considerable eminence in the legal and political world. These men started the "Edinburgh Review," but, owing to an impression of Brougham's indiscretion, he was not invited to write in the first three numbers; after that, he was taken into confidence, and did more work than any other contributor. When the Review had been in existence five years, Brougham wrote to Mr. Constable, the publisher, for one thousand pounds, telling him that he would quickly clear it all off by articles for the serial; and, as a proof of his earnestness, he actually wrote the whole of one number, with the exception of two articles. The papers were upon various subjects: one of them treated on the *operation of lithotomy!* Amongst other papers, he contributed one on the then recently published "Hours of Idleness," by Lord Byron, in which he predicted anything but success for the noble poet. In this he proved, however clever he was as a critic, that he was no prophet; Byron did achieve a wonderful success, and, to revenge himself, wrote his "English Bards and Scotch Reviewers." But, writing for the "Edinburgh" was only the preparation for more serious labour. In 1803 he published his work, in two volumes, on the "Colonial Policy of the European Powers," in which he manifested new capability, and developed fresh talents. He had, meanwhile, acquired a tolerable practice at the Scottish bar, but not sufficient to satisfy his restless spirit; to improve his position he determined to quit Scotland, and was shortly after called to the English bar by the Society of Lincoln's Inn, when he soon attained a good share of practice. Shortly after his settlement in England he was elected a Fellow of the Royal Society; and in 1810 was counsel for a number of London, Liverpool, and Manchester merchants, who were heard in the House of Lords against the orders in council, issued in retaliation of certain decrees of Napoleon, which forbade the continent having any commercial intercourse with the English. On this occasion Brougham made a speech, which extended over two days. But it was not until 1810 that he attained the area where he achieved some of his greatest feats; he then entered the House of Commons for the Borough of Camelford, under the influence of the Earl of Darlington. His speeches in Parliament were chiefly made in connection with Clarkson, Wilberforce, and Grenville Sharpe, directed against the odious slave system. Mainly owing to his exertions, a law was passed in 1811, making it felony for any British subject to engage in the slave traffic. Liverpool had derived immense wealth from this source, and yet, it can scarcely now be imagined that the reason why Liverpool refused to return Brougham at the ensuing dissolution of Parliament, was traceable to this cause. Be this as it may, the inhabitants of that important sea-port returned Mr. Canning by a large majority. During Brougham's four years absence from the House of Commons, the corn laws were enacted, to repeal which, seven years of the energy and spirit of the best men of the kingdom were required, headed by Richard Cobden and John Bright. By the influence of the Earl of Darlington, Brougham was returned, in 1816, for the borough of Winchelsea. In the ensuing session he had an opportunity to display his oratorical powers in defence of tens of thousands of men and women, literally starving for the common necessaries of life, in consequence, as he affirmed, of the starvation laws which had recently passed the House. It was during this mournful time that men and women, who had assembled in the most lawful manner, were cut down by infuriated dragoons at Manchester. It is memorable that the site of this "Peterloo Massacre" is now the site of the Free Trade Hall, built to commemorate the repeal of the odious and iniquitous corn laws.

At this time the various corporate charities were found to be much abused, which excited Brougham's attention. He proved them to be the most scandalous and revolting, and obtained a commission to inquire into and report upon the alleged abuses. Little ultimate good was effected, save the exposure and publicity given to much knavish practice. It is very probable, however, that the fame which attached to him during the discussion of these abuses secured for him the high position which he next occupied, as the defender of Queen Caroline. This was the event of his life. It secured him popularity, and an opportunity which no subsequent divergence from popular interests could efface. His speech upon this occasion is preserved as an instance of fervid brilliant oratory, and produced at the time of its delivery an almost electric effect through the entire kingdom. The next act of Brongham was to bring in a bill for the establishment of schools to provide education for the poor of England and Wales. This bill proposed to centre the chief power of management in the hands of the ministers of the Church of England. In addressing the House of Commons on the subject, he said: "Let the House look at the alacrity, the zeal, the established clergy manifested for the education of the poor. The clergy were the teachers of the poor—not only teachers of religion, but, in the eye of the law, teachers generally. What then, he asked, could be more natural than that they should have control over those who were elected to assist them." He seems to have changed his sentiments in regard to the clergy very speedily. The opportunity was not long wanting to manifest his altered opinion. In 1821 he defended John Ambrose Williams, who had been indicted for a libel on the clergy of Durham. Williams was the proprictor of the "Durham Chronicle," and had published an article in his paper reflecting on the clergy, who would not allow the church bells to be rung on the death of the "murdered" Queen, as she was called. Brougham in his spech manifested the bitterest irony against the men whom he had formerly extolled. The verdict went against Williams, but he was never afterwards called up for judgment.

From this period Brougham devoted himself almost unceasingly to the defence of freedom, and the rights of conscience. In 1825 he was elected Lord Rector of the University of Glasgow, in opposition to Sir Walter Scott—the casting vote being given by Sir James Mackintosh. When the death of George IV. occasioned a general election, Brougham was returned for the large and important constituency of Yorkshire. It was supposed that that county would only return such persons as could boast high birth or splendid connections. The return of Brougham was undoubtedly a great triumph, of which he did not fail to take advantage. In the new ministry, to the astonishment of the whole country, he was made Lord High Chancellor. It is known that Brougham left the House of Commons to preside over the House of Lords, with the utmost pain and reluctance—that his own most earnest desire was not to accept any office which necessitated the abduction of his position as member for Yorkshire, and that he took a position nominally and titularly higher only at the most urgent entreaty and virtual command of his party. Since his removal, now more than thirty years, he has never but once been known to enter as auditor within those walls which had so often echoed with his eloquence. The single exception occurred during the present year, 1860, when he overcame his remarkable reluctance, to hear the financial statement of Mr. Gladstone; being the first time that he had heard that remarkable orator, who now holds the position which he himself so long held unrivalled and undisputed—the greatest orator in the House of Commons.

In his new position Brougham took frequent opportunities to lecture the members of the House of Lords. He often told them that the aristocracy, with all their castles, manors, rights of warren, and rights of chase, and their broad acres, reckoned at fifty years' purchase, "were not for a moment to be weighed against the middle classes of England." His speeches on the reform bill were much praised at the time of their delivery. In 1830, in carrying out various law reform schemes, he introduced a measure for local courts, and subsequently various amendments in the bankruptcy laws. In 1834 the ministry was dissolved; in its reconstruction Brougham took no part—his official life was at an end.

His leisure now enabled him to turn to the world of letters, to which he was always strongly attached. His literary labours may be thus enumerated. First, his essays in the "Edinburgh Review;" in 1803, his treatise on the colonial policy of the European powers; then his eloquent speeches and writings in favour of mechanics' institutions, in connection with Dr. Birkbeck, during the year 1821. In addition to being the principal founder of the Society for the Diffusion of Useful Knowledge, he composed several of the papers published by the Society, as well as contributed to its serial publications. In 1834 he published his expansion of "Paley's Theology," and subsequently his "Lives of the Statesmen of the reign of George III.," four volumes of "Political Philosophy," and "Lives of Men of Science."

In this bird's eye view of the career of this extraordinary man, the reader will have arrived at the conclusion that there must be some secret in his marvellous attainments. That secret his lordship has taken every means to publish to the world. Work is the talisman; work has transmuted his labours into gold; work has been the Alladin's lamp by which his youthful dreams have been more than realized. Perhaps it may be said that he is the most hard-working man in England even now, in his eightieth year; but when he was a young man, his labours were most extraordinary. It is related of him on one occasion, that having practised all day as a barrister, he went to the House of Commons, where he was engaged in active debate through the night, till three o'clock in the morning; he then returned home, wrote an article for the "Edinburgh Review," spent the next day in court, practising law, and the succeeding night in the House of Commons; returned to his lodgings at three o'clock in the morning, and "retired simply because he had nothing else to do." It is known that he was laboriously studying optics in the brief intervals of the queen's trial, one of the most absorbing judicial proceedings of modern times, in which, as we have seen, he was a leading counsel. At other times, when it suited his purpose, he could manifest sympathy for the weakness of humanity. There is an amusing instance related of him while he was chancellor. He had been listening with the greatest attention to the speeches of two counsel on one side, from ten o'clock until half-past two; a third rose to address the court on the same side. His lordship was quite unprepared for this additional infliction, and exclaimed, "What! Mr. A——, are you really going to speak on the same side?" "Yes, my lord, I mean to trespass on your lordship's attention for a short time." "Then," said his lordship, looking the orator significantly in the face, and giving a sudden twitch of his nose—"then, Mr. A——, you had better cut your speech as short as possible, otherwise you must not be surprised if you see me dozing; for really this is more than human nature can endure." The young barrister took the hint, and made a short speech.

Lord Brougham has now passed his eightieth year; yet, only two years ago he devised a National Association for the promotion of Social Science. At the third annual meeting, held in Bradford (1859), in addressing a meeting of the working classes, his lordship said: "That he spoke as a working man himself —he had been all his life a working man. This was the rule he always followed—never to count one hour or one moment his own, to use as a means of amusement or relaxation, even for his instruction, out of the profession to which he belonged, whatever that might be at the time, until the day's work was completely, honestly, and accurately performed. He had been a working man all his life, and what was more, he had all his life lived upon wages. It happened—possibly it was an accident, and therefore did him no credit, but it did happen—that whatever little property he enjoyed, or whatever sums of money had come to him in any way, he had never spent one-half, and had always lived by the sweat of his brow. It might be said that he should at his time of life—and he was a great deal over thirty years of age—take a little rest, and that he had earned a title to a little repose. But it had been said by the great Christian poet, Cowper—

> 'A man unoccupied is not at rest;
> A mind quite vacant is a mind distressed.'

And he had resolved that so long as Providence allowed him to retain his faculties, he would not fall under the description of a man 'unoccupied,' or of a mind 'quite vacant.' He would continue, as far as he was able, to live a 'life of labour,' to which he had so long been accustomed."

One of the newspaper correspondents at the Bradford meeting describes his lordship at his present advanced age:—

"I need hardly say that Lord Brougham was one of the chief objects of interest and admiration at the Bradford meeting. Although a slight deafness, and a little unsteadiness in his gait, testify his advancing years, he is still the Lord Brougham of our early recollections. He still speaks with his characteristic vigour and energy, still laughs as loudly and talks away as rapidly as any of his juniors; he is full of fun and anecdote, and displays all that restless and incessant mental and physical activity for which he was always remarkable. He was, I believe, up and out after twelve o'clock at night, and I understand that this morning he took a walk before breakfast to the grave of Robin Hood, or, to write the name more correctly, Robin Eude, in the Kirklees Park, the seat of Mr. Wickham, M.P. for Bradford, whose guest he has been during the week."

The "Times," in commenting upon the new position of the Edinburgh University, refers to a fresh honour which has since been paid to Lord Brougham:—

"The University of Edinburgh has recently acquired a franchise which cannot be exercised without occasioning considerable trouble and excitement. By the Act for the Regulation of Scotch Universities it is provided that, for the first time, the University of Edinburgh is to have a chancellor. This office, which appears, so far as we can gather from the Act, tc be, like the chancellorships of Oxford and Cambridge very much of an honorary character, it is to be held for life, and filled by the votes of the members of the university council. This council is to consist of the professors, of masters of arts, of doctors of medicine who, as matriculated students, have given regular attendance on classes in any of the faculties of the university, and of the university court, which consists of the Rector, the Principal, the Lord Provost of Edinburgh, and five assessors, appointed in different manners. Of course, there is one man to whom opinion both in Scotland and England points as the proper person to receive all the honour that the University of Edinburgh has to bestow. He was a student at Edinburgh, and distinguished at a time when Edinburgh was, beyond all seminaries in the kingdom, fruitful of great and illustrious men. He has devoted almost every leisure moment of a long and laborious life to the promotion of knowledge in all its shapes; and, himself a scholar, a mathematician, and a physical inquirer of the first order, has been unwearied in his endeavours to raise the standard of knowledge and education throughout the country. In his own profession he has, by the power of industry and talent, long ago risen to the highest post, and as a politician he has filled a conspicuous place at a most momentous period, in the foremost rank of orators and statesmen. Every one will anticipate us when we say there is but one man to whom this description applies, and that that one man is Lord Brougham. How fortunate ought Edinburgh to esteem herself that, in the evening of his life, while he yet possesses those faculties which have for half a century riveted upon him the attention and the admiration of his fellow-countrymen, she has it in her power to offer to her most distinguished alumnus an honour not unworthy even of his acceptance! What claims Lord Brougham may have to the highest place as a statesmen, a jurist, an orator, an author, a philosopher, or a scholar, men may reasonably debate; but as the tried and consistent friend of education, as one entitled to every mark of distinction which the university he has adorned can bestow, he stands altogether without a peer, and therefore we should have supposed without a competitor."

By a recent grant from Her Majesty, the title of Lord Brougham will descend to his brother and his heirs male. The grant of a perpetuity to this title will be felt to be a mark of respect to a man who has deserved the honours of the peerage as fully as any one on whom they have been conferred.

JOHN KITTO:

THE WORKHOUSE BOY, AND AFTERWARDS DR. JOHN KITTO, F.S.A., AUTHOR OF "THE PICTORIAL BIBLE," ETC.

In the social scale we cannot get very much lower than the workhouse. When anybody gets there, it is usually supposed that every resource has failed, and that he is very near "the last scene of all." And yet, even from that comfortless and almost hopeless place, we are about to accompany one of its younger inhabitants upon a journey of usefulness and honour, which might well be envied by some of the greatest and most respected of men.

Our hero, for he was a hero in the true sense, was born at Plymouth in the December of 1804. He had a rough life before him—difficulties of a gigantic character to overcome; it would have been a mercy if he had had a strong healthy constitution. This was not to be. When born, he was so puny and sickly that he was not expected to live many hours; and although great care was taken of him, it was long before he was able to walk. This constitutional weakness prevented him, as he grew up, taking part in the sports and pastimes of other boys. Indisposition to take exercise grew upon him, and was no doubt the source of much after misery. But that which appeared to be so great an evil was providentially turned to a blessing. When other boys were employed in their games, he was to be seen poring over a book behind a hedge or on a sunny bank. Not that any facilities were afforded him to read by his parents; he was not even sent to school until he was eight years of age; his books were borrowed or begged with great difficulty; his home was by no means a home of comfort, but rather a scene of misery and wretchedness; and by the time he had attained his twelfth year, through much sickness and sorrow, he was placed with his father, a stone mason, to act as his labourer.

But this poor boy had to bear other miseries besides his own. His father, soon after his marriage, became a confirmed sot; he was so lost to his position as to regard neither character nor reputation. From being a master waited on by others, he became a servant; worse even than this: to gratify the appetite which consumed him, he frequently violated the laws and found himself in "durance vile"—at one time so seriously, that Kitto wrote: "What will they now say of the felon's son?"

His grandmother, to take him out of this wretchedness, transferred him to her own garret. She, poor woman, had also suffered from the curse of drink. Her second husband, after spending the evening with a friend, was drowned in a pond as he was returning home, helplessly intoxicated. The removal of John to his grandmother's must have been a comfort to his own mother, who was so miserably circumstanced as frequently to work from five in the morning until ten in the evening—"that she might have something to put in the mouths of her babes."

Kitto was with his grandmother from his fourth to his eighth year, who "pinched herself to support" him. Her extreme poverty no doubt prevented her from sending him to school. She took kindly to the poor lad, and for his amusement made many strolls in the neighbourhood. They gathered flowers together, and in the season went nutting; the branches which were out of John's reach she hooked down with her staff. At other times they made excursions to the sea-beach, when his aged relative would be sure to have for him in her pocket a little reserve of ginger-bread, plums, apples, or sugar-stick.

When he had arrived at his eighth year, arrangement was made for his attending school. His attendance, however, was very irregular. The poor old grandmother was too poor to pay the charges, and his father would not spare a few pence for the purpose. When he did save a little from the ale-house, John went to school; when the money was spent in drink, he remained away. It was a great pity some charity school was not found for him; but the father's drinking absorbed all his spare time, and his mother, to find food for her little ones, had to go out early to "char." The schooling that John did get, enabled him to understand a little of "reading, writing, and the imperfect use of figures." His grandmother boasted that he was the best scholar in Plymouth. John knew better, adding, when he heard the remark, "she did it ignorantly, but affectionately."

But if the dear old grandmother could not pay for his schooling, she could teach him at home. She taught him to be a proficient in *sewing*, so that he boasted of having done the best part of a "gay patchwork" for her bed, besides having made "quilts and kettle-holders enough for two generations." The old lady had also a store of stories about ghosts, hobgoblins, fairies, and witches; and a shoemaker, of the name of Roberts, poured into his eager ear, as he sat using his awl, the tales of Bluebeard, Cinderella, Jack the Giant-killer, and Beauty and the Beast. Kitto wrote, in 1832: "Assuredly, never have I since felt so much respect and admiration of any man's talents and extent of information as those of poor Roberts." He soon made the discovery that the shoemaker was not the only repository for such wonders, but that for a copper he could purchase similar astounding marvels at the shop of Mrs. Barnicle. This, of course, was an irresistible temptation. Every spare penny now went to the Barnicle vortex. Plums or ginger-bread presented no attraction like the witchery of a picture-book or a nursery rhyme. Walks and out-door rambles gave place to close reading at home. After the toy-books, John sought amusement in his grandmother's family Bible (which was fortunately profusely illustrated) in her Prayer Book, Pilgrim's Progress, and Gulliver's Travels. "The two last I soon devoured," says he; "and so much did I admire them, that, to increase their attractions, I decorated all the engravings with the indigo my grandmother used in washing, using a feather for a brush. Some one at last gave me a fourpenny box of colours, and between that and my books I was so much interested at home, that I retained little inclination for play; and when my grandmother observed this, she did all in her power to encourage those studious habits, by borrowing for me books of her neighbours." He had soon made the acquaintance of every book in every house in the street. He lived upon books—they were more to him than his food. It was to gratify this love of reading that he made his first literary effort. He thus amusingly narrated the circumstance:—

"My cousin came one day with a penny in his hand, declaring his intention to buy a book with it. I was just then sadly in want of a penny to make up fourpence, with which to purchase the 'History of King Pippin' (not Pepin), so I inquired whether he bought a book for the pictures or the story? 'The story, to be sure.' I then said, that, in that case, I would, for his penny, write him both a larger and a better story than he could get in print for the same sum; and that he might be still further a gainer, I would paint him a picture at the beginning, and he knew there were no painted pictures in penny books. He expressed the satisfaction he should feel in my doing so, and sat down quietly on the stool to note my operations. When I had done, I certainly thought my cousin's penny pretty well earned; and as, at reading the paper and viewing the picture, he was of the same opinion, no one else had any right to complain of the bargain. I believe this was the first penny I ever earned. I happened to recollect this circumstance when last at Plymouth, and felt a wish to peruse this paper, if still in existence; but my poor cousin, though he remembered the circumstance, had quite forgotten both the paper and its contents, unless that it was 'something about what was done in England at the time when wild men lived in it;'—even this was further than my own recollection extended."

His next effort was a drama performed by children. The terms of admission were, "ladies eight pins, and gentlemen ten." It is plain from these first efforts that Kitto thus early had contracted a love for literature which would never be subdued.

These imaginative episodes, however, gave place to more substantial ones. The old grandmother in 1814, attacked by paralysis, went lower down into the depths of poverty; so that, instead of being able to maintain Kitto, she herself had to go and reside with her daughter. Kitto found his father's home no home for him. In order that he might do something for a living, he was sent as an apprentice to a barber, whom Kitto describes as having a face "so 'sour,' that it sickened one to look at it; and which was, beside, all over red by drinking spirituous liquors." This engagement soon came to an end. Kitto was simple enough to leave a woman in charge of his master's razors, that he carried home every night, under the pretext that she wanted the barber; of course, when Kitto returned neither woman or razors were to be seen. His master not only discharged him, but was mean enough to accuse him of complicity with the thief.

There was no other resource now but going with his father to render him any assistance in his power; this enabled him to be a sad witness of the profligate acts of his parent. On the 13th of February, 1817, his father was repairing the roof of a house in Plymouth. John was carrying a load of slates to him; but just as he was stepping from the ladder to the roof he lost his footing and fell a distance of thirty-five feet into the court below. He remained insensible for more than a week, and did not leave his bed for four months. Afterwards, he partially recovered his strength; but the accident deprived him of all sense of hearing. He became as deaf as though he had never had the sense. He subsequently submitted to many surgical operations; but all was in vain—the precious sense was extinguished! Kitto feelingly relates how he learned that he was deaf. He had been in a trance for nearly a fortnight; every sound was hushed; profound silence reigned over all.

"I was very slow in learning," he writes, "that my hearing was entirely gone. The unusual stillness of all things was grateful to me in my utter exhaustion; and if, in this half-awakened state, a thought of the matter entered my mind, I ascribed it to the unusual care and success of my friends in preserving silence around me. I saw them talking, indeed, to one another, and thought that, out of regard to my feeble condition, they spoke in whispers, because I heard them not. The truth was revealed to me in consequence of my solicitude about the book which had so much interested me on the day of my fall. It had, it seems, been reclaimed by the good old man who had lent it to me, and who doubtless concluded that I should have no more need of books in this life. He was wrong, for there has been nothing in this life which I have needed more. I asked for this book with much earnestness, and was answered by signs, which I could not comprehend. 'Why do you not speak?' I cried; 'pray let me have the book.' This seemed to create some confusion; and at length some one, more clever than the rest, hit upon the happy expedient of writing upon a slate that the book had been reclaimed by the owner, and that I could not, in my weak state, be allowed to read. 'But,' I said, in great astonishment, 'why do you write to me? why not speak? Speak! speak!' Those who stood around the bed exchanged significant looks of concern, and the writer soon displayed upon his slate the awful words, 'YOU ARE DEAF!'"

Fearful were now the circumstances of this poor boy. When he left his bed he was useless to his father; his grandmother was too poor to render him any assistance, and he had not a farthing to spend upon a book, which had now become, through his infirmity, a prime necessity of his being. His resort, in this dilemma, was to what he calls a "poor student's ways and means." He went to the shore, where the coasters and fishing-boats discharged their cargoes, wading with other boys for pieces of rope, iron, or any other refuse. Some of them made threepence per day, but Kitto never succeeded better than to make fourpence in one week. This source of profit, poor as it was, soon was closed. One day he gave himself a severe wound by treading on a broken bottle, and there was an end to his hopes from that quarter.

His next effort to obtain the "ways and means" was in quite a different direction. He laid out his remaining twopence on paper, and set about painting heads, houses, flowers, birds, and trees. These he exhibited in his mother's window for sale; they sold, rude as they were, to the extent of about twopence halfpenny weekly. This not satisfying his ambition, he determined to have a stall at the Plymouth fair, from which the proceeds were larger. Then, casting about for other sources of profit, he observed that the labels in the windows of the houses in the outskirts were badly and inaccurately written: "Logins for Singel Men," "Rooms to leet, enquire within." He prepared a number of neat substitutes, in disposing of which he was partially successful. Of course the money thus obtained was spent on books. He used to visit about once a fortnight a bookstall in the market. The owner kindly allowed him to read the books at the stall, and sold him others very cheaply, when he spent the few coppers he had so hardly scraped together. Kitto, in referring to this period, wrote:—

"For many years I had no views towards literature beyond the instruction and solace of my own mind; and, under these views, and in the absence of other mental stimulants, the pursuit of it eventually became a passion, which devoured all others. I take no merit for the industry and application with which I pursued this object, nor for the ingenious contrivances by which I sought to shorten the hours of needful rest, that I might have the more time for making myself acquainted with the minds of other men. The reward was great and immediate, and I was only preferring the gratification which seemed to me the highest. Nevertheless, now that I am, in fact, another being, having but slight connection, excepting in so far as 'the child is father to the man,' with my former self; now that much has become a business which was then simply a joy; and now that I am gotten old in experiences if not in years, it does somewhat move me to look back upon that poor and deaf boy, in his utter loneliness, devoting himself to objects in which none around him could sympathise, and to pursuits which none could even understand. The eagerness with which he sought books, and the devoted attention with which he read them, was simply an unaccountable fancy in their view; and the hours which he strove to gain for writing that which was destined for no other eyes than his own, was no more than an innocent folly, good for keeping him quiet and out of harm's way, but of no possible use on earth. This want of the encouragement which sympathy and appreciation give, and which cultivated friends are so anxious to bestow on the studious application of their young people, I now count among the sorest trials of that day, and it serves me now as a measure for the intensity of my devotement to such objects, that I felt so much encouragement within as not to need or care much for the sympathies and encouragements which are, in ordinary circumstances, held of so much importance. I undervalue them not; on the contrary, an undefinable craving was often felt for sympathy and appreciation in pursuits so dear to me; but to want this was one of the disqualifications of my condition, quite as much so as my deafness itself; and in the same degree in which I submitted to my deafness as a dispensation from Providence towards me, did I submit to this as a necessary consequence. It was, however, one of the peculiarities of my condition that I was then, as I ever have been, too much shut up. With the same dispositions and habits, without being deaf, it would have been easy to have found companions who would have understood me, and sympathised with my love for books and study, my progress in which might also have been much advanced by such intercommunication. As it was, the shyness and reserve which the deaf usually exhibit, gave increased effect to the physical disqualification, and precluded me from seeking, and kept me from incidentally finding, beyond the narrow sphere in which I moved, the sympathies which were not found in it. As time passed, my mind became filled with ideas and sentiments, and with various knowledge of things new and old, all of which were as the things of another world to those among whom my lot was cast. The conviction of this completed my isolation; and eventually all my human interests were concentrated in these points—to get books, and, as they were mostly borrowed, to preserve the most valuable points in their contents, either by extracts or by a distinct intention to impress them on the memory. When I went forth I counted the hours till I might return to the only pursuits in which I could take interest, and when free to return, how swiftly I fled to immure myself in that little sanctuary which I had been permitted to appropriate, in one of those rare nooks only afforded by such old Elizabethan houses as that in which my relatives then abode!"

But this comparative happiness was not long to continue. The dear old grandmother went to reside at Brixton—a severe loss to Kitto. He was now entirely at the mercy of his drinking father, who cared so little for him, that he was soon a pitiable spectacle in the streets, pinched with hunger, shivering in rags, and crawling about with bleeding feet. To save him from this "cold and hunger and nakedness," he was admitted into the Plymouth workhouse—a sad culmination to his literary and artistic dreams!

The governor of the workhouse treated him kindly, permitting him some indulgence. His first task was to learn to make list shoes: in a short time he was a proficient in the business. Within a twelvemonth of his entrance into the workhouse, he commenced to keep a diary, which he "with reverence inscribed to the memory of Cecilia Picken, my grandmother, and the dearest friend I ever had." The diary enters into interesting and minute details of his workhouse life. One entry runs thus:—

"I was to-day most wrongfully accused of cutting off the top of a cat's tail. They did not know me who thought me capable of such an act of wanton cruelty.

"June 2.—I am making my own shoes.

"June 9.—I have finished my shoes; they are tolerably strong and neat.

"August 14.—I was set to close bits of leather.

"August 15.—Said bits of leather that I had closed were approved of, and I was sent to close a pair of women's shoes, which were also approved of.

"November 14.—On Monday had been a twelvemonth in the workhouse, during which time I have made seventy-eight pairs of list shoes, besides mending many others, and have received, as a premium, one penny per week.

"November 20.—I burnt a tale, of which I had written several sheets, which I called 'The Probationary Trial,' but which did not, as far as I wrote, please me."

Many of the most touching entries in the journal relate to the dear old grandmother. Here is one:—

"1819.—Granny has been absent in Dock this two days. Though but for so short a period, I severely feel her absence. If I feel it so acutely now, how shall I bear the final separation when she shall be gone to that 'undiscovered country from whose bourne no traveller returns?' She cannot be expected to live many years longer, for now she is more than seventy years of age. O, Almighty

Power, spare yet a few years my granny, the protector of my infancy, and the—I cannot express my gratitude. It is useless to attempt it."

On April 18 he wrote: "She is dead." The measure of his sorrow was complete. His best friend was gone! After this great loss, his father, for a time at least, seemed desirous to befriend his poor boy, and promised him the twopence that granny had used to give him weekly to get his library books. John was sadly afraid that when the sorrow was blunted by time, that the twopence would be withheld, and then what should he do?

Sometimes his thoughts would go out to the future. His ambition was to have a stationer's shop and a circulating library, with twelve or fourteen shillings a week income. His anxious question was: "When I am out, how shall I earn a livelihood?" He thought he might travel, and that some kind gentleman might take him, even though it were in the humble capacity of a servant, "to tread classic Italy, fantastic Gaul, proud Spain, and phlegmatic Batavia;" nay, "to visit Asia, and the ground consecrated by the steps of the Saviour."

There was a ray of joy let into his heart one day, by the master of the workhouse proposing to him the pleasurable task of writing some lectures to be read to the boys, upon the subject of their duties. Kitto felt the restraint of the workhouse, and yet kindness had partially reconciled him to it. He was, nevertheless, most anxious to quit it. "Liberty," he cried, "was my idol; liberty, not idleness. Methinks when I am out of the house, I breathe almost another air. Like the wolf in the fable, I would rather starve at liberty than grow fat under restraint. There is no fear of my starving in the midst of plenty. I know how to prevent hunger. The Hottentots subsist a long time on nothing but a little gum; they also, when hungry, tie a tight ligature round them. Cannot I do so, too? I will sell my books and pawn my neckerchiefs, by which I shall be able to raise about twelve shillings, and with that I will make the tour of England. The hedges furnish blackberries, nuts, sloes, &c., and the fields turnips; a hayrick or barn will be an excellent bed. I will take pen, ink, and paper with me, and note down my observations as I go—a kind of sentimental tour, not so much a description of places as of men and manners, adventures and feelings."

This tour, it is needless to say, was not made. On the 8th of November, 1821, he was handed over to a much more prosy condition—apprenticed to John Bowden, shoemaker. He was to remain with his new master until he was twenty-one, and he was now seventeen. Kitto had a little reluctance to quit the workhouse at first, and only consented to do so when the advantages of the change were presented to his mind. "The going home at night, the possession of his evenings for himself, the power of reading in his own garret, without molestation, the dropping of the poorhouse uniform, food in plenty, and good clothes—these formed an irresistible temptation." And then, when he was fairly out of the workhouse, he gave expression to his feelings: "I am no longer a workhouse boy—I am an apprentice!"

John's joy, however, was soon changed. His master was a mean-spirited tyrant, who had selected him on account of his deafness—thinking that his infirmity would prevent him making any complaint. John thus records his feelings after being two months with his master:—

"January 19.—O misery, art thou to be my only portion! Father of heaven, forgive me if I wish I had never been born. O that I were dead, if death were an annihilation of being; but as it is not, teach me to endure life: enjoy it I never can. In short, mine is a severe master, rather cruel!" The journal contains many heart-rending passages of the master's heartless cruelty to the poor deaf boy. He often forced him to work sixteen and eighteen hours out of the twenty-four—striking and buffetting him without mercy. His condition was so dreadful, that he twice seriously contemplated suicide. Happily he had the power of writing; his case was heard before the magistrates, and his indentures cancelled. When he returned to his home—the workhouse—he began to turn over in his mind the possibility of doing something besides making shoes. "What might he not do? Might he not write or compose a work? be it poetry or prose might it not immortalise his name? What should hinder the achievement? Might not every obstacle be surmounted, and John Kitto become an author known to fame?"

He wrote, as the result of these thoughts:—"I had learned that knowledge is power; and not only was it power, but safety. As nearly as the matter can now be traced, the progress of my ideas appears to have been this—firstly, that I was not altogether so helpless as I had seemed; secondly, that, notwithstanding my afflicted state, I might realise much comfort in the condition of life in which I had been placed; thirdly, that I might even raise myself out of that condition, into one of less privation; fourthly, that it was not impossible for me to place my own among honourable names, by proving that no privation formed an insuperable bar to useful labour and self-advancement. To do what no one under the same circumstances ever did, soon that ceased to be the limit of my ambition!"

Fortunately, while he was in one of the Plymouth bookshops, he had been noticed by a famed mathematician, Mr. Harvey, who, after learning his history, determined to interest others on his behalf. A circular was drawn up, detailing the incidents of Kitto's birth and life, and suggesting that a small sum of money, raised by subscription, should be appropriated to his use for board and lodgings, until some permanent situation could be procured for him. This appeal was successful. The guardians subscribed five pounds to the fund. In the meantime Kitto boarded with a Mr. Burnard, and had the privilege of using the public library, and devoting all his hours to mental improvement. These hours he used industriously, although he was subject to frequent attacks of illness. It was suggested that he might become a missionary; a position to which he had never hoped to attain in his most excited moments, but when the prospect was opened up to him, it thrilled him with delight, as it presented opportunities of usefulness; and to be useful, he had already learned, was the only way to secure happiness.

About this time Kitto was introduced to a Mr. Groves, a dentist, residing at Exeter, who offered to instruct him in his profession, to board him, and give him for his services, £15 for the first year, and £20 for the second. Kitto happily accepted the offer—and found in the character of Mr. Groves the example of a true Christian, and a valued friend.

In the spring of 1825, a volume of Kitto's letters and essays was published, for which more than four hundred subscribers were obtained. The volume gave evidence of his close and multifarious reading. In it reference is made to Malebranche, Hume, Reid, Stewart, Berkeley, Des Cartes, Locke, and Stillingfleet, Lord Bacon, and Madame de Staël. He descants upon the Tuscan, Doric, and Gothic orders of architecture; criticises the productions of Salvator Rosa, Gainsborough, Titian, and Raphael; and has some noticeable remarks upon the sculpture of antiquity. It was quite evident that Kitto remembered what he had read. But he did not read for amusement merely—he read for the thoughts and facts which the books contained. One day he wrote: "Without books, I should quickly become an ignorant and senseless being, unloving and unloved, if I am not so already. I apprehend that I have sometimes offended my acquaintance, by the importunity with which I have solicited the loan of books. But if I had a house full of books myself, and knew any person to whom they would be so necessary as to me, and who would make so good a use of them as I do, I would not stay to be entreated, nor scruple to lend any, or all of them, in succession, to such a person. What earthly pleasure can equal that of reading a good book? O, dearest tomes! Princely and august folio! Sublime quarto! Elegant octavo! Charming duodecimo! Most ardently do I admire your beauties. To obtain ye, and to call ye mine, I would work day and night; and to possess ye, I would forbid myself all sensual joys!"

At this time, when Kitto was in his twentieth year, Mr. Groves had been contemplating devoting himself to the missionary work, and to this end had been preparing in Trinity College, Dublin. It was proposed to Kitto that he should practise as a dentist, either in Plymouth or in London; but Mr. Groves learning that the printing-offices at several of the missionary stations were in need of willing workmen, and knowing Kitto's spirit and admiration for missionary labour, proposed that he should go out to one of the stations as a printer. He accepted the proposal at once, as the most congenial and desirable work. He was accepted by the London Board, Mr Groves liberally offering to pay towards his board £50 per annum, for two years. In the July of 1825 he was consigned to the care of Mr. Watts, at the Missionary College at Islington, to learn the art of printing. When in the office he soon learned to set the types of the Greek Testament, and Persic, on Henry Martyn's translation. One of the delights which he found in London was an indulgence in his early propensity of visiting and reading at the bookstalls. His industry was not relaxed with his comparatively easy circumstances. "I cannot," he wrote, "accuse myself of having wasted or misemployed a moment of my time since I left the workhouse." He was so methodical in the distribution of his time, as carefully to apportion a task to every part of the day, only allowing himself six hours for sleep; and considered that rather more than he could afford. After spending considerable time in preparation, he finally went out to Malta in 1827, to enter upon the duties of the printing office, which was under the direction of Mr. Jowett and Mr. Schliewz, and was employed in printing tracts in Greek, Arabic, Maltese, and Italian. He entered upon the work with ardour—devoting all his spare time to the study of Asiatic characters.

After a period, owing to the disposition "which would not be controlled," to learn, the Missionary Committee thought his studies interfered with the discharge of his duties in the printing-office; this occasioned a breach, which gradually widened until he resolved to return to England. The Committee evidently did not understand, and certainly did not sympathise, with Kitto in his desires and aspirations. They required a mere printer; Kitto was more—he could originate thoughts worthy of being printed.

On his return to London he resolved various plans to enable him to gain a livelihood, one of which was his original plan: to open a stationer's shop in the neighbourhood of Plymouth. But this project came to nothing. In the meantime his funds were exhausted, and he was once more reduced to the dregs of poverty. Fortunately, at this time a situation was offered him by a gentleman, John Synge, Esq., of Glanmor Castle, County Wicklow, who was printing, at his own private press, "some little works in Hebrew and Greek." He was to have entered upon the duties at the printing office on the 1st of June; but before that time his old friend Mr. Groves had made him a second offer to accompany him to the East, which he at once accepted. This was literally realizing his early dream. He went out as the tutor to the two little boys of Mr. Groves. His instructions to the children embraced Hebrew, scripture, theology, history, geography, writing, arithmetic, and English composition.

On the 12th of June, 1829, the party sailed for St. Petersburg. During his stay in Russia, Kitto did not form a very high opinion of its inhabitants. After staying at St. Petersburg Mr. Groves went to Moscow, which city much pleased Kitto. The next place visited was Astrachan—distant about a thousand miles. They then traversed the entire country, meeting with many adventures on the way, until they arrived at Araxes, the river dividing Russia from Persia. On this journey Kitto was thrown from his horse, but, having adopted the turban the previous day, its thick folds no doubt saved his life. The party entered Bagdad on the 6th of December, 1829, six months after leaving Gravesend. While in Bagdad the plague entered the city. As many as 1000 and 1500 deaths occurred in one day. In two months, 50,000 were supposed to have fallen victims to it. Mrs. Groves was seized on the 7th of May, and died on the 14th, after a week's suffering. Mr. Groves was also threatened, but providentially escaped. This danger was not over before they were exposed to another. On the 27th of April, owing to the river overflowing its banks, 7000 houses were thrown down, and 15,000 people lost their lives! The city seemed doomed, but this was not all. The horrors of a siege followed the death-dealing plague and flood. The Arab Pashas of Mosul and Aleppo, so soon as the waters had subsided, advanced against the stricken city. The siege was carried on for several months, during which time the inhabitants were subjected to all the heart-rending scenes engendered by fiendish war—rapine and famine not being the least. Kitto was confined in the house for five months, during the horrors entailed by death, sword, and pestilence. After collecting all the information possible upon the habits and customs of the East, to illustrate the Bible narratives, he returned to England, in company with a Mr. Newman, in the September of 1832; they arrived at their destination in June 1833—Kitto having acquired considerable information on the journey.

After settling down once more he was introduced to Mr. Charles Knight, who employed him as a regular contributor to the "Penny Magazine"—one of the popular serials, read, it was supposed, by more than a million of people, besides being reprinted in America, and translated into French, German, and Dutch. Mr. Knight also employed Kitto to take charge of the "Penny Cyclopædia." This necessitated his spending seven hours daily in Ludgate Street. Mr. Knight also projected the "Pictorial Bible," being fully assured that Kitto could supply the notes and illustrative matter. This work was commenced in 1835, and completed in May, 1838. During its progress Kitto received £250 a-year, and an additional sum at its completion. The next work upon which he was employed was the "Pictorial History of Palestine and the Holy Land, including a complete History of the Jews." The subsequent work commenced was the "Christian Traveller," a periodical publication. Only three parts were published, owing to Mr. Knight's business becoming embarrassed. Kitto was then engaged by the Messrs. Black of Edinburgh to write a "History of Palestine, from the Patrarchial Age to the Present Time;" he also wrote "Thoughts among Flowers," for the Religious Tract Society. Between 1841 and 1843, he prepared the letter-press of the "Gallery of Scripture Engravings;" and in 1845, "The Pictorial Sunday Book," with 1300 engravings, and an appendix on the Geography of the Holy Land. On the title page of his next work—"The Biblical Cyclopædia"—Kitto's name appears as John Kitto, D.D., F.S.A. The pauper surely never dreamed of such a height! He received the diploma of Doctor of Divinity from the University of Giessen; and in 1845 he became a Fellow of the Royal Society of Antiquaries. From this period his industry was incessant—working almost constantly from four in the morning until nine in the evening, producing in succession a series of standard works which will ever remain to attest his labour and research. In the December of 1850, Lord John Russell wrote him: "The Queen has directed that a grant of £100 a year should be made to you from her Majesty's Civil List, on account of your useful and meritorious literary works." This well-earned bounty he did not enjoy very long, his intense exertion bringing on a serious illness, which, despite the best attention, remission of his labours, and the pleasure of a journey into Germany for the restoration of his health, terminated in his death, in the November of 1854. He was interred in the cemetery of Cannstatt, in Germany, followed to his resting-place by a large concourse of the residents. Thus terminated the life of this pauper boy! more glorious in the results of his life than if he had been born to the heritage of a noble name and an ample estate. His works would have done him infinite honour had he had the advantages of the most liberal education, the companionship and encouragement of the learned; but how much more do they redound to his honour when his infirmity, and all the disadvantages of his early position are considered! What boy, or what man, reading the life and trials, and ultimate triumphs of the workhouse boy, will not be nerved with earnest resolve and fixed resolution to imitate him in his eagerness in the pursuit of knowledge, and to leave the world somewhat better than he found it.

HUGH MILLER:

STONEMASON; AFTERWARDS GEOLOGIST, AUTHOR, LECTURER, AND NEWSPAPER EDITOR.

THE newspapers of 1856 contained notices of the death of one of the most eminent men of the age. One writer thus wrote: "Science and letters have to deplore the painful and untimely loss of one of the most remarkable men of his time and country. Yesterday morning Mr. Hugh Miller was found lying lifeless on the threshold of his bedroom, in his house at Portobello. His health had been disordered for some time past, and his sleep broken by fits of nightmare. About midnight on Tuesday, it would seem, he had risen in one of those paroxysms, and snatching up a revolver which lay loaded by his bed-side, made for the door of his chamber. There the pistol went off, and the ball, piercing his breast, he dropped dead upon the spot. The story of the life which has come to so sad an end needs not now be told. His own graceful and graphic pen has made the world acquainted with the circumstances of his birth and boyhood, his self-instruction in a wide circle of knowledge, and his rise from a lot of toil and obscurity to a position of comparative ease and acknowledged eminence. He was born at Cromarty, on the 10th of October, 1802, and had worked for fifteen years as a stonemason, when, about 1835, he was appointed manager of a bank in his native town. His first work, 'Scenes and Legends of the North of Scotland,' was followed rapidly by his 'Old Red Sandstone,' and his 'Letter to Lord Brougham on the Auchterarder Case;' so that his reputation, both as a successful cultivator of geology, a skilful controversialist, and a brilliant and eloquent writer, was already made when he took up his residence in Edinburgh about sixteen years ago. His contributions to the 'Witness' were for some time large and frequent, and at once established that journal in the confidence of the ecclesiastical party to whose interests it devoted itself. Latterly, as the heat of controversy abated, he wrote more sparingly in its columns. His health, shaken by over exertion, now began to fail, and his physicians ordered him to seek repose and change of scene. His eyes were turned southward, and the result was his 'First Impressions of England and its people.' The publication of the well-known 'Vestiges of Creation' soon afterwards called forth his 'Footprints of the Creator.' The last book which he lived to finish was the autobiographical sketch on which he bestowed the title of 'Schools and Schoolmasters.' He had for some time been labouring, only too industriously, on a new work on geology. His lecture, two winters ago, in Exeter Hall, on 'The

Mosaic Periods;' his paper, read the summer before last to the British Association at Glasgow; and his lectures which were in course of delivery on 'The Noachian Deluge,' were, we believe, portions of the volume he was hurrying to completion when he was so suddenly struck down by the hand of death."

And what were the circumstances of the birth and boyhood of this remarkable man? Briefly these: he was born at Cromarty, in 1802; he came from a race of bold and hardy mariners. His father was a rough sailor, but a kind man. An anecdote is related of him, that when he was a boy he was sent to drown a litter of puppies, but he found the task impossible; so he tucked them up in his kilt and took them home, saying, "I couldna drown the little doggies, mother! and I brought them to you."

After serving his country in the navy faithfully and honourably, he was at the time of Hugh's birth master of a sloop. One sad stormy day this sloop, the "Friendship," lay insplinters on the bar of Findhorn; another vessel, however, was obtained, which in ten years after put to sea during the lull of a storm; but, sharing a worse fate than its predecessor, no vestige of crew or vessel was ever seen more!

This tragic event induced Hugh's two uncles to compensate in some measure for the severe loss which he had sustained. Before his father's death he had been sent to a "dame school," where he learned to read the Catechism, the Proverbs, the New Testament, and the Bible. The inducement to read was chiefly owing to the stories which reading was the key to. The stories of the Old and New Testament were soon mastered; then followed the usual round of "Jack the Giant Killer," &c., to the "Odyssey;" and, as a matter of course—the "Pilgrim's Progress." Then followed some harder reading: "The Scots Worthies," "Naphthali," "The Cloud of Witnesses," &c. "Wallace, the Hero of Scotland," was a special attraction.

The dame at the dame's school having exhausted her store upon Hugh, he was transferred to the grammar school of Cromarty. The dominie, however, took more kindly to his own ease and comfort than teaching; the consequence was, that if a boy preferred play to work—why, he was allowed to follow his inclination. The schoolmaster put Hugh into Latin—a change not much relished, as he soon desired to give up "The Rudiments" and go back to his English stories. Some of the Cromarty inhabitants not liking the small progress their sons made under the schoolmaster, established a subscription school on their own account. The teacher was clever, and competent for his duties; but, owing to intemperate habits, he had soon to give up his teaching. His successor was a licentiate of the Church of Scotland; he had to leave, however, in consequence of mixing up in a theological controversy. The third teacher gave up in despair. All this time, no doubt, Hugh and his companions had fine opportunities to make rural excursions, and indulge their strong propensities for out-door exercise.

Miller, in his "Schools and Schoolmasters"—one of the most interesting pieces of autobiography ever written—describes the natural wonders of Cromarty. "The Cromarty Sutors," he says, "have their two lines of caves—an ancient line, hollowed by the waves many centuries ago, when the sea stood, in relation to the land, from fifteen to thirty feet higher along our shores than it does now; and a modern line, which the surf is still engaged in scooping out. Many of the older caves are lined with stalactites, deposited by springs that, filtering through the cracks in their passage, acquire what is known as a *petrifying*, though, in reality, only an encrusting quality. And these stalactites, under the name of 'white stones made by the water,' formed of old—as in that Cave of Slains specially mentioned by Buchanan and the chroniclers, and in those caverns of the Peak so quaintly described by Cotton—one of the grand marvels of the place. Almost all the old gazetteers sufficiently copious in their details to mention Cromarty at all, refer to its 'Dropping Cave' as a marvellous marvel-producing cavern; and this 'Dropping Cave' is but one of many that look out upon the sea from the precipices of the Southern Sutor, in whose dark recesses the drops ever tinkle, and the stony ceilings ever grow." Sir George Mackenzie of Coul, anxious to see the sort of stones of which the caves were composed, sent a commission to the minister of the parish for specimens. He, in his turn, employed a poor man, a nailor, to explore the caves. It so happened, however, that the nailor's wife had been accidentally drowned, and, if report spoke true, was subsequently seen at night-fall in various lone places. By no means anxious to give his wife an opportunity to meet him in the deep recesses of the cave, the nailor had prudently confined himself to the entrance, and, as the result, brought home a heap of rubbish—but not a particle of stalactite, In this emergency Hugh's uncles were appealed to—who were delighted at the opportunity of thus forwarding the interests of science; providing themselves with torches and a hammer, they set out for the caves; Hugh, of course, forming one of the party. "In the deepest recesses of the caves, where the floor becomes covered with uneven sheets of stalagmite, and where long spear-like icicles and drapery-like foldings, pure as the marble of the sculptor, descend from above, or hang pendant over the sides, we found in abundance magnificent specimens for Sir George. The entire expedition was one of wondrous interest; and I returned next day to school, big with description and narrative, to excite, by truths more marvellous than fiction, the curiosity of my class fellows." So wrote Hugh, in after years.

He failed to interest his companions to the extent of inducing them to devote their play hours to the exploration of the caves. There was a solitary aspect about them, which did not conform to their buoyant hilarity; they preferred their old play-ground, it being almost within hail of their homes. There was one little fellow, however, who had won the confidence of Hugh, who was his constant companion in his rambles, whose curiosity was largely excited about the caves. With this companion, and armed with John Feddes's hammer, they started for the Doocot Cave, one fine spring morning. Miller, in his own graphic way, thus narrates the adventure:

"I stood on the beach opposite the eastern promontory that, with its stern granite wall, bars access for ten days out of every fourteen to the wonders of the Doocot, and saw it stretching provokingly out into green water. It was hard to be disappointed, and the caves so near. The tide was a low neap, and if we wanted a passage dry shod, it behoved us to wait for at least a week; but neither of us understood the philosophy of neap tides at that period. I was quite sure I had got round at low water with my uncles not a great many days before, and we both inferred that, if we but succeeded in getting round now, it would be quite a pleasure to wait among the caves inside until such time as the fall of the tide should lay bare a passage for our return. A narrow and broken shelf runs along the promontory, on which, by the assistance of the naked toe and the toe-nail it is just possible to creep. We succeeded in scrambling up to it, and then, crawling outwards on all-fours—the precipice, as we proceeded, beetling more and more formidable from above, and the water becoming greener and deeper below—we reached the outer point of the promontory; and then, doubling the cape on a still narrower margin—the water, by a reverse process, becoming shallower and less green as we advanced inwards—we found the ledge terminating just where, after clearing the sea, it overhung the gravelly beach, at an elevation of nearly ten feet. Adown we both dropped, proud of our success; up splashed the rattling gravel as we fell; and, for at least the whole coming week—though we were unaware of the extent of our good luck at the time—the marvels of the Doocot Cave might be regarded as solely and exclusively our own. For one short seven days—to borrow emphasis from the phraseology of Carlyle—'they were our own, and no other man's.'"

After exploring minutely the wonders that lay "all before them," they thought it strange that the tide, while there was yet a full fathom of water beneath the brow of the promontory, ceased to fall, and then, after a quarter of an hour's space, began actually to creep upwards on the beach. Hoping there might be some mistake in the matter, which the evening tide would rectify, they continued to amuse themselves. Hour after hour passed, and yet the tide still rose. "We made," says Hugh, "desperate efforts to scale the precipices, and on two several occasions succeeded in reaching shelves midway among the crags where the sparrowhawk and the raven build; but though we had climbed well enough to render our return a matter of bare possibility, there was no possibility whatever of getting farther up: the cliffs had never been scaled before, and they were not destined to be scaled now. And so, as the twilight deepened, and the precarious footing became every moment more doubtful and precarious still, we had just to give up in despair. 'Wouldn't care for myself,' said the poor little fellow, my companion, bursting into tears, 'if it were not for my mother; but what will my mother say?' 'Wouldn't care neither,' said I, with a heavy heart; 'but it's just backwater, we'll get out at twall.' we retreated together into one of the shallower and drier caves, and, clearing a little spot of its rough stones, and then groping along the rocks for the dry grass that in the spring season hangs from them in withered tufts, we formed for ourselves a most uncomfortable bed, and lay down in each other's arms." Hugh's companion had only the real evils of their position to deal with, but he had imaginary ones—much more serious in their effects. About a month previous he had seen the body of a drowned seaman, which, as all drowned persons long exposed to the water, presented a very awful sight. While they were in the cave Hugh continually fancied he saw the corpse. Towards midnight they crept down in the uncertain light, to ascertain if the tide had not fallen sufficiently to yield them a passage. The waves were where the tide-line rested twelve hours before. A vessel was observed crossing the wake of the moon, but all their efforts to arrest its progress were fruitless. There was nothing to be done but once more seek their comfortless bed within the cave. They had scarcely dropped to sleep ere both were roused by a loud shout. There was a brief pause, and then two boats, strongly manned, shot round the western promontory. The whole town had become alarmed by the intelligence that two little boys had straggled away in the morning to the rocks of the Southern Sutor, and had not found their way back. All ended well, notwithstanding fearful forbodings. Some enormously bad verses, so Hugh said, were composed upon the adventure, which found admiring auditors at the various tea-tables of Cromarty, and had the further honour of being recited at the town boarding-school examination by a pretty young lady.

Notwithstanding the small amount of education possessed by Miller, owing chiefly to the squabbles and incapacity of the schoolmasters, the last of whom he deemed a pedant and coxcomb, Hugh, at seventeen years of age, became a stonemason's apprentice. His uncles desired to send him to college, and would have done so, but he objected, not considering that he had any fitness for any of the professions. His first day in the Cromarty stone-quarry, he thus describes:—

"A heap of loose fragments, which had fallen from above, blocked up the face of the quarry, and my first employment was to clear them away. The friction of the shovel soon blistered my hands; but the pain was by no means very severe, and I wrought hard and willingly, that I might see how the huge strata below, which presented so firm and unbroken a frontage, were to be torn up and removed. Picks, and wedges, and levers were applied by my brother workmen; and, simple and rude as I have been accustomed to regard these implements, I found I had much to learn in the way of using them. They all proved inefficient, however, and the workmen had to bore into one of the inferior strata, and employ gunpowder. The process was new to me, and I deemed it a highly amusing one; it had the merit, too, of being attended with some such degree of danger as a boating or a rock excursion, and had thus an interest independent of its novelty. We had a few capital shots; the fragments flew in every direction, and an immense mass of the diluvium came toppling down, bearing with it two dead birds that in a recent storm had crept into one of the deep fissures to die in the shelter. I felt a new interest in examining them. The one was a pretty cock goldfinch, with its hood of vermillion, and its wings inlaid with the gold to which it owes its name, as unsoiled and smooth as if it had been preserved for a museum. The other, a somewhat rarer bird, of the woodpecker tribe, was variegated with light blue and a greyish-yellow. I was engaged in admiring the poor little things—more disposed to be sentimental, perhaps, than if I had been ten years older, and thinking of the contrast between the warmth and jollity of their green summer haunts, and the cold and darkness of their last retreat—when I heard our employer bidding the workmen lay by their tools. I looked up, and saw the sun sinking behind the thick firwood beside us, and the long dark shadows of the trees stretching downwards towards the shore.

"This was no very formidable beginning of the course of life I had so much dreaded. To be sure, my hands were a little sore, and I felt nearly as much fatigued as if I had been climbing among the rocks; but I had wrought and been useful, and had enjoyed the day fully as much as usual. It was no small matter, too, that the evening, converted, by a rare transmutation, into the delicious 'blink of rest' which Burns so truthfully describes, was all my own. I was as light of heart next morning as any of my brother workmen. There had been a smart frost during the night, and the rime lay white on the grass as we passed onwards through the fields; but the sun rose in a clear atmosphere, and the day mellowed as it advanced, into one of those delightful days of early spring, which give so pleasing an earnest of whatever is mild and genial in the better half of the year. All the workmen rested at mid-day, and I went to enjoy my half-hour alone on a mossy knoll in the neighbouring wood, which commands through the trees a wide prospect of the bay and the opposite shore. There was not a wrinkle on the water, nor a cloud in the sky, and the branches were as moveless in the calm as if they had been traced on canvas. From a wooded promontory that stretched half way across the frith, there ascended a thin column of smoke. It rose straight as the line of a plummet for more than a thousand yards, and then, on reaching a thinner stratum of air, spread out equally on every side, like the foliage of a stately tree. Ben Wyvis rose to the west, white with the yet unwasted snows of winter, and as sharply defined in the clear atmosphere as if all its sunny slopes and blue retiring hollows had been chiselled in marble. A line of snow ran along the opposite hills; all above was white, and all below was purple. They reminded me of the pretty French story, in which an old artist is described as tasking the ingenuity of his future son-in-law, by giving him as a subject for his pencil a flower-piece composed of only white flowers, of which the one-half were to bear their proper colour, the other half a deep purple hue, and yet all be perfectly natural, and how the young man resolved the riddle and gained his mistress, by introducing a transparent purple vase into the picture, and making the light pass through it on the flowers that were drooping over the edge. I returned to the quarry, convinced that a very exquisite pleasure may be a very cheap one, and that the busiest employments may afford leisure enough to enjoy it."

As the work progressed he was struck with the

varying appearance of the solid rocks upon which the workmen were employed. In addition to the novelty of labour, he found ample time for thought, in the fresh objects that were continually meeting his view. He was at this time laying the foundation of the future geologist. After working some time in the Cromarty quarries, Miller began to work across the Moray Frith. Here new wonders met his astonished gaze. Geological deposits, rich in the deepest interest, were everywhere around. The observations he then made, prompted only by the interest of the passing hour, were the ground-work of much of his future eminence. When the labour season was over, Hugh, in the company of a cousin, made a tour in the Highlands. During the three months recess he renewed some old acquaintanceships and formed new ones; and when spring came again, went once more to his stone-cutting. The failure of his master, however, before midsummer, threw him and the rest of the men out of employment. His next engagement brought him into contact with the Bothy system, the first night of which he passed in a hay-loft, the only place of shelter he could find. The position was so new and uncomfortable that hecould not sleep. About midnight he got up to look out of the window, which opened upon a dreary moor, a ruinous chapel, and solitary burial-ground. His attention was aroused by observing a light amid the grave-stones, and presently a low wailing scream came upon his ear. In a moment after, the door of the mansion-house was thrown open, and the servants ran out to claim the assistance of the workmen: a poor creature—mad Bell—had broken from her confinement. Their services were not needed, as two men were already dragging her to her cottage, who proceeded to bind her to the damp earth. Miller and a comrade successfully remonstrated. The mad woman, as if a gleam of reason had flitted across her mind, turned her face upon the two youths, exclaiming: "Blessed are the merciful, for they shall obtain mercy."

This work coming to an end, Miller determined to try his fortune in Edinburgh. He found work when he arrived there, in the vicinity of Niddry Mill, where he first became practically acquainted with combinations amongst workmen. The strike in which they were then engaged he believed would not succeed in obtaining the object of the men. A monster meeting was projected, to be held on Bruntsfield Links, at which Hugh attended. But the spirit of the meeting did not accord with his views—he was glad to get away. At this time Edinburgh was the centre of a literary galaxy which has never been surpassed at any period in the history of the Scottish metropolis. There were Jeffrey, and Wilson, and Dugald Stewart, and Walter Scott—names that will be known while the English language is spoken. Miller was so unfortunate as not to see any of these celebrities: one notable man, however, he both saw and heard—Dr. M'Crie, the biographer of Knox and Melville.

After stone-cutting for about two years in and about Edinburgh, Hugh found himself with symptoms of disease of the lungs and chest, brought on by his employment; he determined to return to Cromarty to recruit. For some months after his return he laboured under the illness which proves fatal to so many stonemasons. In the meanwhile he employed himself in cutting tablets and tombstones. He afterwards visited Inverness for the same purpose, where he obtained excellent employment. It was at this place that he put forth his first literary venture—a small volume of poems, serviceable only in bringing him into contact with some literary men.

The stone-cutting proving so prejudicial to Hugh's health, it was determined that some other employment should be obtained for him. A branch of the Commercial Bank having been opened in Cromarty, he was fortunate enough to be appointed accountant. Having obtained a little instruction at the Linlithgow Bank, Hugh, with very little practice, became very expert in the duties of his new position; and yet he found time also to send forth his "Scenes and Legends of the North of Scotland."

The second year of his engagement at the bank he made Lydia Mackenzie Fraser Mrs. Miller; he wrote, also, at this time, for "Wilson's Tales of the Borders," and "Chamber's Journal." Subsequently, the House

o. Lords had made their decision in the celebrated Auchterarder case, which called forth a pamphlet fiom Hugh Miller's pen. It was entitled, "A Letter from one of the Scotch People, to the Right Honourable Lord Brougham." It met with immense success. The classic Gladstone pronounced favourably on its merits. A second pamphlet was equally well received.

The free-church party were at that time on the look-out for an editor for their paper. They were not long in making the discovery that the man that wrote the pamphlets, was the man to edit the "Witness." Miller accepted the offer that was made to him, and closed his accountantship at the Cromarty Bank. Then commenced his intense life of literary labour, in which he brought into full play his peculiar genius and the experience of his life. Subsequently he appeared as a lecturer, the Duke of Argyle occupying the chair.

When he had nearly finished "The Testimony of the Rocks," his greatest work, his medical adviser forbade, for a time at least, any more literary labour. Miller had become subject to dreams and wakeful appearances, so that frequently he left his bed more wearied than when he entered it. To relieve these distressing symptoms, Mrs. Miller invited a friend to pass one evening with them. The time passed genially and pleasantly. Mr. Miller entertained them at tea by reading Cowper's "Castaway," and the sonnet to Mary Unwin. After spending some time in his study he took a bath, which had been recommended. Next morning his body was found lifeless on the floor! the feet upon the study rug, the chest pierced with the ball of a revolver, which had fallen into the bath by his side!

This was a sad, mournful ending in the meridian of Hugh Miller's mental power! Impressively does the lesson come to the student, who, careless of the limited physical power with which he is endowed, seeks to attain, by midnight labour and excessive mental pressure, results in weeks, which would fairly occupy months, or even years. Had Hugh Miller devoted only half his time to literature, and the other half to those exercises which brace the will as well as the muscles, he might, and doubtless would, have been living this day, to diffuse the riches of the rarest intellect, to warn back oppression and the oppressor, to open up pages of the primeval world, and to inculcate a taste for science and literature, wherever books are read and the human voice heard.

"Miller broke down," says the "Spectator," "because he was disobeying the laws of the creation in which he lived. He was concentrating the whole force of his nature in one pursuit, and suffering himself to be carried away by the excitement into which he had worked himself. He was necessarily arrested. It is imperative that the laws of the creation be obeyed, it is *not* imperative that they be 'understood.' Man, indeed, may for his own benefit work out a better intellectual comprehension of the laws under which he lives, but he must do it consistently with obedience. He cannot snatch a further revelation, nor will nature permit excess, even when the object of the excess is laudable or pious. Whether understood or not in the critical sense, the law goes on relentless, and all who stand across its path are mowed down."

Some little time ago the "Inverness Courier" had this notice :—

"The foundation stone of the monument to be erected at Cromarty, in memory of Hugh Miller, was laid on Wednesday afternoon. Everything was done by the inhabitants that could render the ceremony impressive, and to exhibit the sincere pride which they feel in being able to refer to our distinguished countryman as a native of their town, born and brought up among themselves. Probably not less than five or six hundred persons were present. The monument will consist of a pillar about fifty feet high, surmounted by a statue of Hugh Miller, to be sculptured by Mr. Handyside Ritchie. The base is of old red sandstone, taken from the shore quarry, the first scene of Mr. Miller's labours, and of his geological researches. The rest of the work will be completed in a more durable stone, and of a yellowish colour, obtained from the quarry at Davidston. The following inscription is to be engraved upon the base :—

SAMUEL DREW:

SHOEMAKER'S APPRENTICE AND SMUGGLER; AFTERWARDS MASTER OF ARTS, AND THE FIRST METAPHYSICIAN OF HIS TIME. AUTHOR OF WORKS ON THE IMMORTALITY OF THE SOUL AND THE RESURRECTION OF THE BODY, ETC.

THE instances are so numerous, of great men being in their youthful years poor and subjected to privation, unfriended and uninstructed, that the reader of biography almost looks upon that condition of early life as necessary to future greatness. There can be no doubt that overcoming difficulties is a training and an education, which no amount of mere scholastic teaching can supply; and the boy who succeeds in throwing from him habits and practices formed in the company of dissolute companions, has laid the foundation of a life of usefulness and honour. If our admiration is excited at the narration of some deed of daring or perilous adventure, cited as an instance of the pith and prowess of Englishmen, how ought we to treasure every example of perseverance under difficulties, especially, as in the case of Samuel Drew, those difficulties being overcome, a position of intellectual greatness was attained, not surpassed by the most gifted scholars of any age?

Samuel Drew was born near St. Austell, in Cornwall, March 3, 1765. His father was a husbandman, and followed, also, the occupation of "steaming;" but neither means of living secured his family against the chilling influences of poverty. But still, he contrived to send his two boys, Samuel and Jabez, to a day-school at St. Austell. Jabez was evidently in love with the instruction he received; but Samuel, the subject of this sketch, preferred to absent himself from the school as often as opportunity permitted. His mother partially supplied the deficiency, by giving him reading lessons at home; and his brother, also, gave him some little instruction in writing. His mother appears to have been an invaluable woman, whose simple teaching left an impression that remained with him his life long. Of one incident he thus speaks: "I well remember, in my early days, when my mother was alive, that she invariably took my brother and me by the hand, and led us to the house of prayer. Her kind advice and instruction were unremitting; and even when death had closed her eyes in darkness, the impression remained long upon my mind, and I sighed for a companion to accompany me thither. On one occasion, I well recollect, we were returning from the chapel, at St. Austell, on a bright and beautiful starlight night, when my mother pointed out the stars as the work of an Almighty Parent, to whom we were indebted for every blessing. Struck with the representation, I felt a degree of gratitude and adoration which no language could express, and through nearly all the night enjoyed ineffable rapture."

Rude and callous as Samuel was, the death of his mother much affected him. His best friend was gone. By the time he was eight years old he was placed to work as a *buddle-boy*, for which he received three halfpence per day. The example and immorality of the boys amongst whom he worked, did him serious injury. Samuel's father was a religious man; but owing to his engagements to preach to strangers, he had no time to devote to his own household; thus Samuel and his brother were neglected.

In the year 1776, and before he had finished his eleventh year, Samuel was apprenticed to a shoemaker, residing about three miles from St. Austell. His condition there is best expressed in his own words: "My new abode," he wrote, "at St. Blazey, and new engagements, were far from being pleasing. To any of the comforts and conveniences of life I was an entire stranger, and by every member of the family was viewed as as underling, come thither to subserve their wishes, or obey their mandates. To his trade of shoemaker my master added that of farmer. He had a few acres of ground under his care, and was a sober, industrious man; but, unfortunately for me, nearly one half of my time was taken up in agricultural pursuits. On this account, I made no proficiency in my business, and felt no solicitude to rise above the farmers' boys with whom I daily associated. While in this place, I suffered many hardships. When, after having been in the fields all day, I came home with cold feet, and damp and dirty stockings, if the oven had been heated during the day, I was permitted to throw my stockings into it, that they might be dry against the following morning; but frequently have I nad to put them on in precisely the same state in which I had left them the preceding evening. To mend my stockings, I had no one; and frequently have I wept at the holes, which I could not conceal; though, when fortunate enough to procure a stocking-needle and some worsted, I have drawn the outlines of the hole together, and made what I thought a tolerable job.

"During my apprenticeship many bickerings and unpleasant occurrences took place. Some of these preyed with so much severity on my mind, that several times I had determined to run away, and either enlist on board of a privateer, or a man-of-war. A kind and gracious Providence, however, invariably defeated my purposes, and threw unexpected obstacles in the way, at the moment when my schemes were apparently on the eve of accomplishment.

"In some part of my servitude, a few numbers

of the 'Weekly Entertainer' were brought to my master's house. This little publication, which was then extensively circulated in the west of England, contained many tales and anecdotes which greatly interested me. Into the narratives of adventures connected with the then American war, I entered, with all the zeal of a partisan, on the side of the Americans. The history of Paul Jones, the 'Serapis,' and the 'Bon Homme Richard,' by frequent reading, and daily dwelling upon them in the almost solitary chamber of my thoughts, grew up into a lively image in my fancy, and I felt a strong desire to join myself to a pirate ship; but, as I had no money, and scarcely any clothes, the idea and scheme were vain. Besides these entertainers, the only book which I remember to have seen in the house, was an odd number of the History of England, about the time of the Commonwealth. With the reading of this I was at first pleased; but when, by frequent perusal, I had nearly learned it by heart, it became monotonous, and was shortly afterwards thrown aside. With this, I lost not only a *disposition* for reading, but almost *ability* to read. The clamour of my companions and others engrossed nearly the whole of my attention, and, so far as my slender means would allow, carried me onward towards the vortex of dissipation.

"One circumstance I must not omit to notice, during this period of my life, as it strikingly marks the superintending providence of God. I was sent one day to a neighbouring common, bordering on the sea-shore, to see that my master's sheep were safe, and together. Having discharged my duty, I looked towards the sea, which, I presume, could not be less than two hundred feet below me. I saw the sea-birds busily employed, providing for their young, flying about midway between the sea and the elevation on which I stood, when I was seized with a strange resolution to descend the cliff, and make my way to the place where they had built their nests. It was a desperate and dangerous attempt; but I determined to persevere. My danger increased at every step; and at length, I found that a projecting rock prohibited my further progress. I then attempted to retreat, but found the task more difficult and hazardous than that I had already encountered. I was now perched on a narrow ledge of a rock, about a hundred feet below the edge of the cliff, and nearly the same height above the ocean. To turn myself round, I found to be impossible: there was no hand to help, no eye to pity, no voice to soothe. My spirits began to fail. I saw nothing before me but inevitable destruction, and dreaded the moment when I should be dashed in pieces upon the rocks below. At length, by creeping backwards about one-eighth of an inch at a step, I reached a nook where I was able to turn, and happily succeeded in escaping the destruction which I had dreaded."

This was not his last adventure that nearly terminated with the loss of life. He had a certain amount of shrewdness and cunning in his composition that predisposed him for speculation and adventure. This was, no doubt, induced to a large extent by the dissatisfaction he felt at the menial drudgery to which he was subjected by his mistress. This naturally induced him to seek companionship *from* home, there being no love or attraction *at* home. The result was that he formed the acquaintance of the idle and dissolute, and became, as a consequence, vicious and morally debased. At this time Cornwall was celebrated for the number of smugglers to be found on the coast. It would have been strange indeed if Samuel, with his love of adventure and course of reading, had not connected himself with these domestic freebooters. Of course his absence on these occasions was without the knowledge or consent of his master. But the boy who was only deterred from joining Paul Jones because he had no money or clothes, would not hesitate to run a cargo of French goods or foreign spirits, without much fear either of master or revenue officer. Samuel's respect for his master would be considerably diminished from the fact that he took no means to teach him his business; this conjoined to the treatment of his mistress, who seemed to view him as the most abject menial, would necessarily render him callous and intractable. One of his early associates remarked: "I believe Sam was a difficult boy to manage; but he was made worse by the treatment he received. I was once in the shop, when, for a very small offence, his master struck him violently with a last, and maimed him for a time. Such usage only made him sturdy, and caused him to dislike his master and his work." This treatment determined him to leave his master; when he did so, his funds where only sixteenpence halfpenny! He subsequently thus described his adventure: "I thought of travelling to Plymouth, to seek a berth on board a King's ship. Instead of taking the short road, where I feared my father might fall in with me, I went on towards Liskeard, through the night, and feeling fatigued, went into a hayfield and slept. My luggage was no incumbrance, as the whole of my property, besides the clothes I wore, was contained in a small handkerchief. Not knowing how long I should have to depend on my slender stock of cash, I found it necessary to use the most rigid economy. Having to pay a halfpenny for passing either a ferry or toll-bridge, feeling my present situation, and knowing nothing of my future prospects, this small call upon my funds distressed me; I wept as I went on my way; and, even to the present time, I feel a pang when I recollect the circumstance.

"The exertion of walking, and the fresh morning air, gave me a keener appetite than I thought it prudent to indulge. I, however, bought a penny loaf at the first place I passed where bread was sold, and, with a halfpennyworth of milk, in a farmer's house, ate half of my loaf for breakfast. In passing through Liskeard, my attention was attracted by a shoemaker's shop, at the door of which a respectable-looking man, whom I supposed to be the master, was standing. Without any intention of seeking employment in this place, I asked him if he could give me work; and he, taking compassion, I suppose, on my sorry appearance, promised me employ the next morning. Before I could go to work tools were necessary, and I was obliged to lay out a shilling on these. Dinner, under such circumstances, was out of the question; for supper I bought another half-pennyworth of milk, ate the remainder of my loaf, and for my lodging had again recourse to the fields. In the morning I purchased another penny loaf, and commenced my labour. My employer soon found that I was a miserable tool; yet he treated me kindly, and his son took me beside him in the shop, and gave me instruction. I had now but one penny left, and this I wished to husband till my labour brought a supply; so for dinner I tied my apron-string tighter, and went on with my work. My abstinence subjected me to the jeers of my shop-mates, thus rendering the pangs of hunger doubly bitter. One of them, I remember, said to another, 'Where does our shopmate dine?' and the response was, 'Oh! he always dines at the sign of the mouth.' Half of the penny loaf which I took with me in the morning I had allotted for my supper; but before night came, I had pinched it nearly all away in mouthfuls through mere hunger. Very reluctantly, I laid out my last penny, and with no enviable feelings, sought my former lodging in the open air. With no other breakfast than the fragments of my last loaf, I again sat down to work. At dinner time —looking, no doubt, very much famished—my master kindly said, 'If you wish, I will let you have a little money on account;' an offer which I very joyfully accepted. This was, however, my last day's employment here. Discovering that I was a runaway apprentice, my new master dismissed me, with a recommendation to return to the old one; and while he was talking, my brother came to the door with a horse to take me home."

He returned, however, on condition that he should not be expected to resume work with his old master, with whom arrangements were subsequently made, and Samuel's indentures cancelled. After staying at home for a few months, work was obtained for him with Mr. Williams, at Millbrook. This place was more congenial to Samuel's tastes and disposition. It was remarkable for the stir and bustle which pervaded it, being a naval station of some importance. He was also more comfortable in his situation; there were a number of worknen employed, the work being neat and various—a great contrast to the solitary state and rough work of his former situation. Owing to his being, as he calls himself, "a wretched tool at the trade," his average weekly earnings was not more than eight shillings. He had great need, therefore, not only to exercise diligence in his calling, but the most rigid economy. He used in after years to say, that Liskeard was not the only place where he *had tied his apron-string tighter for a dinner*.

He remained in this situation about a year. His shopmates regretted his leaving. One of them said afterwards: "I very well remember that in our disputes, those who could get Sam Drew on their side always made sure of victory; and he had so much good humour and drollery that we all liked him, and were very sorry when he went away."

The reason of his removal was owing to one of his smuggling adventures, which nearly terminated fatally. "Notice was given throughout Crafthole, one evening about the month of December, 1784, that a vessel laden with contraband goods was on the coast, and would be ready that night to discharge her cargo. At nightfall Samuel, with others, made towards the port. One party remained on the rocks, to make signals and dispose of the goods when landed; the other, of which he was one, manned the boats. The night was intensely dark, and but little progress had been made in discharging the vessel's cargo, when the wind rose, with a heavy sea. To prevent their vessel being driven on the rocks, the seamen found it necessary to stand off from the port, thus increasing the hazard of the boatmen. Unfavourable as these circumstances were, all seemed resolved to persevere; and several trips were made between the vessel and the shore. The wind continuing to increase, one of the men belonging to the boat in which Samuel sat had his hat blown off, and in striving to recover it, upset the boat. Three of the men were immediately drowned: Samuel and two or three others clung to the boat for a considerable time; but, finding that it was drifting from the port, they were obliged to abandon it, and sustain themselves by swimming. They were now about two miles from the shore, and the darkness prevented them from ascertaining its direction. Samuel had given himself up as lost, when he laid hold of a mass of sea-weed, which afforded him a temporary support. At length he approached some rocks near the shore, upon which he and two of the men, the only survivors of seven, succeeded in getting; but they were so benumbed with cold, and so much exhausted with their exertion and swimming, that it was with the utmost difficulty they could maintain their position against the force of the sea, which sometimes broke over them. Their perilous situation was not unperceived by their companions; yet their calls for help, if heard, were for a long time disregarded. When the vessel had delivered her cargo, and put to sea, a boat was despatched to take them off; and now, finding in what condition Samuel and his wrecked companions

Samuel Drew's perilous Adventure with the Smugglers.

were, after having been three hours in the water, and half of that time swimming about, the others endeavoured to compensate, by a show of kindness, for their previous inhumanity. Life being nearly extinct, the sufferers were carried to a neighbouring farm-house, and the inmates compelled by threats to admit them. A fire was kindled on the hearth, and fresh faggots piled on it, while the half-drowned men, who were placed in a recess of the chimney, unable to relieve themselves, were compelled to endure the excessive heat which their ignorant companions thought necessary to restore animation. One of the party, supposing too, that fire within would not be less efficacious than fire without, and believing brandy to be a universal remedy, brought a keg of it from the cargo landed, and, with the characteristic recklessness of a sailor and a smuggler, knocked in the head with a hatchet, and presented them with a *bowlful*. Whether," said Mr. Drew, subsequently, " we drank of it or not, I do not know: certainly not to the extent recommended, or I should not now be alive to tell the tale. My first sensation was that of extreme cold. Although half-roasted, it was a long while before I felt the fire, that burnt my legs, and occasioned wounds, the marks of which I shall carry to my grave. After leaving the farm-house, I had to walk about two miles through deep snow, to my lodgings. When I think of the complicated perils of that night, I am astonished I ever survived them."

When he heard of the adventure his father exclaimed: "Alas! what will be the end of my poor unhappy boy?" In order to secure him against any future like temptation, he procured him employment with a saddler in St. Austell, who was commencing the shoemaking business. He went to this new situation in the January of 1785, being then in his twentieth year. At this period he says: "I was scarcely able to read, and almost totally unable to write. Literature was a term to which I could annex no idea. Grammar I knew not the meaning of. I was expert at follies, acute in trifles, and ingenious about nonsense. My master was by trade a saddler, had acquired some knowledge of bookbinding, and hired me to carry on the shoemaking for him. He was one of those men who will live anywhere, but will get rich nowhere. His shop was frequented by persons of a more respectable class than those with whom I had previously associated, and various topics became alternately the subjects of conversation. I listened with all that attention which my labours and good manners would permit, and obtained among them some little knowledge. Sometimes, when disputes ran high, I was appealed to; this acted as a stimulus. I examined dictionaries, picked up many words, and, from an attachment which I felt to books, which were occasionally brought to the shop to be bound, I began to have some view of the various theories with which they abounded. The more I read the more I felt my own ignorance—the more invincible became my energy to surmount it. Every leisure moment was now employed in reading one thing or other. Having to support myself by manual labour my time for reading was but little, and to overcome this disadvantage, my usual method was to place a book before me while at meat, and at every repast I read five or six pages. The custom has not forsaken me at the present moment."

He continues: "After having worked with this master several months, a neighbouring gentleman brought Locke's 'Essay on the understanding,' to be bound; I had never seen or heard of this work before. I took an occasion to look into it, and I thought his mode of reasoning very pleasing, and his arguments exceedingly strong. I watched all opportunities of reading for myself, and would willingly have laboured a fortnight to have the books. I had then no conception they could be obtained for money. They were, however, soon carried away, and with them all my future improvement by their means. The close and decisive manner of Mr. Locke's reasoning made on my mind an impression too deep to be easily effaced; and though I did not see his essay again for many years, yet the early impression was not forgotten, and it is from this accidental circumstance that I received my first bias for abstruse subjects.

"Locke's Essay set all my soul to think, to fear,

and to reason from all without and from all within. It gave the first metaphysical turn to my mind; and I cultivated the little knowledge of writing which I had acquired, in order to put down my reflections. It awakened me from my stupor, and induced me to form a resolution to abandon the grovelling views which I had been accustomed to entertain. In my new situation I found myself surrounded with books of various descriptions, and felt my taste for the acquirement of information return with renewed vigour, and increase in proportion to the means of indulgence, which were now placed fully within my reach. But here some new difficulties occurred, with which I found it painful to grapple. My knowledge of the import of words was as contracted as my ideas were scanty: so that I found it necessary to keep a dictionary continually by my side whilst I was reading, to which I was compelled constantly to refer. This was a tedious process. But in a little time the difficulty wore away, and my horizon of knowledge became enlarged."

What were the books that Drew read at this time little is known. No doubt, like other readers, he read pretty much all that came in his way. The first book, however, which he owned was the "Pilgrim's Progress," by the glorious dreamer. Its perusal afforded him, as it has afforded tens of thousands, constant and increasing delight.

About this time Samuel commenced business on

his own account. He had only fourteen shillings of his own; a friend, however, who had urged him to commence, said, "I'll lend you five pounds upon the security of your good character, and more if that is not enough; and I'll promise not to demand it till you can conveniently pay me." Samuel, on taking this important step, determined to adopt Dr. Franklin's maxims in his "Way to Wealth." He worked eighteen hours out of the twenty-four, and sometimes longer; his friends found him plenty of work, but until the bills could be sent to his customers he had no means to employ a journeyman. At the end of the year he had the satisfaction to know that he stood clear, the five pounds repaid, and a tolerable stock of leather on hand. Industry and economy had removed the necessity of going to bed supperless to avoid rising in debt; in addition to which, he was now enabled to gratify his desire for the acquisition of knowledge. The assistance which he was able to obtain in his business enabled him to devote to study the ordinary leisure of a common workman; this was all he desired. He says: "In this situation, I felt an internal vigour prompting me to exertion, but was unable to determine what direction I should take. The sciences lay before me. I discovered a charm in each, but was unable to embrace them all, and hesitated in making a selection. I had learned that,

> 'One science only will one genius fit,
> So vast is art, so narrow human wit.'

"At first I felt such an attachment to astronomy, that I resolved to confine my views to the study of that science; but I soon found myself too defective in arithmetic to make any proficiency. Modern history was my next object; but I quickly discovered that more books and time were necessary than I could either purchase or spare, and on this account history was abandoned. In the region of metaphysics I saw neither of the above impediments. It appeared to be a thorny path; but I determined, nevertheless, to enter, and accordingly began to tread it." On being asked, subsequently, if he had not studied astronomy, he said: "I once had a very great desire for it, for I thought it suitable to the genius of my mind, and I think so still: but then,

> 'Chill penury repressed the noble rage,
> And froze the genial current of the soul.'

Dangers and difficulties I did not fear, while I could bring the powers of my mind to bear upom them, and force myself a passage. To metaphysics I then applied myself, and became what the world and my good friend Dr. Clarke call, a METAPHYSICIAN."

Besides this study he had contracted a love for the discussion of the absorbing politics of the day. The American war was at that time occupying a large part of public attention. Drew entered so deeply in the discussion that he could not have been more interested if his livelihood had depended upon the issue. The neighbours crowded into his shop, and he went into his neighbours' with no other intention than to discuss the news. To make up for this loss of time he had frequently to work until midnight. One night, when he was so engaged, some youngster shouted through the key-hole of the door, "Shoe-maker! shoemaker! work by night, and run about by day!" "Had a pistol," said Drew, "been fired off at my ear, I could not have been more dismayed or confounded. I dropped my work, saying to my-self, 'True, true! but you shall never have that to say of me again.' I have never forgotten it; and while I recollect anything, I never shall. To me it was as the voice of God, and it has been a word in season throughout my life. I learned from it not to leave till to-morrow the work of to-day, or to idle when I ought to be working. From that time I turned over a new leaf. I ceased to venture on the restless sea of politics, or trouble myself about mat-ters which did not concern me."

"During several years," he further wrote, "all my leisure hours were devoted to reading or scribbling anything which happened to pass my mind; but I do not recollect that it ever interrupted my business, though it frequently broke in upon my rest. On my labour depended my livelihood—literary pursuits were only my amusement. Common prudence had taught me the lesson which Marmontel has so happily expressed: 'Secure to yourself a livelihood independent of literary success, and put into the lottery only the overplus of time. Woe to him who depends wholly on his pen! Nothing is more casual. The man who makes shoes is sure of his wages—the man who writes a book is never sure of anything.'"

The books he read at this time were Milton, Young, and Cowper; Pope's Ethical Epistles he frequently perused, and Goldsmith's works he highly valued, having committed to memory the whole of the "Deserted Village." The knowledge he thus received he would frequently turn over with his own workmen, rendering that plain and palpable which was difficult and abstruse. In April, 1791, he married the daughter of Jacob Halls, of St. Austell, on which occasion it is recorded that his wedding coat was "as good as new, of a plum colour, with bright buttons, very little worn, and quite a bargain." He was now esteemed as a respectable tradesman, and had exercised his ability as a local preacher amongst the Wesleyans, amongst whom he had become very popular.

His first literary effort was a poetical epistle to his sister, which was followed by several other metrical compositions. His manner of study he has himself related: "During my literary pursuits I regularly and constantly attended my business, and do not recollect that one customer was ever disappointed by me through these means. My mode of writing and study may have in them, perhaps, something peculiar. Immersed in the common concerns of life, I endeavour to lift my thoughts to objects more sublime than those with which I am surrounded, and, while attending to my trade, I sometimes catch the fibres of an argument, which I endeavour to note, and keep a pen and ink by me for that purpose. In this state, what I can collect through the day remains on any paper which I have at hand, till the business of the day is despatched, and my shop shut, when, in the midst of my family, I endeavour to analyse such thoughts as had crossed my mind during the day. I have no study—I have no retirement—I write amidst the cries and cradles of my children, and frequently, when I review what I have written, endeavour to cultivate the 'art to blot.' Such are the methods which I have pursued, and such the disadvantages under which I write." He usually sat on a low nursing chair by the kitchen fire, with the bellows on his knees for a desk!

Samuel was first induced to become an author in consequence of a friend, a young surgeon, imbibing the principles of Voltaire, Rousseau, Gibbon, and Hume. With this gentleman Samuel had debates from time to time, the groundwork being the newly published "Age of Reason," by Paine. These discussions ultimately resulted in the gentleman's renouncing his infidel opinions, and his acceptance of the truth of revelation. Drew having committed the arguments to paper, as the debate proceeded, at the conclusion submitted the MS. to two competent friends, who advised their immediate publication, which was done. The publication of this pamphlet secured him many warmly attached friends. His next venture was an elegiac poem, which, owing to local circumstances, became very popular. But poetry was certainly not Samuel's *forte*. At this time the Rev. Richard Polwhele, Vicar of Manaccan, Cornwall, had issued a little work: "Anecdotes of Methodism," which was a very severe and unwarranted attack upon that body of Christians. Samuel answered the book. The result was one of the severest and justly merited castigations that a religious libeller ever received. Polwhele was not only silenced, but he afterwards became a warm friend and admirer of Drew. When Samuel published his great work, "Essay on the Soul," which was the next printed after the "Reply," Polwhele reviewed the work in the "Anti-jacobin Review." This spontaneous act redounded to his credit as a scholar and a Christian. Drew, by his publications, had now established himself as an author of some repute. A visit to "the metaphysical shoemaker" was deemed an essential by all strangers. Drew was not much puffed up by this public notice. He said: "These gentlemen certainly honour me by their visits; but I do not forget that many of them merely wish to say, that they have seen the cobbler who wrote a book."

Drew was next engaged upon his largest work—his essay on the "Identity and Resurrection of the Human Body." This occupied a considerable amount of time, was written and rewritten, and was, before publication, submitted to the criticism and examination of the members of the London Philological Society. Eight hundred copies were at once subscribed for, the author receiving five hundred copies for the copyright. When it was published only one or two reviews appeared. This, as it was subsequently found, was not owing to any slight on the part of the editors of the serials of the time, but owing to the absence of persons capable to enter into the spirit of the work. One London bookseller actually wrote to Drew requesting him to review his own work. To this request he made answer: "Such things may be among the tricks of trade, but never will I soil my fingers by meddling with them. My work shall honestly meet its fate. If it be praised, I shall doubtless be gratified—if censured, instructed; if it drop still born from the press, I will endeavour to be contented." It was soon after the publication of this work that Mr. Drew was elected a member of the Manchester Philological Society. The next year witnessed Drew withdrawing from shoemaking with the intention of devoting himself exclusively to literature. His first work was in connection with Dr. Coke, whom he assisted in finishing his "Commentary on the Bible," his "History of the West Indians," and other works.

In 1806 Drew commenced to write for the "Eclectic Review," on the recommendation of Dr. Clarke. In 1812, he competed for the Burnet prize on the "Being and Attributes of the Deity." He was not successful, however. The first prize was awarded to Dr. Brown, then Principal of Marischal College; and the second prize to Dr. Sumner, afterwards Bishop of Chester. Drew's Essay was afterwards published in two octavo volumes, and an edition of a thousand copies sold.

It will now only be needful, in this rapid sketch of this wonderful self-taught man, merely to indicate his subsequent labours. First, then, he was engaged to write a "History of Cornwall," and a "Life of Dr. Coke," at that Divine's special request; then he assumed the entire editorship of the "Imperial Magazine," published by Mr. Fisher, in Liverpool, where Drew then resided. In 1821, the degree of A. M. was conferred upon him by Marischal College, Aberdeen. This mark of favour and appreciation of ability, was alike honourable to the College and to Drew. In 1831, the council of the London University solicited him to allow himself to be nominated as Professor of Moral Philosophy in that institution. He declined, on the ground of his desire to settle down in his own native county for the remainder of his days. His incessant literary employment had materially weakened a constitution which must at one time have been as strong as iron. During the summer of 1831, he visited his native place; he had fixed this as the time to retire from his editorial labours, but for the benefit of his children resolved to continue for two years more—a resolve which no doubt helped to hasten his final departure. After *endeavouring* to fulfil faithfully his engagements for a little while longer, illness overtook him. He died, as he desired, in his native county, on the 29th of March, 1833. The inhabitants of St. Austell, in remembrance of their distinguished townsman, erected in the parish church a tablet bearing the following inscription:—

"To the Memory of SAMUEL DREW, a native of this Parish, whose talents as a Metaphysical writer, unaided by education, raised him from obscurity into honourable notice, and whose virtues as a Christian won the esteem and affection of all who knew him. He was born March 3rd, 1765. Lived in St. Austell until January, 1819, and, after an absence of fourteen years, during which he conducted a literary journal, he returned to end his days in his native county, as he had long desired, and died at Helston, March 29th, 1833. To record their sense of his literary merit and moral worth, his fellow-townsmen and parishioners have erected this tablet."

So ended the life of one of England's greatest worthies! No, not ended: his life is still stored up in the books he wrote, which are as imperishable as his name. He has left a torch, in the bright example of his life, which will cheer many a desponding student in the monotony of his daily tasks; and when the humble Christian is assailed by the sophistries of the infidel and the sceptic, he will find his best defence in the unanswered arguments of the giant shoemaker. Cornwall has reason to be proud of such a son, and England, that she was privileged to give birth to such a man.

THOMAS COOPER,

SHOEMAKER; AFTERWARDS POET, NEWSPAPER EDITOR, AND ORATOR.

"I was born," says Thomas Cooper, "at Leicester; but my mother, being left in a state of widowhood in my infancy, removed me to Lincolnshire, her native county. She procured me bread by the labour of of her own hands, and I have often known her give me the last bit of food in our humble home, while she herself fasted. I frequently knew, in childhood, what it was to go shoeless, and to wear ragged clothing. My constitution was enfeebled by early and continued illness, and to this circumstance, perhaps, it was owing—rather than to any natural bent of the mind —that I became very early devoted to reading, drawing, and music. My beloved mother inflicted hardships on herself in order to afford me encouragement; she frequently gave me her last penny for a circulating library book, a sheet of paper, a black-lead pencil, or a bit of water-colouring; and, as I advanced in boyhood, she purchased me, with much self-denial, one of the old-fashioned but sweet-toned instruments called a dulcimer, on which I learned to play with considerable skill. In this manner, surrounded with poverty, but wrapt up in a happy attachment to books, and drawing, and music, often varied by a ramble on the hills and among the woods above Gainsbro', in search of flowers, I passed the earlier portion of my existence. At fifteen years of age, after many promises of patronage had been broken, my poor mother was compelled to send me to the stall to learn the humble trade and craft of a shoemaker. I plied the awl and bent over the last until I was three-and-twenty years of age; and if I can look on any period of my life with unmingled pride and pleasure, it is on that portion of it which I passed in this sedentary employment. My young enthusiasm found a vent in the composition of poetry, for some time after I was thus placed at an occupation which only employed the hands without filling the mind; but the perusal of a memoir of Samuel Lee, Professor of Hebrew in the University of Cambridge, and an example of genius and perseverance triumphing over all the difficulties of lowly birth, soon animated me to encounter the labour of acquiring languages, together with the mathematics. I formed a written resolution to acquire, in a given time, the elements of Latin and Greek, and of geometry and algebra, and to commit the whole of 'Paradise Lost' to memory, together with the seven best plays of Shakspeare. My resolve was exceeded in some respects, but failed in others. I committed to memory three books of Milton and the whole of 'Hamlet;' and these treasures I still retain. I went through a course of geometry and learnt something of algebra, and, in addition to the Latin and Greek, I mastered the elements of Hebrew and French; to these philological acquirements I have, in succeeding periods of my life, added some knowledge of the Italian, German, and other tongues, but less perfectly than my earlier studies. During the youthful period in which I was striving after elementary knowledge, I had to contend with want and deprivation, sometimes in a severe degree. I could not earn more than ten shillings a week at my trade, and my poor mother, who began to advance in years, was often too much enfeebled to work. We were thus compelled to share a scanty pittance, barely sufficient to keep us in existence. Yet I look back to that time with pride and pleasure. In the summer mornings I used to rise at three or earlier, and walk miles, among the woods and over the hills, reading every inch of the way, and returning to my labour at the hour of six, not quitting my stall till nine or ten in the evening found me so far wearied with exertion that I frequently swooned off my seat. In the winter, because poverty prevented my enjoyment of a fire, I used to place a stool upon a stand to rest my book, and a lamp upon it, and with a bit of old rug under my feet, and my mother's old red cloak over my shoulders, I used to keep up a gentle kind of motion, so as to keep off cold and sleep at the same time. In this mode I used to pass the winter hours from nine or ten to twelve at night, and from three or four to seven in the morning, my mind being too enfeeverd after learning, to permit my sleeping long, even if I had remained in bed. During those laborious hours, in addition to my pursuits in languages, I read over the production of some of the most colossal intellects my country has ever produced—such as Hooker, and Cudworth, and Stillingfleet, and Warburton. Oh! those were happy hours, I am proud of them!

"On recovering from a severe illness, brought about by severe study, a valued friend persuaded me to leave the humble trade which I had followed for nearly eight years, and to enter on the profession of a schoolmaster. I did so, and formed a prosperous school at Gainsborough. Shortly before I was thirty years of age, I left that town for Lincoln, still pursuing my calling as a schoolmaster. I joined the Mechanics' Institute there, a thriving establishment, under the patronage of Lord Yarborough; I taught Latin and French classes, gratuitously, in the institution, and was enthusiastically attached to my engagement. In conjunction with two other young men, I also projected a choral society; and during four years I devoted myself most unremittingly to its management as secretary. My mind thus became familiar with the choral majesty of Handel, the sweetness of Haydn, the varied richness of Mozart, and the sublimity of Beethoven.

"It was at Lincoln that I first became connected with a newspaper. I had been listening to some very eloquent and instructive lectures on chemistry, delivered at the Institute by a Mr. Murray, and asked my stationer whether the lectures would be reported in any of the public papers. He replied, that he would send a paragraph descriptive of the lectures to the 'Stamford Mercury,' if I would write one. That paragraph led to my connection with that paper. Mr. Richard Newcomb, a gentleman for whom I shall always feel a grateful attachment, gave me a situation as reporter for Lincoln, my salary being successively advanced from £20 to £40, £60, and £100 a year. Eventually he removed me to Stamford, with the understanding that I was to remain there and to assist him in the editorship of his paper, at a salary of £300 per annum.

"Owing to family circumstances, I was induced to leave Samford and ventured to London, depending chiefly on the promises of help given me by a literary baronet who then represented Lincoln, and in whose interest I had sedulously laboured for some years. For seven anxious weeks that baronet kept me in cruel suspense, pretending that he had placed a manuscript romance in the hands of his own publisher. I afterwards learned that this was a wholesale falsehood; and he had only been mocking me when he returned that manuscript, complimenting me on its merits, but affecting to regret that his publisher had too many things on hand to undertake to bring it out. For eleven months I subsisted almost by casuality in London. My library, which was a choice one, amounting to five hundred volumes, I sold, volume by volume, for bread. Sometimes I obtained a little employ on the magazines; but when I had earned five pounds, I usually received no more than one. Mr. Lumley, the bookseller, was one of the kindest friends I found in town; he employed me on various occasions, especially in the pleasing though laborious work of copying at the British Museum library. At length when I was on the point of being reduced to extreme difficulty—having actually pawned my cloak and several other articles —I received a letter, offering me the editorship of the 'Greenwich Gazette, or Kentish Mercury.' I remained upon that paper, at a salary of £3 per week, until the prospect of retrieving it from ruin was gone. It has since become extinct. One fortnight after I had given notice to leave that situation —by one of those sudden and unlooked-for incidents which I have so often experienced in life, as to impel me to the belief that a high and ever watchful Power presides over our ways—I received an offer of a situation as reporter to the 'Leicestershire Mercury.' There were several reasons which operated strongly to induce me to accept this offer."

Some of his reasons were political, and others maternal; it was his birthplace, and his aged mother was still living there. In a few weeks after his settlement at Leicester, he was requested by the proprietor of the paper to attend and report a political lecture. When he left that lecture, he first became acquainted with the destitution then prevailing amongst the operatives. It was about eleven o'clock at night; when, hearing the looms still going, he observed to some of the working men who had been at the meeting:—

"Bless me, do these poor people frequently work so late?"

"Aye, and gladly, when they can get it to do," was the reply.

"And what may their earnings be?" was the next question.

"On the average about seven shillings; and three goes for frame-rent and other charges, so that they have about four shillings left."

"Well," was the reply, "four shillings per day is a decent wage."

"But we mean four shillings per week," was the rejoinder.

On inquiry, Cooper found this to be the case. Actual knowledge of this distress induced him to make the poor workers' cause his own. One framework-knitter, on whose veracity he could repose his life, had suffered the deepest privation for weeks, but suffered silently. At length, when every article which could be so disposed of had been taken to the pawnshop, himself, his young wife, and infant reached the verge of starvation. Unable longer to conceal his extremity, he laid a note upon Cooper's desk at eleven o'clock one night, and ran out of the shop. That note depicted his destitution, and informed Cooper that on the previous morning, when he awoke, with his young wife lying by his side, her first language, accompanied with heart-breaking sighs, was—

"Sunday come again, and nothing to eat;" while the infant sought her breast, but there was no nutriment for it: Nature's fountains were dried up by starvation! Another stockinger went one morning into Cooper's house, and, sitting down with a despairing look, exclaimed, with an oath—

"I wish they would hang me! I have lived on cold boiled potatoes, which were given me, for the last two days, and this morning I have eaten a raw potato from sheer hunger! Give me a bit of bread and a cup of coffee, or I shall drop!" Such was the wretchedness and suffering to which the operatives had been reduced. This suffering induced Thomas Cooper to commence political lecturer. Amongst other places he was invited to lecture in the Potteries. He arrived at Hanley for the purpose, on the 13th of August, 1842. On the next day he addressed three meetings. His text in the evening was, "Thou shalt do no murder." After the meeting, he was invited to address the colliers next morning, who were then on strike. The result of the meeting at Hanley was disastrous. The colliers, excited to a high degree on the following night, broke into the house of an obnoxious clergyman, became furious by drinking the wine in his cellar, set fire to his and other houses, and committed various acts of violence.

Mr. Cooper was arrested on the charge of aiding and abetting this riot. He proved on his trial that he was on his way to Manchester at the time of the outbreak. He was acquitted of this charge, but remanded on two other indictments. In his defence he referred to the moral means by which he sought to elevate the people. "I have," he said, "delivered familiar and elementary lectures on geography, astronomy, history, phrenology, and other popular subjects. I have endeavoured to humanize, and civilize, and refine my own class. I never saw a pike, a gun, or a dagger, among the Leicester Chartists. I never had an offensive weapon of the kind in my possession during my whole life. I never let off a gun or a pistol in my life, nor do I know how to prepare either instrument for firing."

On the second trial of Cooper, he made a most able and eloquent defence. The famous Judge Erskine sat on the bench. The trial lasted ten days. The case for the prosecution was conducted by the Solicitor-General, Sir William Follett. The result was the imprisonment of Cooper for two years and eleven weeks; during which time, owing to being placed in a damp cell, he was afflicted with neuralgia, rheumatism, and other torments. While in prison he wrote his "Purgatory of Suicides." In the preface Mr. Cooper says: "I am poor, and have been plunged into more than two hundred pounds debt by the persecution of my enemies; but I have a consolation to know that my course was dictated by heartfelt zeal to relieve the sufferings and oppressions of my fellow men. Sir William Follett was entombed with pomp, and a host of titled great ones, of every shade of party, attended the laying of his clay in the grave; and they purpose now to erect a monument to his memory. Let them build it: the self-educated shoemaker has also reared his; and despite its imperfections, he has a calm confidence that, though the product of poverty, and suffering, and misery, it will outlast the posthumous stone block that may be erected to perpetuate the memory of the titled lawyer."

William Howitt, in the "Eclectic Review," thus speaks of the "Purgatory of Suicides:" "We have here a genuine poem, springing out of the spirit of the times, and, indeed, out of the heart and experience of one who has wrestled with and suffered for it. It is that of a soul full of thought, full of a burning zeal for liberty, and with a temperament that must and will into action. The man is all bone and sinew. He is one of those *terræ filii* that England, more than all the other nations of the earth put together, produces. One of the same class as Burns, Elliot, Fox, the Norwich weaver-boy, to say nothing of the Arkwrights, Smeatons, Brindleys, Chantreys, and the like, all rising out of the labour-class of the thinkers and builders-up of English greatness. What is moreover singular, is, that he is another of the shoemaker craft—that craft which has produced such a host of men of talent, as Hans Sachs, George Fox, Drew, Gifford of the 'Quarterly,' and others." "Till three-and-twenty," he says of himself, "he bent over the *last* and *awl*, struggling against weak health and deprivation, to acquire a knowledge of languages, and his experience in after life was, at first, limited to the humble sphere of a schoolmaster, and never enlarged beyond that of a laborious worker on a newspaper."

In two months after the "Purgatory of Suicides" was published, Cooper sent forth a work in two volumes: "Wise Saws and Modern Instances;" this was succeeded by "The Baron's Yule Feast." Subsequently, Mr. Cooper was engaged on Douglas Jerrold's newspaper, to write a series of articles on "The Condition of the People of England," making a tour through the manufacturing districts to collect materials.

In 1846 he delivered, in the National Hall, "Two Orations against taking away Human Life under any Circumstances;" and subsequently, in the same place, lectures upon almost every subject of history, science, morals, and government; and in the various literary institutions in London and the provinces, lectures upon men of genius, history, and poetry, &c. He has also composed two songs, estimated by competent judges to display real musical taste. One of his productions, which does not bear his name—"The Triumphs of Perseverance," published by Darton and Co., London—is one of the most nervous and eloquent incentives to industry in the language. It is a book which should be put into the hand of every youth, and read by every young man, who complains of want of time for self-improvement.

It is as an orator, however, that Mr. Cooper leaves the most indelible impression. His public discourses he styles—and very properly—*Orations*. He realises, in the magnificence of his periods, the grandeur of the ancient orator, rather than the modern speaker. After listening to him for two hours upon the "Genius of Milton," detailing at the outset every important incident of his life, with ample reference to the times in which he lived, and the circumstances by which he was surrounded, the audience is amazed by hearing him recite, with becoming dramatic action, the whole of the first book of Milton's "Paradise Lost," and this without a pause!

"It will be seen that Thomas Cooper is still a hard worker—the especial fate of the author in London. The labour he performs would be a large amount for a man of strong habit and robust health, but in

Thomas Cooper's case this labour is performed with a constant struggle with ill health, debility, and neuralgia, the fruit of jail confinement. The difficulty with which he pursues his lecturing from this cause would perhaps, however, never be suspected by those who listen to the fervent addresses which often, for two hours together, he pours out."

In his earlier years Mr. Cooper had deistical impressions; as he says, "for two years I rejected revelation." This state of mind was superinduced by reading the plausible infidel works which were in vogue at that period; a perusal of the "Memoirs of Henry Martyn," and an acquaintance with Paley's "Evidences," which he read thrice, so that he could repeat the substance of the work, served to fix in him a belief of the historical evidence of Christianity. That evidence he has never since doubted. Subsequently, however, he adopted the Socinian views, and taught in his lectures the doctrines of Strauss' "Life of Christ." He has renounced these views. At the present time he is engaged lecturing throughout England upon the various forms of infidelity and scepticism, and on the Sabbaths, preaching twice or thrice in various dissenting chapels.

Recently he has addressed a letter to the "Freeman," in which he says:—"I have little that is new to communicate to you, save and except that for four months I have been a teetotaler. I broke off smoking more than a year and a-half ago, and vowed never to smoke more. But when friends urged their total abstinence doctrines upon me I resisted, under the persuasion that, with my life of labour, a draught of bottled stout, or a 'night cap' of spirit and water was necessary, absolutely necessary for me, if I meant to continue to work hard and keep tolerable health. Last summer, however, on revisiting some dear friends in Northumberland and Durham, characterised by holy lives and prayerful habits, I felt self-condemned, because I saw they were grieved with me. I reflected that Paul would not 'eat flesh, or drink wine, or do anything whereby his brother stumbled or was offended, or was made weak;' and I said within myself—'I must not grieve the children of God.' Yet, I thought, Paul would not have killed himself outright in order to avoid giving offence to his brethren, So I said again, 'I will try, in right good earnest, whether I can abstain, and yet be as strong as heretofore.' And I have tried, and I hereby declare that I believe I am stronger and better without alcoholic drinks; and, by God's help, I will be a teetotaler as long as I live. I lecture usually every night, and most commonly preach three times on Sundays, and I find I am well enough to go on; and have no need to say, 'I am wearied.' I could enlarge on the happy feelings resulting from the consciousness that slavish habits are broken; but I refrain, begging pardon for having said so much about myself instead of my work."

WILLIAM JAY:

THE EMINENT BOY-PREACHER, AND DISTINGUSIHED DIVINE.

WE may be sure that he was a beardless boy when he commenced his career: we learn this from an anecdote related by himself in his autobiography. He had been preaching at Melksham on the Sunday: on the following morning he called upon an old gentleman from London, a very wise man—in his own opinion. He did not receive Jay very courteously, but said rudely, he had no notion of *beardless* boys being employed as preachers. "Pray, sir," said Jay, "does not Paul say to Timothy, 'Let no man despise thy youth!' And, sir, you remind me of what I have read of a French monarch, who had received a young ambassador, and complainingly said, 'Your master should not have sent me a beardless stripling!' 'Sir,' said the youthful ambassador, 'had my master supposed you wanted a beard, he would have sent you a goat.'"

On the subject of the ancestors of Jay we are not much enlightened: a matter of small moment. Jay has said facetiously, in the words of Bacon, that "they who derive their worth from their ancestors resemble potatoes, the most valuable part of which is underground." He used to relate, that when one of Lord Thurlow's friends was endeavouring to make out his relationship to the secretary Cromwell, whose family had been settled in the county adjoining Suffolk, he replied, " Sir, there were two Cromwells in that part of the country, Thurlow the secretary and Thurlow the carrier; I am descended from the latter." This is almost as good as the anecdote related of the man, who, being asked some questions about his pedigree, answered that " he was not particularly sure, but had been credibly informed that he had three brothers in the ark."

Jay's father was a stonsmason. Neither his father nor mother were persons of much education; they were, however, upright, conscientious, kind, tender, charitable, and were much esteemed in the neighbourhood. The family attended the ministry of a Presbyterian, who was described as a dry and dull preacher, but very kind and generous. He gave Jay the two first books he could call his own—Watt's " History of the Old and New Testament," and Bunyan's " Pilgrim's Progress." At this time he was receiving the humble education afforded at the village school. But he was not apt in receiving instruction. One of his sisters said the family thought William would never learn to read; but when he did master the art, he was very anxious to acquire additional knowledge. He was, perhaps, learning more at this time than his teachers would give him credit for. The impressions of the beautiful scenery around his home sank into his heart and memory, during his solitary walks, never after to be effaced. At this time he had a reputation for being a good boy, with a desire to do right: he had not, as he relates, any immoralities. On one occasion, however, while he was at play, he uttered a falsehood, accompanying the untruth with an oath, to carry his point. This wicked act so preyed upon his conscience that he shortly after retired to his own room, to repent in solitude and to ask God's forgiveness. He was apprenticed to his father's business, stone-cutting, when he was about fourteen years of age, and worked with his father at the building of Fonthill House, the celebrated residence of Mr. Beckford, which cost in its erection £273,000; the pictures, library, and furniture were valued at more than a million! On one occasion, after his day's work, he went to hear a Mr. Turner preach in a private dwelling; the singing and the sermon upon that occasion made a deep impression upon him, so that he scarcely slept for weeping and for joy. Next morning there was another service at seven o'clock, at which he was the first attendant. Mrs. Turner, the preacher's wife, opened the door, and kindly taking him by the hand, said, "Are *you* hungering for the bread of life?" Subsequently, this excellent woman met him on his way from work on several occasions, and conversed with him as only a good kind woman can. One evening, after hearing a sermon by Mr. Turner on family worship, Jay returned home and besought his father to undertake it. On his refusing on account of inability, he offered to perform it himself. The offer was accepted with tears, and he became a kind of domestic chaplain.

Just at this time the excellent Cornelius Winter came to preach at Tisbury. Jay formed one of the congregation, whose countenance so impressed the preacher as to be remembered twelve months after, when he again officiated in the same place. This second occasion was on a week evening, when there sat Jay with his flannel jacket and his white leather apron, just as he had returned from work. After the sermon the minister sought an interview with him, desiring the doorkeeper to ask "Billy Jay" to come to him in the parlour after the service. When he did so, the good man knelt down and prayed with him, and subsequently offered to admit him amongst a small academy of young men that he was educating. The invitation was happily accepted. He went to Marlborough, where for some years he was under the instructions of that "celestial creature Cornelius Winter," as Bishop Jebb called him.

It may be both interesting and instructive to insert a specimen of Jay's literary ability at the time of his joining the academy. There is only one specimen extant, and, contrasted with the after productions of

Jay, it is a very curious document indeed. It is inserted, of course, verbatim.

"To Mr. Winter, Marlborough.

"Tisbury, January 30th, 1785.

"DUTIFULL FREIND—this comes with my kind loved to you hoping It will find you in good health as it Left me and all my friend at tisbury thanks be to god for his mercy and Goodness in preserving us to this present moment in health and strength, health is the honey that Sweetens every temporal mercy to be well in body is a great blessing but to be well in Soul is a much greater Blessing than this what is the body when compar'd with the Soul it is no more than the Candles Slender Light to the great illuminary the Sun in its meridian Splender and beauty.

"I received your Letter and was very thankfull for your kindness to me in it. You Desired to hear from me Mr. Serman's return and if I could write you something of my Christen Experience. my experience is that I Desire to Love the Lord above all and Desire to Live more to his Glory and honour. I hope I can Say that he is the Cheiftest to my Soul of ten thousand and altogether Lovely I Desire to know nothing but Jesus and Desire to be found in him not having on my own Righteousness which is pulluted with sin and impure but the Righteousness which is of god which is for all and upon all that Believe in him. my father says he will find me in cloths as much as he is able. I can come at any time when you think proper. So I conclude with my father and mother's Love to you I am your humble servant

"WILLIAM JAY."

It will be apparent that few persons could go to the academy more deficient of general knowledge than Jay. But he had the essential thirst for information, which ensured application when the opportunity was presented. At the academy he soon made progress under the direction of his tutor, by whom he was appointed at various times, with the other pupils, to visit the surrounding villages to exhort and in various ways to forward the spiritual interests of the people. Jay was little more than sixteen when he preached his first sermon, selecting as his text, "If so be ye have tasted that the Lord is gracious." After this he preached very frequently, so that he delivered, as he tells us, more than a thousand sermons before he had attained his twenty-first year!

Jay was not unconscious, from the fact of the many applications for the "boy preacher," that he possessed talents of which he had previously taken no account. He had, however, the good sense to know if he was to make any figure in the world he must remember a remark in the "Life of Watts:" "The reason why the ancients surpassed the moderns was their greater modesty. They had a juster conception of the limitation of human powers; and, despairing of universal eminence, they confined their application to one thing, instead of expanding it over a wider surface."

After the needful preparation at Mr. Winter's, Jay was engaged by the celebrated Rowland Hill to preach for a season at the Surrey Chapel, London—a formidable engagement for so young a man. The place, though so large, was soon crowded to excess; and when he preached his last sermon, the yard before the adjoining dwelling-house was filled with the lingering multitude, who would not disperse until he had bidden them farewell from the window. Before he left London, he had several offers to become the pastor of various chapels. With singular good sense he declined the invitations, with the wise intention of securing more preparation before entering upon any important permanent interest. For this purpose he accepted a small charge at Christian Malford, near Chippenham. His salary was to be £35 a year, with the additional consideration of being boarded gratuitously by one of the tradesman of the place. His design, however, in going to the village was frustrated: his books were few; there was no public library to which he could have access, and his salary was too small to allow him to purchase new ones; also, as a farther impediment to his improvement, he was constantly urged to preach abroad, and he lacked the moral courage to say "No."

After leaving Christian Malford, which the circumstances of the case compelled him to do, Lady

Maxwell, who owned the chapel at the Hotwells at Bristol, invited him to occupy that pulpit. He stayed there twelve months, during which time the chapel was always crowded; and, what must have filled him with great joy, he heard of several conversions as the result of his preaching, three of whom subsequently became preachers themselves, and were ordained over congregations, and ultimately died in the faith. Some difficulty arising with Lady Maxwell's sub-governess, who had the management of affairs in her lady's absence, induced Jay to withdraw from the charge. At this time he fortunately received an invitation from the Independent Church at Bath, then destitute by the death of the Rev. Thomas Tuppen. This invitation he accepted, and soon found himself in his new position completely at home. His ordination shortly followed; when he might now be said to have made his permanent choice. Subsequently the chapel was thrice enlarged, and even then it was too small to meet the wishes of the members who desired sittings.

Shortly after his establishment at Bath, he married a most excellent and amiable woman, who was in his after life, and under all circumstances, a true helpmate. Jay speaks of her in terms the most enthusiastic, and doubtless ever loved her with the utmost warmth of his ardent nature. Both Jay and his wife suffered from continued illness at different periods of their lives. He speaks of his own illness as resulting from a weak constitution and from study, which had at times been much protracted. For a lengthened period he had been subject to constant headaches, which rendered both his preaching and his preparatory studies painful. At times, his sight was so confused that he was almost rendered unconscious of outward things. The medical men to whom he applied used all the means which their skill and experience suggested, which only resulted, however, in bringing him almost to the brink of the grave. In this emergency he was recommended by the slave's friend, Mr. Wilberforce, to consult Dr. Bailie, whom he spoke of as his friend and physician. The result of his advice was the adoption of habits which ultimately tended to the restoration of his health. In the first place, he contracted the custom of being seldom in bed after five in the morning; this was not because he could not sleep, but because he felt it a duty to practice this self-denial. He felt that the practice was morally right, as it redeemed time and aided duty; and also that it was physically right, as it was wholesome and healthful. Then, in addition, he was exceedingly temperate in his food; he used, in his later years at least, water only. He was careful, also, not to add to his wants by any fictitious appetites. The wretched habits of snuff-taking and smoking he carefully avoided, and during any temporary headache, or disturbance of his general health, exercised himself in the garden or in any open air relaxation, which soon brought back the desired healthy tone.

The works he published during his protracted life were read with the utmost avidity by members of various denominations. His first literary venture was a sermon on "The mutual Duties of Husbands and Wives," which went through six editions, and was much commended at the time. This was succeeded by a volume of sermons, also favourably received; and subsequent volumes of sermons—"Short Discourses for the Use of Families," went through repeated editions, and procured for him the diploma of D.D. This title he never used except on one occasion, when he left a case of manuscripts at a large inn. It answered the purpose of preserving the papers, and from that circumstance he argued the use of such honours. After the volumes of sermons he published two biographical works—"The Life of the Rev. Cornelius Winter," and "Memoirs of the Rev. John Clarke." He also published two volumes of "Morning Exercises for the Closet," which soon reached a tenth edition; these were followed by two more volumes of exercises for the "Evening." Many, if not the whole of these works, were reprinted in America; and one complete collected edition of the entire was published at Baltimore. The rich, refined, and elegant Mr. Beckford, during the time that Jay was preaching in Bath, took an opportunity to hear him, without being aware of the fact that the preacher had been employed as a lad in assisting to rear his princely home. Afterwards he left a noble tribute to Jay's power. He said: "This man's mind is no petty reservoir, supplied him by laborious pumpings; it is a clear, transparent spring, flowing so freely as to impress the idea of its being inexhaustible. In many of these passages the stream of eloquence is so full, so rapid, that we are fairly borne down and laid prostrate at the feet of the preacher, whose arguments in these moments appear as if they could not be controverted, and we must yield to them. The voice which calls us to look into ourselves, and prepare for judgment, is too piercing, two powerful, to be resisted; and we attempt, for worldly and sensual considerations, to shut our ears in vain."

Jay records the circumstance of preaching at the opening of Hanover Chapel, on which occasion the Duke of Sussex was present. He adopted his usual custom to retire before the service, for prayer and contemplation; so that when he entered the pulpit he delivered his message with his accustomed freedom. The fear of man had no snare for him. He did not, as a rule, write out his sermons, yet, as the opportunity presented, he committed his thoughts to paper. It was the advice of Mrs. Hannah Moore, at her first interview with him, to write much. "It matters not, comparatively," said that extraordinary woman, "on what a young composer first writes; by the constant use of his pen he will soon form a style; and by nothing else will he attain it." She also recommended writing with as much *celerity* as possible, regardless of trifling inaccuracies. "These," she said, "should not be suffered to check and cool the mind. These may be safely left for correction in review, while advantage is taken of the heat of composition, to go on to the end; it being better to produce the whole figure at one fusion, than to cast successively various parts, and then conjoin them."

On the 31st day of January, 1841, Mr. Jay completed his fiftieth year of ministering. On that occasion the members of his congregation presented him with a silver salver, with the following inscription:—

"Presented, together with the sum of six hundred and fifty pounds, to the Rev. William Jay, by the members of the church and congregation assembled in Argyle Chapel, Bath, and by other friends, on the completion of the fiftieth year of his happy and useful pastorate, as a tribute of Christian esteem, affection, and gratitude. January 30, 1841." The younger members of the congregation also presented him with a handsome gold medal and a silver salver. Subsequently, the servants of the families composing the congregation presented him with a silver sugar-basin, stating simply, "that it came from many attached female servants in connection with the church and congregation." Mr. Jay wrote the contributors affectionate letters, and presented each of them with a volume of his sermons.

The life of this good man came to a close on the 27th day of December, 1853, when his spirit left it earthly clay to join the good who had gone before. Thus ended the lengthened life and valuable career of the stonemason's apprentice—honoured and esteemed by the whole Christian world. How fittingly may we close this sketch in the words of the poet:—

> "Honour and shame from no condition rise;
> Act well your part—*there* all the honour lies

JOHN PHILPOT CURRAN:

THE CELEBRATED ORATOR AND LAWYER.

IRELAND is celebrated for its famous orators. For wit, and the power to move the passions, they are unrivalled. The present generation, however, bears no comparison with the generation long ago carried to the "narrow house." The wit and eloquence of the modern Irish orator seem tame and vapid to the springy freshness of an O'Connel or a John Philpot Curran.

"Little Jacky," as the subject of our sketch used to be called, saw the light in the small town of Newmarket, in the county of Cork. He is described in his boyhood to have been a light-limbed, short, brown boy. Loving his mother—as if it were possible that any true-hearted boy could do otherwise—the tales she told him he treasured in his memory. She became his inspiration; he afterwards boasted, when surrounded with friends and in the noon-tide of his fame, that to his affectionate and intelligent mother all his success and merit must be attributed. When Curran had attained a first position at the bar, and perhaps after being present in the court and hearing her son plead with his accustomed eloquence, she said,

"O Jacky, Jacky, what a preacher was lost in you!"

Kind and considerate as this excellent woman was, owing to her large family, she could not bestow special attention upon any member, so that "Master Jacky" was left pretty much to his own resources. He early became acquainted with all the means of amusement both in the town and in the country around; he was a prime favourite at all the wakes and dances, and anticipated with great delight the Newmarket fair, which was held four times a year. On one occasion Newmarket was visited by the time-honoured exhibition of "Punch and Judy," which attracted much attention; but owing to the sudden illness of the proprietor, the pleasure of the sight-seers seemed speedily about to come to an end. In this emergency Curran offered his services as showman, and acquitted himself to the satisfaction of the on-lookers. Indeed, it is said that he would have proved quite a treasure to the Punch and Judy man had he not, in the exuberance of his spirits, dared to burlesque the parish priest. He got so roughly handled for his profane treatment, that all taste for showmanship was taken out of him.

One day, while playing marbles, there occurred an incident upon which his future eminent position mainly depended. He had been very successful at play, and was, as a consequence, full of hilarity and fun. Mr. Boyce, the rector of the parish, was a cheerful spectator of the game, and was particularly delighted with Curran's vivacity and sparkle. Determining to develope the power, of which he had discovered the germ, he induced "Jacky," by bribes of kind words and sweet cakes, to visit him at the rectory, where he taught him to read, gave him a knowledge of grammar, and made him acquainted with the rudiments of the classics. Subsequently he sent him to Middleton school.

The school was under the direction of Mr. Carey, an excellent classical scholar. From this school he went to Trinity College, when he was not seventeen years old. He was an inmate of the college, which saved him from absolute want, and enabled him to devote himself with assiduity to his studies. In three years after entering the college he obtained a scholarship by his steady and persevering industry. He subsequently aspired to a fellowship, but from some unexplained reason, relinquished the hope. His classical acquirements were very considerable. He could quote from the classics at all times with the happiest effect. His biographer, Phillips, says that he saw him in a Holyhead packet during a fearful storm, while all on board were dreadfully sea-sick, deliberately take out of his bag a pocket edition of Virgil, by which he charmed himself into security.

While he was at Trinity College he was frequently before the board, charged with some slight irregularity. On one occasion the crime was laid to his charge of wearing a dirty shirt: in his defence he told his accusers the story of Barry Yelverton, afterwards Lord Avonmore. "I wish, mother," said Barry, "I had eleven shirts." "Eleven, Barry, why eleven?" "Because, mother, I am of opinion that a gentleman, to be comfortable, should have twelve." Barry and Curran had *two* between them.

Curran was intended for the church; his mother was sanguine enough to think that one day he would become a bishop. He had himself no such thoughts; so that when he had obtained his degrees at Trinity College, he started for London with a light heart and quite as light a purse. When he arrived in the metropolis, he contrived to enter the Middle Temple, and also contrived to live—*how*, is the unsolved question. Probably he wrote for the papers and magazines, and so eked out a subsistence, and prevented himself from starving. He managed, however, to pass the legal terms, and come out a full-fledged barrister. While he was in London, Curran did not consider that his law studies were sufficient to occupy his attention: in the first place, he had an impediment in his speech, which had obtained for him at school the *soubriquet* of "Stuttering Jack;" this he set himself earnestly to amend. One of his plans was to declaim daily before a looking-glass, selections from Junius, Bolingbroke, and Shakespeare. He was also a constant attendant at debating clubs. One of the most celebrated, at which he made his *debut* as a public speaker, is in existence at the present day, close to Temple Bar, in Fleet Street. Curran thus tells the story of his first effort: "When I had gained some reputation as an advocate, a friend flatteringly told me one day that he thought oratory was born with me. I denied it, and said that it was not born until at least twenty-three years afterwards. The story of its birth, as regards me, is this: I was one night at the debating society, when I was appointed to speak to a certain subject. I arose, in the pride of conscious ability, and said, 'Mr. Chairman'—I became nervous; the sound of my own voice startled me; I grew pale; my heart must have bounded into my throat, for certainly I could not heave out another word. The fact is, I fancied at the moment, although there was not more than a dozen in the room, that I was to address a grand assembly, and that every eye was intently riveted on me, as a kind of moral centre, from which they expected the purest rays of intellect to beam upon them. The thought unnerved me; I was bewildered; in short, I concluded by sitting down. After this they called me 'Orator Mum.' I attended the society notwithstanding, and after some time I could say 'ay' or 'no,' boldly enough. It happened, I think, about three weeks or a month after my first essay at speech-making, that I went to the debating club; my spirits were unusually high, for I had dined that day with two friends on a leg of mutton. Well, as I said, I went to the club, and on entering the room I found a ghostly-looking fellow, with an extremely dirty shirt, speaking at a rapid rate. I could not help smiling at his ludicrous blunders. He remarked me, and challenged me, as 'Orator Mum,' to a discussion. Excited by the taunt, I got upon my legs, and dressed him better than ever he was dressed before. I was loudly applauded, and the president invited me to supper. Such was the birth of my oratory, and ever since I never was at a loss for a reply."

During the second year of his residence in London, he married his cousin, Miss Creagh, of Newmarket —a most unwise, and, as it subsequently proved, a most unfortunate act. In 1775 he returned to Ireland, and was called to the Irish bar, penniless and without patronage. Yet he took his seat amongst the junior barristers with the utmost confidence of ultimate success, and experienced the usual fate of attending the courts without a brief. But even at this time he attained a degree of celebrity. If he was not called upon to exhibit his oratorical powers in the law courts, he had his revenge by seeing always ar und him a willing and eager crowd of listeners in the halls, whom he amused by his wit, and delighted by his eloquence. After attending the Cork Assizes he returned to Dublin, very little improved in his circumstances. He was so poor at this time that he could not pay the rent of his very humble lodgings; this was the more embarrassing, as his landlady would not wait for a change of fortune.

One morning Curran left home in the utmost dejection of spirits. He had no dinner for his family, and he had no money for his rent. The day was passed miserably, as usual, when on returning home, he was surprised to find on his study-table a large brief, with twenty guineas wrapped inside, and the name of "old Bob Lyons" inscribed upon it. We may be sure the rent was immediately paid, and "old Bob" invited to a good dinner. That brief was the commencement of his fortunes. "Bob" afterwards gave him business that amounted to eleven hundred pounds. Then the time speedily arrived when no important cause was tried in any part of Ireland in which he was not engaged.

While he was struggling to make a position at the bar, he was the subject of a heartless attack by Judge Robinson, who is described as having a sour, cynical disposition, and who attained his elevation to the bench by meanness and corruption. In the course of one of his speeches in court, Curran, in combating the opinion of the opposite counsel, said, "he had consulted all his law books, and could not find a single case in which the principle contended for was established." "I suspect, sir," said the judge, "that your law library is rather limited." To this remark, Curran, after eyeing him for a moment, indignantly replied: "It is very true, my lord, that I am poor, and this circumstance has certainly rather curtailed my library; my books are not numerous, but they are select, and I hope have been perused with proper dispositions; I have prepared myself for this high profession rather by the study of a few good books than by the composition of a great many bad ones. I am not ashamed of my poverty, but I should of my wealth, could I stoop to acquire it by servility and corruption. If I rise not to rank, I shall at least be honest; and should I ever cease to be so, many an example shows me that an ill-acquired elevation, by making me the more conspicuous, would only make me the more universally and the more notoriously contemptible!"

After being five years at the bar, Curran entered the Irish House of Commons, and attained there an equal celebrity to that which he had acquired in the law courts.

In the height of his fame, Curran returned one day from the courts, where he had been practising, and found to his astonishment a venerable stranger in his rooms, making himself freely at home. A glance showed him that it was the good Mr. Boyce. "You are right," said he, as he rushed into his arms, "you are right, sir; the chimney-piece is yours, the pictures are yours, the house is yours; you gave me all I have —my friend, my father!" After dinner Mr. Boyce accompanied his protegée to the House of Commons, of which he was a member, and heard him with delighted feelings make one of his eloquent and powerful speeches.

At the death of Mr. Pitt, the political party to which Curran was attached, came into office. He was made Master of the Rolls, which position he filled for six years, and then retired upon a pension of £2,700 per annum, and finally closed his eventful life on the 14th of October, 1817, in the sixty-eighth year of his age.

After his death the celebrated Irish barrister Phillips thus wrote of him: "His place at the Irish bar has not even been approached since his departure. There is no man, not merely next him, but near him. I have heard the best efforts of the ablest amongst them; and though they were brilliant in their way, it was as the brilliancy of the morning star before the sunbeam. One, perhaps, is witty, sarcastic, argumentative—another, fluent, polished, plausible—a third, blunt, vehement, and energetic—but, there is not one like him, at once strong, persuasive, witty, eloquent, acute, and argumentative, giving to every argument the charm of his imagery, and to every image the magnificent simplicity of his manner—not one, who, when he had touched all the chords of pity, could so wrinkle up the cheek with laughter, that the yet undried tear was impeded in its progress—not one who, when he had swept away the heart of his hearer, left at the same time such an impression upon his memory, that the judgment, on reflection, rather applauded the tribute which, at the moment of delivery, had been extorted from the feelings!"

SAMUEL CROMPTON:

THE INGENIOUS BOY, INVENTOR OF THE SPINNING MULE, AND ONE OF ENGLAND'S GREATEST BENEFACTORS.

THE results of perseverance are seen, not only in individual progress and personal success, but in the happiness and prosperity of towns, of districts, of countries. Some ingenious mechanic, to further his own ends, may devise a machine which may save him from many tedious hours' labour; the machine not only answers his individual ends, but is an invention for all time, to save so much manual labour to the human family. No more remarkable instance is to be found than in the life of Samuel Crompton, the inventor of the "Spinning Mule." His discovery gave an immense impetus to the industry of the people of Lancashire, causing insignificant villages to spring into large and important towns.

Samuel Crompton was born on the 3rd of December, 1753. His ancestors had occupied distinguished positions both in the commercial and legal world. His parents resided at Firwood, in the township of Tonge, near Bolton; they were farmers, but, as was the custom of the time, the leisure of the family was devoted to carding, spinning, and weaving. George Crompton, the father of Samuel, died at the early age of thirty-seven. He and his wife, Elizabeth (better known as Betty) Holt, of Turton, were religious people, regularly attending the services at the Chapel-in-the-fields, now known as All Saints' Church, Little Bolton.

Fortunately for Samuel, his mother was a prudent and exemplary woman, she had decision and energy in her character; some thought her self-willed and imperative, but no mother could have been kinder or more solicitous for her son's welfare than Betty Crompton was for her son Samuel. The school that this good woman sent her boy to was kept by one William Barlow, who had quite a reputation for his skill in writing, arithmetic, book-keeping, geometry, mensuration, and mathematics; he was styled "a witch in figures." No doubt this school afforded Samuel all the education that he received, and that his attendance was not protracted to any lengthened period, as his mother would be anxious to avail herself of his earliest capable services. During this period, Samuel says, his mother practised to the very letter the injunctions of Scripture, many times subjecting him to a beating, not for any fault, but because "she *so* loved him"—an excess of kindness from which she might have been excused.

When Samuel was in his sixteenth year he was occupied at the loom at his mother's house. For six years previous there had been a great demand for cotton goods, and especially for imitations of the muslins sent from India. The efforts of the manufacturers to produce these goods at home were fruitless. A little advance had, however, been made in the means of producing the cloth; Kay, of Bury, had invented a mode of throwing the shuttle by a simple contrivance, by which the weaver could make twice as much cloth; and Hargreaves, a weaver of Stand-hill, near Blackburn, had invented the jenny. But both Kay and Hargreaves were driven from their country by the ignorant prejudices of their fellow workmen, who conceived that their inventions would throw them out of employ. While Samuel was working at home on one of these machines he was also *learning to think.* His mother exacted a certain amount of work daily. His leisure, however—for he had some hours of relaxation—was devoted to making a violin, which he soon learned to play, contracting a love for the instrument which never afterwards left him. This, and the few books which were at his command, filled up the spare time not given to his daily work.

When he was in his twenty-first year he commenced the construction of his "Mule," which took him five years to perfect. He thus briefly relates the experience of these years :—" The next five years had this addition to my labour as a weaver, occasioned by the *imperfect* state of cotton spinning, viz., a continual endeavour to realize a more perfect principle of spinning; and. though often baffled, I as often renewed the attempt, and at length succeeded to my utmost desire, at the expense of every shilling I had in the world." All this experimenting was done at "over hours," and many hours which should have been spent in bed were devoted to the "improvements." The lights and noises at all sorts of untimely hours heard and seen at the old Hall, originated a report that it was haunted. This was no doubt the fact, but it was with Samuel's restless spirit, which would not be laid until his object was attained. The only tools he had to work with were a few sacredly preserved by his mother, once the property of his father, and which were used by him in the construction of a church organ. Every spare shilling was devoted to adding to their number; for this purpose Samuel frequently hired himself and his darling violin to the manager of the Bolton Theatre for one shilling and sixpence per night, so that he might purchase some needed tool for his inventions. The "Mule" was chiefly constructed of wood, but parts of it were of iron, as it has subsequently been ascertained that he frequently visited a small way-side smithy in the township, where he "used to file his bits of things." In a paper which John Kennedy, Esq., read before the Manchester Literary and Philosophical Society in 1830, he informs us that "Crompton's machine was called the 'Hall-in-the-wood wheel,' or muslin wheel, because its capabilities rendered it available for yarn for making muslins; and finally it got the name of the 'Mule' from its partaking of the two leading features of Mr. Arkwright's machine and Hargreaves's spinning-jenny."

When Crompton was just on the eve of completing his machine, in 1779, the Blackburn spinners and weavers were excited to riot against machinery, which they ignorantly supposed would destroy their means of living. Every jenny for miles round Blackburn was destroyed, excepting such only as had less than twenty spindles. Samuel, during this outbreak, took his machine to pieces and concealed the parts in the loft or garret, not daring to put them together for some weeks after. In the course of the same year, however, it was all complete, and yarn spun upon it, which was used for the manufacture of muslins of a very fine description.

The first profits of the "Mule" were spent upon a silver watch, made expressly for Samuel by a watchmaker in Bolton. This watch was his constant companion for fifty years. Soon after, Samuel set up house on his own account in a cottage attached to the old Hall, taking home Mary Pimlott, who made him an excellent wife and judicious adviser. She is said to have been gifted with an additional sense, "something like Scotch second-sight, by which she could tell a rogue in an instant, and warn her family to have nothing to do with him." Samuel now worked upon his "Mule" with the utmost secrecy, and astonished the manufacturers by the *fineness* and *firmness* of the yarn he produced. Everything at this time had a promising and cheery look for a happy future.

Samuel was then only twenty-seven years of age, and the inventor of a machine which from the first hour of its completion altered the entire system of cotton manufactures in the country. It was now seen that the much-coveted India muslins could be made at home. We may well suppose, therefore, that the neighbouring manufacturers were very anxious to penetrate the secret of Samuel's invention. This, of course, he was very unwilling to disclose. The old Hall was besieged as a consequence, by persons near and from a distance; some to purchase yarn, others desirous of learning something of the wonderful new wheel. All sorts of stratagems were used to obtain admission to the house; and when this was denied, many climbed up to the windows outside, by the aid of harrows and ladders, to look in at the machinery.

A screen was erected to defeat this espionage; but that was not always successful. One man is said to have ensconced himself for some days in the cock-loft, watching Samuel at work through a gimlet-hole pierced through the ceiling.

Under these circumstances it seemed impossible to retain the secret of his machine. In one of his papers he refers to this period: "During this time I married, and commenced spinner. But a few months reduced me to the cruel necessity either of destroying my machine altogether, or giving it up to the public.

To destroy it I could not think of; to give up that for which I had laboured so long was cruel. I had no patent, nor the means of purchasing one. In preference to destroying, I gave it to the public." He trusted to the manufacturers to remunerate him; and they made, indeed, a sort of one-sided bargain with him. The agreement was thus drawn up: "We whose names are hereunto subscribed, have agreed to give, and do hereby promise to pay unto, Samuel Crompton, at the Hall-in-the-wood, near Bolton, the several sums opposite to our names, as a reward for his improvement in spinning. Several of the principal tradesmen in Manchester, Bolton, &c., having seen his new machine, approve of it, and are of opinion that it would be of the greatest public utility to make it generally known, to which end a contribution is desired from every well-wisher of trade." According to one statement Samuel derived £50 for giving up his "Mule;" while another authority sets the amount at £106. Crompton said himself: "I received as much by way of subscription as built me a new machine with only four spindles more than the one I had given up; the old one having forty-eight, the new one fifty-two spindles." How miserable this result, when the advantage rendered is taken into account!

But more shameful still—even those parties that had promised a wretched dolement, when the "Mule" had left Crompton's hands, sought by any or every means to evade the payment. He wrote: "At last

I consented, in hope of a generous and liberal subscription. The consequence was, that from many subscribers, who would not pay the sum they had set opposite their names when I applied to them for it, I got nothing but abusive language, given to me to drive me from them, *which was easily done*, for I never till then could think it possible that any man (in such situations of life and circumstances) could pretend one thing and act the direct opposite. I then found it was possible, having had proof positive." This disgraceful conduct on the part of the manufacturers tended to sour the temper of Samuel for the remainder of his days.

Some time before the year 1785, Crompton removed from the old Hall to the farm-house at Oldhams, about two miles from Bolton. His new "Mule" was erected in the upper story, and to prevent the crowds who flocked to see the new wheels gaining admission to the apartment, Samuel contrived a secret fastening for the door. One of the visitors was no less a person than the first Sir Robert Peel, then a member of the firm of Peel, Ainsworth, and Co., Bolton. On the first visit he found Crompton absent, when he chatted with his wife, and presented his son George with half a guinea. On Mrs. Crompton going into her dairy for a bowl of milk for her guest, Mr. Peel took the opportunity to ask the boy where his father worked. He was just pointing out the secret contrivance for fastening the door latch, when his mother returned and warned him by a look that he was doing wrong. It is creditable to the Peel family to know that old Mr. Peel's visit was made with the intention of inducing Mr. Crompton to accept a lucrative situation in his employ, and subsequently a partnership in his concern.

Samuel unfortunately saw fit to decline both these offers. Doubtless, had he acceded to the overture, he would have been saved from much after sorrow; but he had been disappointed once, and his faith in promises was considerably lessened. He continued, therefore, in his own loft, hoping at least to secure as much success as his neighbours; but in this he was doomed to be disappointed. No sooner did he teach any new hands the use of his machines than they were bribed to leave him by some of the manufacturers. Crompton thus bitterly records this additional injustice: "I pushed on, intending to have a good share in the spinning line, yet I found there was an evil which I had not foreseen, and of much greater magnitude than giving up the machine, viz., that I must always be teaching green hands, employ none, or quit the country; it being believed that if I taught them they knew their business well. So that for years I had no choice left but to give up spinning, or quit my native land. *I cut up my spinning machine for other purposes.*" On another occasion, feeling most acutely the injustice which was done him, he seized his axe and broke his carding machine in pieces, saying, "They shall not have this too." The axe used in this work of almost justifiable destruction is preserved as a relic at the present time.

In 1800, however, some gentlemen of Manchester got up a subscription for Crompton, under the impression that he had been hardly used. Before it was completed the country was suffering from the high price of food, owing to a failure of the crops. This almost destroyed the scheme. Between four and five hundred pounds was all that was handed over to enable Samuel to increase his little manufacturing establishment.

It must not be assumed that his inventive talents were exclusively devoted to the invention of manufacturing machinery. About the year 1803 he built an organ in his house in King Street, Bolton, where he had removed. It was afterwards bought for the use of the New Jerusalem Church. At this church Crompton took the entire charge of conducting the singing. There are several music books preserved that contain tunes composed by him, and "pricked" with his own hand. The choir thought so highly of his services that they presented him with a silver cup, upon which his portrait was engraved; he afterwards made a pentagraph, by which he added the profiles of all the members of the choir.

In 1811 Samuel commenced collecting information of the results of his invention. He found, after visiting the manufacturing districts of England, Scotland, and Ireland, that there were between four and five millions of mule spindles in use; two-thirds of the steam power then employed in cotton spinning was applied to turn the mules. The value of the buildings and machinery employed in Samuel's invention was computed at between three and four millions sterling; and, as a proof that the invention had not thrown hands out of employ, it was found that 70,000 persons were directly engaged upon the mules, and 150,000 more in weaving the yarn thus spun. It was ascertained that the aggregate number of persons depending upon Crompton's invention was 660,000! This was in 1811: what must the number be in 1860? When Samuel was in Scotland the Glasgow manufacturers were desirous of giving him a public dinner: their intention was frustrated by his modesty. When the time came, to use his own words: "rather than 'face up,' I first hid myself, and then fairly bolted from the city."

The result of the statistics was embodied in a petition to Parliament; a committee was empowered to examine the allegations of the petition, which reported favourably, after examining various witnesses and documents. The report to the House concluded thus: "Your committee beg leave to observe, that the petitioner appears to them to be highly deserving of a national reward." Samuel was in the lobby of the House of Commons on the 11th of May, conversing with Sir Robert Peel and Mr. Blackburne on the subject, when the Chancellor of the Exchequer, Mr. Perceval, joined them. His first words were—"You will be glad to know that we mean to propose twenty thousand pounds for Crompton; do you think that will be satisfactory?" Samuel did not hear the reply, as, from motives of delicacy, he walked away.

In a moment after, before he had left the lobby, he heard a rush of people, and cries that Mr. Perceval had been shot. The assassin, Bellingham, had completed his deadly purpose; in an instant England had lost a faithful servant, and Samuel a valuable friend. On the 24th of June the House voted him five thousand pounds—a large sum unquestionably; and yet, taken into consideration with the benefits the nation had derived from the invention of the mule, it was a miserable pittance. Crompton had proved before the committee of the House of Commons that he had contributed £300,000 per annum to the revenue, solely from duty on cotton wool imported into the country to be spun on his machine! Mr. M'Culloch designated the grant to Samuel as "a pittance hardly adequate to defray the expenses of the application." In the sessions of 1826 or 1827, a second application was made to Parliament, but was unsuccessful in procuring another grant. So far as Samuel was individually concerned, this was not of much consequence, as he died in his house in King Street, Bolton, on the 26th of June, 1827, in his seventy-first year. In the language of his biographer, "Let us hope that his memory may yet be revived, and his name worthily honoured, not only in his native parish, but reflected thence over the world; which his invention has done so much to civilize; and that history may yet inscribe the neglected name of SAMUEL CROMPTON on one of the brightest pages of her annals."

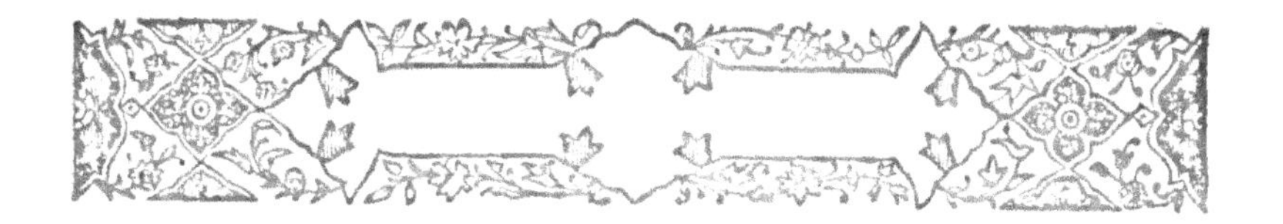

ELIHU BURRITT:

THE LEARNED BLACKSMITH.

A FEW years ago there was gathered within the walls of the lecture hall of the Manchester Athenæum, the *élite* of the city, attracted by the fame of the gentleman announced to lecture upon the "Philosophy of Labour." He was introduced by one of the Directors, who passed a high eulogium upon his character and genius, and who, in the warmest terms, gave him a public welcome to that important city. Elihu Burritt—for he was the lecturer—then stood forth, and delivered in terms the most chaste and classic, an admirable exposition and defence of labour, replete with poetic simile and the wisest maxims. If ever man has earned a right thus to speak it is this man, who may well be described as "the apostle of labour."

Elihu Burritt's father was a shoemaker, and was blest, in common with Elihu's mother, with a most benevolent and kind disposition. His early home was the refuge of the poor and the weary. He remembers, as one of his earliest acts, arranging the seats and chairs round the fire, for the poor people who came from a distance to church. He also fondly remembers the expression of his father's face, as he conducted to the best seat an old idiotic pauper, called "Aunt Sarah." All persons who had met with misfortune were admitted to a relationship with the family. The lame, the halt, the blind, the dumb, if they were males, became uncles; if females, aunts. Elihu remembers his father, when weary from the fatigue of attending the market ten miles distant, turning many times two or three miles out of his way, in order that he might leave in the home of some poor sick sufferer, a few oysters, oranges, or other small present. Elihu's mother was a fitting helpmate to her husband; "she was the best friend her children had on this side of Jesus Christ, exhibiting all the father's benevolence, with an unruffled placidity of manner truly beautiful." In such a school, and with such teachers, no wonder that Elihu stands out at this day as the embodiment of benevolence, and the high priest of brotherly kindness. But this excellent father was removed from his labours while his famous son was yet in his earliest years. That son has now the satisfaction of knowing that after a hard day's work in the forest or in the fields, he sat for half the night by his father's bedside, during his last illness, ministering in all those kindly acts prompted by affection. At this time he had few opportunities of obtaining knowledge. There was a chapel library, to be sure, to which he had access; but the books were very few, and only changed once in four months. The few historical books which he obtained, however, he read with avidity.

When he was sixteen years of age, he apprenticed himself to a blacksmith, residing with his brother Elijah, who had opened a school in his native town, having left Georgia in consequence of some of his anti-slavery notions. By this brother's advice, when his apprenticeship expired in his twenty first-year, he became a student in his school for six months. In this course he had no other end in view than being able to manage a surveyor's compass, and, perhaps, learn to read Virgil in Latin. As a blacksmith, he could earn six shillings per day; therefore he justly considered that his schooling cost him that amount of money. This, of course, would incite him to the utmost industry. At the end of the half year, he was well satisfied with the progress he had made—he had gone through Virgil in Latin, had read several French works, and was well versed in mathematics. In order to make up for the time spent in school, he determined to undertake the united labour of two men, that he might receive double wages, to do which he had to work fourteen hours each day. Still, absorbing as this labour was, he found time to read a little of Virgil, or French, in the morning or evening. He found also, at this period, that he could, without much difficulty, read Spanish. In addition to which he determined to obtain an acquaintance with the Greek language. To this end he procured a Greek grammar which would just lie in the crown of his straw hat; so that while he was at work he could glance at the page, and thus commit part of a Greek verb to memory. In this manner he worked with brain and hands until autumn. The progress that he made rendered him dissatisfied with his position: the more he learned the more he desired to learn. Leaving his furnaces, therefore, he determined to appropriate his earnings to the pursuit of knowledge. He spent the winter at New Haven, where he devoted himself to intense study. He thus records the course he adopted:—

"As soon as the man who attended to the fires had made one in the sitting-room, which was at about half-past four in the morning, I arose, and studied German till breakfast, which was served at half-past seven. When the boarders were gone to their places of business, I sat down to Homer's Iliad, without a note or a comment to assist me, and with a Greek and Latin lexicon. A few minutes before the people came into their dinners, I put away all my Greek and Latin, and began reading Italian, which was less calculated to attract the notice of the noisy men who at that hour thronged the room. After dinner I took a short walk, and then again sat down to Homer's Iliad, with a determination to master it, without a master. The proudest moment of my life was when I first possessed myself of the full meaning of the first fifteen lines of that noble work. *I took a triumphal walk in celebration of that exploit.* In the evening I read in the Spanish language until bedtime. I followed this course for two or three months, at the end of which time I read about the whole of the Iliad in Greek, and made considerable progress in French, Italian, German, and Spanish."

When the winter was over he once more put on the leather apron, resolving to double his diligence to "make up for lost time." The fame of his learning having reached his home before him, he received an offer on arriving there, which he accepted, of the mastership of a grammar school in a neighbouring town. He occupied this position for about a year, attending most sedulously to his own studies as well as to the studies of the scholars under his care. His health suffering from the confinement, he was compelled to give up the charge, and resume once more the healthful exercise of the forge. After some time he formed the resolution to obtain a knowledge of the oriental dialects; the chief difficulty, however, seemed to be to get the books needed for the study. Elihu entertained the idea of working his passage over to England to obtain them, and actually walked to Boston, a distance of a hundred and twenty miles, for the purpose. When there he heard of an antiquarian library at Worcester, where he determined to go and obtain work as a journeyman, in order that he might have the opportunity of consulting the books. As he was about to leave the city, a feeling of unwonted depression and weariness came over him. He was exhausted in body by fatigue: he was lame, and so poor, that all his store was one dollar and his watch. In this wretched plight he limped along the streets of the city in no very enviable mood. When he reached Boston bridge, on his way to Worcester, he was overtaken by a boy with a waggon, that he found was going to his destination. As it was still forty miles away, Elihu induced the boy to allow him to ride. When they arrived at the end of the journey, the question arose how the boy should be compensated. Burritt, under his then circumstances, could not dispense with the dollar, as that was all his available cash; so he determined to part with his old watch. The boy was informed that it was useless as a watch, but as he could afford to have it properly repaired, it would be worth more than the ride; and at some future time he must give him the difference. On these not very hard terms the watch was accepted. Elihu soon got employment as a journeyman blacksmith. One day when he was at work at the anvil, the waggon-boy entered the smithey and handed him a few dollars, telling him with a smiling face, that "the watch had been mended, and was going cleverly." Subsequently Burritt again became possessed of the watch. He was travelling on the railway from Worcester to New Britain, when one of his fellow passengers, a handsome well dressed young man, thus accosted him:—"You have forgotten me,

Mr. Burritt, but I have not forgotten you. You remember the boy to whom you gave the watch? I am he—a young man now, a student of Harvard College." After mutual pleasant greetings, Burritt said: "And about that watch; what has become of it? for to tell you the truth, I was much attached to it, and should like to have it back again." "That you shall," replied the young man, "you *shall* have it back. I sold it; but I know where it is, and it shall be yours." The watch was soon recovered, and afterwards decorated Burritt's printing office.

The Worcester antiquarian library could not be used by Burritt, much to his sorrow. The library was only open to the general public a certain number of hours each day, and those hours he was employed at the forge. Under this difficulty he continued his study of Hebrew without assistance. Every spare moment was devoted to its study. In the winter mornings he rose early; and while the mistress of the house was preparing breakfast by lamplight, he would stand by the mantel-piece with his Hebrew Bible on the shelf, and his lexicon in his hand; he partook of all his meals in this way. This incessant study, however, was not indulged in with impunity. He suffered much from headache—the remedy for which was two or three additional hours of hard work at the forge, with a little relaxation from study. Burritt kept a diary, from which we learn the amount of mental labour incurred. One specimen of the appropriation of the spare time of a week will serve for the whole :—

"Monday, June 18th: Headache; forty pages Cuvier's Theory of the Earth, sixty-four pages French, eleven hours forging. Tuesday: Sixty-five lines of Hebrew, thirty pages of French, ten pages Cuvier's theory, eight lines Syriac, ten ditto Danish, ten ditto Bohemian, nine ditto Polish, fifteen names of stars, ten hours forging. Wednesday: Twenty-five lines Hebrew, fifty pages of astronomy, eleven hours forging. Thursday: fifty-five lines Hebrew, eight ditto Syriac, eleven hours forging. Friday: Unwell; twelve hours forging. Saturday: Unwell; fifty pages natural history, ten hours forging. Sunday: Lesson for Bible class."

Subsequently, Burritt became acquainted with the Turkish, Ethiopic, and Persian languages. He translated many of the Icelandic Sagas for the American serials, and received repeated invitations to lecture in the chief American cities, as well as overtures for a provision to secure him against the necessity of labour. The last he resolutely refused. He did not care to owe anything to patronage, and therefore continued at his forge. Indeed, he held that the condition of an apprentice, or workman, was most favourable to the attainment of knowledge. When the day's work is done there is no care or thought on the mind to interfere with study. Burritt himself furnished an example of what may be the result of application during the workman's own time.

It does not appear that he had any ultimate design in his vast acquirement of languages; in the order of Providence, however, devoting himself to the one grand idea—the universal brotherhood of all the nations of the earth, his labours have resulted in the greatest benefits to the human family. Returning from Europe after spending some time there in the cause of peace, he was welcomed home by a public meeting of the inhabitants of the state of Massachusetts. On that occasion the Rev. Warren Burton said:—"About twelve years ago there came from a little town in Connecticut, on foot, travelling one hundred and twenty miles to Boston, a young man about twenty-six years of age. He, while labouring at the anvil many hours of the day, and as thousands and tens of thousands and millions of other mechanics can do, and I hope will do, spent the leisure hours of the morning and evening in study.

"He found that he had exhausted little Connecticut, and he sought where he could find more books that would open to him those lofty and hidden treasures of literature which his heart and head coveted; and he sought the nearest point where he supposed a vessel might be found, bound to the eastern continent, that there—amid those old cities, and laid up amid those mighty libraries—he might find the books his own country could not supply. On reaching Boston he found, to his disappointment, no ship going out. He knew nobody. He was in the largest human wilderness into which he had ever wandered. There, depressed in heart, and equally depressed in pocket, he knew not what to do, which way to turn, or whom to ask. Passing through Cornhill, and accidentally stepping into some of the antiquarian book stores—I think into Barnum's—his eye fell on the catalogue of the antiquarian library of this city. Here, he said, is what I want. And towards Worcester he turned his steps on foot. He became wearied; he became lame; he became despondent. And in this state a boy with a waggon came along, and, making inquiry whither he was going, found he was bound for Worcester. The boy consented to let him ride, the young man offering his old silver watch in pay.

"He came to Worcester. He knew nobody; nobody knew him. Everything was strange. He had not the key to open that library door. All he could do was to go, with his humble attire, as I have been told, to a blacksmith's shop, and, putting his foot upon the anvil, and his hand upon the bellows, asked the foreman whether he would like to hire some one very cheap. The master at first employed him for very low wages. And there he laboured, and laboured on for months. And there he found access to the treasures his heart coveted. And now, after having entered on this great enterprise of peace—having scattered his OLIVE LEAVES broadcast over one continent, and with a strong arm flung them three thousand miles to another, so that they alighted there, after having crossed the ocean, and marched them to one common centre, as it were, under the guidance of their distinguished men—after having accomplished what others did not dream of, he now comes back to you, borne in the hollow of the hand of Providence, and he is in our midst. What a change! What a contrast!"

Speaking of himself, Burritt remarks :—"All that I have accomplished, or expect or hope to accomplish, has been, and will be, by that plodding, patient, and persevering process of accretion which builds the ant-heap—particle by particle, thought by thought, fact by fact. And if I ever was actuated by ambition, its highest and farthest aspiration reached no further than the hope to set before the young men of my country an example in employing those fragments of time called "odd moments." And I should esteem it an honour of costlier water than the tiara encircling a monarch's brow, if my future activity and attainments should encourage American working-men to be proud and jealous of the credentials which God has given them, to every eminence and immunity in the empire of mind. These are the views and sentiments with which I have sat down night by night for years, with blistering hands and brightening hope, to studies which I hoped might be serviceable to that class of the community to which I am proud to belnog. This is my ambition; this is the gaol of my aspirations. But not only the prize, but the whole course, lies before me, perhaps beyond my reach. 'I count myself not yet to have attained' to anything worthy of public notice or private mention: what I may do is for Providence to determine. With regard to my attention to the languages (a study of which I am not so fond as of mathematics), I have tried, by a practical and philosophical process, to contract such a familiar acquaintance with the head of a family of languages, as to introduce me to the other members of the same family. Thus, studying the Hebrew very critically, I became readily acquainted with its cognate languages; among the principal of which are the Syriac, Chaldaic, Arabic, Samaritan, Ethiopic, &c. The languages of Europe occupied my attention immediately after I had finished my classics; and I studied French, Spanish, Italian, and German, under native teachers. Afterwards I pursued the Portuguese, Flemish, Danish, Norwegian, Icelandic, Welsh, Gaelic, Celtic. I then ventured on further east, into the Russian empire, and the Sclavonic opened to me about a dozen of the languages spoken in that vast domain, between which the affinity is as marked as that between the Spanish and Portuguese. Besides those, I have attended to many different European dialects still in vogue. I am now trying to push on eastward as far as my means will permit, hoping to discover still further analogies among the Oriental languages, which will assist my progress."

In connection with his study of the Celtic language Mr. Burritt relates an interesting circumstance. One day while looking over the books at the public library, he lighted upon a grammar and dictionary of the Celto-Breton language, which had been presented by the Royal Antiquarian Society of Paris. In turning over the leaves of the dictionary it struck him that it would be a very fine exercise for him to try and write a letter in that language to the president of the Royal Antiquarian Society. When this thought first crossed his mind he did not know a single word of the language, but with him, to will such an undertaking was to perform it. He immediately began the task, and in less than three months it was accomplished. A letter was written in the Celto-Breton tongue, and duly forwarded to Paris, in August, 1838. About a year afterwards a gentleman residing in Worcester called upon Elihu, whom he found busily employed at the anvil, and handed him a large parcel, addressed, "Mr. Elihu Burritt, Worcester, Massachusetts, U.S." This was from the Royal Antiquarian Society of Paris, and, along with a letter from the secretary, not in ancient Celto-Breton, however, but in good modern French—acknowledging the receipt of Mr. Burritt's letter, contained a copy of the yearly Transactions of the Society, in which, among other interesting documents, that letter, followed by a translation into French, had been inserted. Burritt speaks of this incident as one of the most gratifying which has occurred to him in connection with his studies, and certainly it was one of the most wonderful, seeing that, for want of proper books, he had to hunt up his words in the dictionary, which was merely the Celto-Breton and French portion, and consequently not very available for his purpose. In looking for a Celtic word, he had sometimes to go before he could find it. But Mr. Burritt was not a man to be arrested by any such obstacles. He had made up his mind that "it would be a very good thing to show the French *savans* what a real Yankee could do." And no doubt he rather astonished them with his Celtic epistle from New England.

In concluding this brief sketch of this wonderful man, it may be mentioned that for several years past he has wholly given up the study of languages, having found work of a more practical nature. The great business to which he has devoted himself is the spread of peace amongst all the nations of the earth. To this end he has formed a "League of Universal Brotherhood," the basis of which may be found in the "pledge" put forth at its formation by Burritt:—"Believing all war to be inconsistent with the spirit of Christianity, and destructive of the best interests of mankind, I do hereby pledge myself never to enlist or enter any army or navy, or to yield any *voluntary* support or sanction to the preparation for, or prosecution of, any war, by whomsever or for whatsoever purposes declared or waged. And I do hereby associate myself with all persons, of whatever country, condition, or colour, who have signed, or shall hereafter sign this pledge, in a 'LEAGUE OF UNIVERSAL BROTHERHOOD;' whose object shall be to employ all legitimate and moral means for the abolition of all war, and all the spirit and all the manifestations of war throughout the world; for the abolition of all restrictions upon international correspondence and friendly intercourse, and of whatever else tends to make enemies of nations, or prevents their fusion into one peaceful brotherhood; for the abolition of all institutions and customs which do not recognise and respect the image of God and a brother in every man, of whatever clime, colour, or condition of humanity."

DOUGLAS JERROLD:

SAILOR BOY, SATIRIST, DRAMATIST, NOVELIST, AND PHILOSOPHER.

"His bitterness was but to make things sweet,
And sprang from love of all the tried and lowly,
He felt so yearningly for lives that slowly
Toil through their flinty ways with hopeless feet.
His trenchant wit—the truest of our age—
His soul-deep warrings relaxation gave;
As foam is but the fringing of the wave,
The ornament that decks its noble rage!
Like some physician, steadfast to an end,
Which end, he trusts, may fuller life secure,
His tonic-thoughts, unsweet at first, endure,
And health and vigour to our nation lend.
In this life's fight—the last of wrong his goal!
With tender freshness ever in his soul."

The kind, witty, trenchant, laughter-loving, tear-evoking Douglas—who has not heard of him?

Of Samuel, the father of Douglas, less is known. He, however, in his time, literally "played many parts." Had the reader, in 1806, been at Wilsby, in Kent, he might have made the acquaintance of the elder Jerrold, who at that time owned the theatre, set up in a barn, under the protecting wing and on the estate of Sir Walter and Lady Jane James, the great people of Angley. Samuel Jerrold, like all other mortals, had had his fortunes and misfortunes. One of his misfortunes was to lose his wife, and one of his fortunes was to marry again at Wicksworth, in Derbyshire, a Miss Reid, who is described as a young lady of great energy and spirit. The husband, however, was older than his mother-in-law. Still, the match was a prudent one, because a happy one, and brought prosperity to the theatrical concern. On the 3rd of January, 1803, while she was in London, Mrs. Samuel Jerrold gave birth to our hero, who received the name of Douglas, in compliment to his grandmother's maiden name.

"The sheep-bells," writes Blanchard Jerrold, "that made the softly-rounded hills about Cranbrook ever musical, and the rude theatre in the suburbs of the little town, were little Douglas's earliest recollections. In 1806, when in his third year, he was a strong, rosy, white-haired boy, as Mr. Wilkinson, who had just arrived at the little theatre, to tempt fortune upon its humble boards, is still alive to testify. That intense love of nature, that thirst which the grown man felt for the freshness of the breeze, and that glow of heart with which he met the sunshine in after-life, appear to have first moved his soul as an infant. The memory of the sheep-bell, I have said, was his earliest impression; for the sweetness of the rich pasturages and leafy lanes, the swelling distances of grove, and hill, and valley, were all summed up, in his memory, in this pastoral music. Led by his grandmother, with whom he chiefly lived, for careful walks along the cleaner paths, he gathered the abundant wild flowers of Kentish hedges, and trotted early home to bed, that the old lady might be at her humble post of money-taker at the Wilsby theatre.

When Master Douglas passed into his fourth year, in 1807, his father became the lessee of the Sheerness theatre. At this theatre many important personages visited; amongst others the Russian admiral, whose bespeak resulted in the welcome sum of £42 18*s*. Lord Cochrane was also a frequent visitor, who always insisted upon paying double. No doubt the management was not materially inconvenienced by his lordship's bounty. Little Douglas, however, the little white-haired boy, who ran about the theatre, looked with feelings of awe and veneration at the naval hero. In after years Douglas did him good service with his pen.

At this time, in various ways, little Jerrold was made useful. In the performance of the *Stranger*, he appeared as one of the children of that melancholy man; he was also carried on the stage in "Rolla," by the celebrated Edmund Kean. But still he had no special liking for the stage, and in after-life he did not care to go behind the scenes. A certain Mrs. Reid, who took upon herself the duties of bringing Douglas up, was careful that no spot should be seen upon his collar, that no button should be wanting upon his clothes.

"Mr. Wilkinson, who remained a member of the Sheerness company till 1809, having joined it at Sheerness at Christmas, 1807—some months, probably, after the close of the Cranbrook campaign—was engaged early in 1809, when Douglas was six years of age, to teach him reading and writing. He combined the duties of teacher with those of actor till the close of that year's season, when he left Sheerness for Scotland. At this time 'little Douglas' showed a remarkable love for reading; and years afterwards, when the good old lady was blind and bedridden, she would tell stories of how she used to lock up 'the dear child in his own room, with his books, before she went to take money at the theatre. And the 'dear child,' grown to manhood's estate—hazy acreage very often! —would tell his stories of the bright summer evenings when he was locked up like a pet bird, and when he looked down into the streets to watch his free playmates pass, chirruping, to and fro, to their games. He loved his books undoubtedly; but the key was turned in the lock, and his spirit chafed to know it."

Blanchard Jerrold, in his admirable life of his father, says that Douglas, "from his little prison in the High Street, might, however, watch the fleet at anchor off the town. And in those days, when the men about the thoughtful boy were all naval heroes—when the glories of the British tar was the unfailing theme upon his father's stage, the great ships lay there, to him fairy floating palaces. Already his half-brother was a sailor, and his grandmother had relatives in the service of his Majesty. The stories that were told him by his garrulous grandmother were of Prince William, the royal sailor; of Nelson, and Collingwood. The passionate reader of the 'Death of Abel' and of 'Roderick Random' (his first books), at an age when most boys devote their free energy to the niceties of 'knuckling down,' or to the mysteries of rounders; he turned from the dwarfed pictures of life, as presented on the stage, to the great, real drama afar off, of which he caught the faint but thrilling echoes. In his walks with his grandmother, who insisted that he should wear pattens in dry as in wet weather, neighbours would stop to watch the little fellow read the names over the shops, or the bills in the shop windows; and Jogrum Brown declares that his master's boy, Douglas, was a stout, well-made, white-haired, and rosy-cheeked child, graver than other children, and somewhat unusually ready to 'show fight.'"

When the first schoolmaster Wilkinson left Sheerness, in the pursuit of his fortunes, his pupil Douglas was handed over to the care of a Mr. Herbert, who had the honour of keeping the best school in Sheerness, and directing the ideas of about a hundred scholars, and who now—for he still lives—bears testimony to Master Douglas as a boy to whom he had not, at any time, need to speak an angry word; and was particularly studious. But the routine of a day school, with its meagre teaching, was not sufficient to fill the large heart of Douglas. Wistfully and longingly did he gaze from out his temporary prison-windows at the noble ships sinking below the horizon, on their way to victory. At this time, great visions would come over him of Nelson afloat under victorious bunting, of flying Frenchmen and gallant boarding-parties, of prizes in tow, and the grateful cheers from English shores glowed in his heart. That ardent temper, that white-hot energy which pulsed through him in after-life, and made his utterances all vehement, whether right or wrong, showed in the boy whose daily walks were in the midst of gallant sailors scarred by war—come home to be glorified by their countrymen. He also would bear his part, and add by his prowess to the glory of England. And yet, with these valorous sentiments, the games of boys, and the company of boys, were not his delight, The only game he ever mastered was backgammon. He was, however, engaged in the serious business of directing, as their leader, the Blue Town juveniles. His leadership was so earnest, that the interference of heroes of a larger growth became necessary. The Blue Town of those days was a very loose place. "Jack-ashore" was always "Jack-a-prise." Hence the mouth of the Medway was the scene frequented by Jews, by landsharks, and the endless pimps, whose business it was to filch Jack of his hard-earned wages and prize money.

It was here that Douglas learned to hate the French; to thrash them being the aspiration of his life. He had no future that was not connected with the sea. And very soon, on the 22nd of December, 1813, he was on his way to join the guard-ship "Namur," lying at the mouth of the river. He joined as a first-class volunteer, and was not a little proud of his uniform.

"Life on board a man-of-war in 1813," writes Blanchard Jerrold, "even on board a guard-ship at the Nore, was no holiday work. I have often heard my father dwell upon the great emotion with which he first ascended the gangway to the deck of one of his Majesty's ships. The great floating mass had the pomp and power of a kingdom about it—a kingdom in which he, a child eleven years of age, was to play a part not quite obscure. The good Captain Austen received him kindly, and petted him throughout the year and one hundred and twenty-three days which he passed under his command. Still, life at the Nore was not the naval career to which Captain Austen's midshipman aspired. He liked well enough to pass hours in the captain's cabin, to read Buffon through and through, and to get up theatricals, aided by the pictorial genius of foremast-man Clarkson Stanfield, afloat in the same ship. He was near home, too, and this had its charm. He was permitted also to keep pigeons; and he loved to see his flight of birds swooping round the fleet. The sounds of war afar off, however, smote incessantly upon his ear, and made him eager for active service. The life on board the 'Namur' was dull; the position of a midshipman in her not a very hopeful one—as, in the fortunes of 'Jack Runnymede,' first-class volunteer Douglas William Jerrold, promoted long afterwards to pen, ink, and paper, ventured to set forth. To this picture of a guard-ship, when Runnymede, caught by a press-gang, was put on board, must be added the figure of the faithful limner, as he walked the deck with his dirk at his side, and clad in that remarkable compromise between a gentleman and a footboy, which in those days distinguished the midshipmen in his Majesty's service from their betters or inferiors."

From the comparative monotony of the guard-ship, Douglas was transferred to the brig "Earnest." Active service at sea was now to be the order of the day. At this time the glory of the great Napoleon was about to culminate. The tragic events of Waterloo were about to dim the lustre of that *prestige* which had been won on many a hard-fought field. The "Earnest" was to take part in the final catastrophe. She was to convoy transports with troops and stores to Ostend. During this trip Midshipman Jerrold experienced the usual troubles of all youngsters at sea. His hammock was stolen, so that for six weeks he had to sleep on the floor; in addition to which he got into disgrace with the captain for being too lenient with his men. But all this was nothing to the fine boy, full of glorious enthusiasm. He was at sea, taking part in the hostilities against the French. With that thought in his mind, and the fine sight of the transports surrounding the little brig, these annoyances were not worthy of being entertained for a moment. The "Earnest" entered Ostend harbour only five days before the battle of Waterloo, and then returned to the Nore. After a stay of only two days the little brig was off to sea again. While on this voyage the weather became heavy, so that the "Earnest" had to anchor at Cuxhaven or at Heligoland; where, writes Blanchard Jerrold, "I suspect that the midshipman of the brig, in whom we are interested, fell into sad disgrace. He had gone ashore with Captain Hutchinson, and was left in command of the gig. While the commander was absent, two of the men in the midshipman's charge requested permission to make some trifling purchase. The good-natured officer assented, adding,—

"'By the way, you may as well buy me some apples and a few pears.'

"'All right, Sir,' said the men; and they departed."

The captain presently returned, and still the seamen were away on their errand. They were searched for, but they could not be found. They had deserted. Any naval reader whose eye may wander over this page will readily imagine the disgrace into which Jerrold fell with his captain. Upon the young delinquent the event made a lasting impression, and years afterwards he talked about it with that curious excitement which lit up his face when he spoke of anything he had felt. He remembered even the features of the two deserters, as he had most unexpectedly an opportunity of proving.

The midshipman had long put his dirk aside, and washed the salt from his brave face. He had become a fighter with a keener weapon than his dirk had ever proved, when one day, strolling eastward from the office of his own newspaper, to the printing premises of Messrs. Bradbury and Evans, in Whitefriars, he was suddenly struck with the form and face of a baker, who, with his load of bread at his back, was examining some object in the window of the surgical instrument-maker, who puzzles so many inquisitive passers-by, near the entrance of King's College. There was no mistake. Even the flour dredge could not hide the fact. The ex-midshipman walked nimbly to the baker's side, and, rapping him sharply upon the back, said:—

"I say, my friend, dont you think you've been rather a long time about that fruit?"

The deserter's jaw fell. Thirty years had not calmed the unquiet suggestions of his conscience. He remembered the fruit and the little middy, for he said:—

"Lor! is that you, sir?" The midshipman went on his way laughing.

On the 30th of June, the "Earnest" was back at

Texel. Here Jerrold was witness to one of those dreadful floggings which have of late years excited the public disgust. The after-recollection of the punishment of Michael Ryan for theft always made him heart-sick; and probably incited him, in after-years, to write with his distinguishing vehemence against the "cat."

On the 8th of July, 1815, the "Earnest" was ordered to the Downs, there to receive on board one ensign, forty-seven invalided soldiers, two women, and two children, who were to be conveyed to Sheerness. This ghastly cargo was a remnant of the battle of Waterloo: the raw stumps and festering wounds gave the young middy a lively sense of the horror of war. Subsequent years failed to erase a vivid recollection of the stench from and groans of the sufferers. When this duty was performed, the "Earnest" had discharged her last trust. Europe was preparing for a long peace, in which a gun-brig could be of no manner of use. Orders came therefore that the ship's company should be paid off. Accordingly, on the 21st of October, 1815, the Middy Douglas Jerrold stepped on shore, and his service in the Navy was at an end. His son insists, however, that he remained through life at heart a sailor. "He loved the sea—was proud of British oak."

"Yet he spoke with horror of the hardships of a sailor's life. That a boy should 'rough it' was an idea he frequently and earnestly put forth. He believed that the roughing process gave manliness to a boy's nature—that it steeled him to fight the world. Yet he saw in the life of a 'middy' something too rough to be good—something that might make a very brutal man. His admiration for the midshipman who had fought his way to command, and had kept the gold of his original nature in him—who had developed into a bluff, daring man, with that wondrous touch of feminine tenderness which belongs to sailors of the better class—his admiration for this triumph of nature over adverse conditions, was boundless. Of Nelson he would talk by the hour, and some of his more passionate articles were written to scathe the Government that left Horatio—Nelson's legacy to his country—in want. It was difficult to persuade him, nevertheless, that a man did wisely in sending his son to sea. A friend called on him one day to introduce a youth, who smitten with love for the salt, was about to abandon a position he held in a silk manufacturer's establishment, for the cockpit. 'Humph!' said the ex-midshipman of the 'Earnest;' so you're going to sea. To what department of industry, may I enquire, do you now give your exertions?' 'Silk,' briefly responded the youth. 'Well, go to sea, and it will be worsted.'"

After his two years' sea-service, Douglas was received once more in the arms of his old grandmother. Fortune was not dealing kindly with his father—the peace was certain ruin to the Sheerness Theatre. Certain alterations which Mr. Samuel Jerrold had been induced to make in the theatre, which amounted to the re-erection of the entire building; the unjust dealings of the men to whom he committed the work, with losses at Southend, compelled him to relinquish management altogether. The final blow was struck when the Government resolved to claim the land upon which the theatre stood. Then it was that the brave young wife went forth to London to pave the way for the family, leaving her children and her now aged husband to brood upon their misfortunes. At the close of the year the family left Sheerness never to return.

"About seven o'clock in the morning, on the first day of the year 1816, the Chatham boat arrived in London. A sharp, damp, and foggy dawn very appropriately ushered in to Mr. Samuel Jerrold the three or four sad years he was destined to spend within the sound of Bow Bell. His son Douglas, whose coat had been stolen from the cabin, and who, therefore, trudged for the first time, along London streets hardly prepared for the fog or the cold, probably felt neither the sharpness of the wind nor the suffocating tendency of the fog. The scene was new to him, and all that is new is welcome to the young. Holding his sister by the hand, he walked the streets for some minutes on his own responsibility, while his father stepped aside to comfort himself with a draught of purl. The young middy might well try thus early, even for a few minutes, the effect of walking alone in

London! A house in Broad Court, Bow Street, received the family—a humble lodging enough; but the general peace, and the confiscation of the land upon which the theatre stood, had ruined them utterly. Fortune, food, had to be sought. This Broad Court, with its dingy houses; its troops of noisy, ragged boys, its brawls and cries; was the first impression of the great city. Here, too, for the first time, Douglas came to hob-and-nob with the stern realities of the world. As yet he had passed a youth not remarkable for its vicissitudes, and he had been two years in His Majesty's navy, in the position, and with the prospects of a gentleman."

But what was he to do now that he was in London? He had thought of a little work for himself—not likely, at that time at least, to result in any profit. Meeting one of his father's former actors, of whose abilities he seems to have had a very high estimation, he said: "Oh, Mr. Wilkinson! your are sure to succeed, and I'll write a piece for you." Rather presumptuous this!

Yet the boy spoke earnestly. He felt that there was the strength in him to produce. He was measuring himself by others; and possibly—it is the custom of youth—was dwarfing the capacities of the successful men about him as much as he over-estimated his own power. In after years, he could hardly suppress his disgust for the assumptions of young men or boys. "It appears to be a habit," he would say, "among young fellows, to think they're frogs before they're tadpoles." For his keen eye saw the fall that was coming to every man who started in life with the idea that at one spring he would carry the world with him. This bitter feeling was the fruit of long sorrow. For many years his passionate soul suffered agony, as day by day opportunities flew by—as time after time, utterings were cast into print, and left unnoticed. The deep religion that, to him, lay in the true outpouring of every human soul, kept a burning desire in his heart, making him irascible, fierce; because the expression of this religion was, for the moment, denied him. Yet he had the sailor's manful bearing too—the sailor's hearty spirit in him. If he had left the sea, and the dangers of the sea, he could still find pleasure in banding together the boys of his neighbourhood, and leading them to a fierce conflict against a rival band in Broad Court; and he always liked to see something of the combative spirit in boys. "I can remember," writes his son, "that, when I was a child about seven years old, he knelt one day upon the lawn behind his house in Thistle Grove, Chelsea, and, calling me to him, gave me a lesson in sparring. I was, of course, afraid to strike out; but he repeatedly shouted to me to hit hard, and aim at his head. Years afterwards he would relate with obvious glee, how certain of his boys, with their schoolfellows had repeatedly thrashed a whole village of French urchins. The pugnacious element was peculiar in him decidedly. It is clear, unmistakable in all his writings; it gave a zest to his conversation. It extended to physical prowess; for he, borne down by rheumatism, was heard, in a moment of anger, to threaten the eviction through the window of a gentleman standing six feet. He would wander in after-life through the most lonely places at any hour of the night, calm as in his own study. I call to mind an occasion on which, when walking home with him, a gardener, a square, strong man, hustled me as he passed. The father turned upon him, and bade him 'take care of the child.' The man replied with a gross impertinence. In a minute the father's hat and stick were in my trembling hands, and a hard blow would have been dealt in a minute had not the burly workman, cowed by the fierceness of his opponent, slunk away." This spirit, irrepressible in the man, must have been very fierce in the boy, when the blood was hot. It must have made him eager to enter the lists—to be independent. The poverty of his parents at this time was a new stimulus to him, and when he was apprenticed to Mr. Sidney, a printer in Northumberland Street, Strand, he went to his work with hearty good will. The naval uniform was thrown away, the dirk was given to good Mrs. Reid, to be treasured by her, and a dress suited to the new position was put on eagerly.

"There was something congenial to the young apprentice in the business of a printer. It brought him, in some degree, into connection with books. It would be his duty, at any rate, to set up the thoughts, the teachings of others; and, biding his time, and reading hard, to put the stick aside some day, and take up the pen. This was his burning hope when he went every morning at daylight to Mr. Sidney's printing offices; and as books fell in his way, the hope became a passion. I have often heard him describe his work at this period of his life, with honest pride. He would tell me how he had risen with the first peep of day to study his Latin grammar alone, before going to work; how he had fallen upon Shakespear, and had devoured every line of the great master; and how, with his old father, who was a thoughtful, if a weak man, he had sat in the intervals of his labour, to read a novel of Sir Walter Scott's, obtained, by pinching, from a library. He used to relate a story, with great delight, of a certain day on which he was useful in several capacities to his father. The two were alone in London: Mrs. Jerrold and her daughter were in the country. The young apprentice brought home, joyfully enough, his first earnings. Very dreary was his home, with his poor weak father sitting in the chimney corner; but there was a fire in the boy that would light up that home; at any rate, they would be cheerful for one day. The apprintice, with the first solid fruits of industry in his pocket, sallied forth to buy the dinner. The ingredients of a beefsteak-pie were quickly got together, and the purchaser returned to be rewarded with the proud look of his father. To earn the pie was one thing, but who could make it? Young Douglas would try his hand at a crust! Merrily the manufacture went forward; the pie was made. Then the little busy fellow saw that he must carry it to the bakehouse. Willingly went he forth; for, with the balance of his money, it had been agreed that he should hire the last of Sir Walter's volumes, and return to read it to his father while the dinner was in the oven. The memory of this day always remained vivid to him. There was an odd kind of humour about it that tickled him. It so thoroughly illustrated his notions of independence, that he could not forbear dwelling again and again on it among his friends. 'Yes, sir,' he would say, emphatically, 'I earned the pie, I made the pie, I took it to the bakehouse. I fetched it home; and my father said, Really the boy made the crust remarkably well.'"

When Jerrold was in his fourteenth year he had formed the determination to write. He had already begun to compose little bits of prose and poetry. The book which was his constant companion was Shakespear. He has often been heard to say, that when he was a young man, nobody could quote a line from the works of the immortal bard, to which he could not instantly add the next line. "Young men now-a-days," he would often repeat, "read neither their Bible nor their Shakespear enough."

"In 1818 (his fifteenth year), I presume," writes Wilkinson, "he wrote his first piece. It was sent in to Mr. Arnold, of the English Opera House, and it remained in the theatre for two years. It was probably never read. After some difficulty, he got it back. In the year 1821, Mr. Egerton, of Covent Garden Theatre, becoming manager of Sadler's Wells Theatre, and I having a short time to spare between the closing of the Adelphi and the opening of the Lyceum, he wished me to engage with him for a few weeks, which I did, but on condition of his purchasing the farce which had been returned from the English Opera House, and producing it on the first night of my engagement, giving me the character intended for me. The original title of this piece was 'The Duellists'—a weak title, I thought, for Sadler's Wells; so I re-christened it, calling it 'More Frightened than Hurt.' It was performed, for the first time, on Monday, the 30th of April, 1821, in its author's eighteenth year." It was received, according to the play-bills', with rapturous applause. "It was," continues Mr. Wilkinson, "highly successful, and however meanly the author may have thought of it in after days, it had merit enough to be translated and acted on the French stage; and, oddly enough, some years after it had been produced in France, Mr. Kenney being in Paris, saw it played there, and, not knowing its history, thought it worth while to re-translate it; and he actually brought it out at Madame Vestris's Olympic Theatre, under the name of 'Fighting by Proxy,' Mr. Liston sustaining the character originally performed by me."

"It has been said wisely, that Douglas Jerrold's first printed works appeared in the 'Sunday Monitor,' then edited and printed by his employer, of Lombard Street; but this is not the fact. The author of 'More Frightened than Hurt,' following the almost invariable tendency of young men with something to say, first tempted the judgment of the public by bits of fugitive verse; and this in 'Arliss's Magazine,' a periodical long since forgotten. From the moment when he came in contact with journals, he began to cast off sonnets, epigrams, and short quaint papers. It is true that the young compositor, having an order to see 'Der Freischutz,' went to the theatre, and became so possessed with the harmony of the work, that he wrote a critical paper on it, and dropped the composition into Mr. Bigg's letter-box. He passed an anxious night, we may be certain, when this adventurous step had been taken. And that was a bright morrow when the editor handed him his own article to compose, together with an address to the anonymous correspondent, asking for further contributions. His way from the case to the writer's desk was bridged, though years might pass before he should be able finally to pass from the mechanical drudgery to the intellectual pursuit. It was true that Jerrold's first article in the 'Monitor' was a criticism on 'Der Freischutz,' but it is not true that this article was his first appearance in print."

Subsequently, his sisters remember the boisterous delight with which he would occasionally bound into the house with a little publication in his hand, shouting, "It's in, it's in!"

Our limits will not permit us to do more than thus accompany Douglas to the confines of his literary pilgrimage. Otherwise, it would be a pleasant task to follow him through his life of work; to enjoy the rich flavour of his comedies—ever "pointing a moral and adorning a tale;" again to laugh at his exquisite word-painting in "Punch;" and admire once more the manly and patriotic spirit which ever fired his breast in the defence of the wronged and the injured, despite the threats or cajolings of friend or foe.

On the 8th of June, 1857, without a struggle, peacefully as a child falls asleep in its nurse's arms, this brave, strong, self-reliant man—worker for all men, and for all time, fell into his long rest, with a smile upon his face.

'Yet mourn not idly o'er his grave—the words he left behind
Were something more than empty sounds that die upon the wind;
Their echoes through men's hearts shall ring, as onward years shall roll,
And men will own the master-hand, and say, 'God rest his soul.'"

DAVID LIVINGSTONE:

THE POOR FACTORY LAD; NOW DR. LIVINGSTONE, THE FAMOUS AFRICAN EXPLORER.

It is a very old saying, but a very true one, "that truth is stranger than fiction." Who can imagine changes, in fairy land even, greater than those effected by the marvels of science? Fairies, genii, gnomes, dwarfs with golden hair, wonderful lamps, enchanted wands and rings, have all been rivalled long ago by electricity and by steam. Why, that daring "Puck" never conceived a time so short to put a girdle round the earth, as we can now encircle it with a stream of electricity! But what was the girdle worth when "put round?" and what is our stream of electricity worth? The one is the toy of a child, the other a powerful instrument in the hands of a giant. Many years agone, so it is said, visits could be paid to strange old men and women, who had, amongst other curiosities—stuffed alligators and dried bats being the chief—a marvellous magic mirror, which, after certain cabalistic words had been pronounced, would reflect the image of some dear friend or loved relation for a single instant, and would then vanish. Now, by the aid of photography, our fathers and mothers and loved relatives can peep at a glass four inches square, prepared not with any enchantment, but with a little collodion, sold by most chemists, and their loved images will be reflected and retained for many coming years. And then again, all the stories of converting cinder-girls into princesses, porters and market-men into grand viziers and chief magistrates, by the touch of a wand or the exercise of a wish—why, that is not so marvellous as the reality. Look at this fact in illustration:—David Livingstone was a poor factory lad; he is now one of the most successful travellers, and for his scientific attainments the learned societies of all countries have vied to do him honour. He is a gold medallist and corresponding member of the Royal Geographical Societies of London and Paris, and Doctor of Civil Laws of the University of Oxford.

David's great-grandfather fell at the memorable battle of Culloden: that is something to be proud of; his grandfather, like many men of a past race, was intimately acquainted with all the legends and stories which formed the foundation of Sir Walter Scott's "Tales of a Grandfather," and other thrilling narratives. David was a willing and a delighted listener to the recital of these legends. His grandmother, also, had stores of Gaelic songs, which she sang for the amusement of our hero, and which she believed had been composed by captive islanders, languishing hopelessly among the Turks. David's grandfather could trace the family tree for six generations; he could state incidents, and give interesting particulars of the various members for so long time back. David remembers with pleasure one fact in connection with his family. A poor islander, one of his ancestors, who was renowned in the district for great wisdom and prudence, when he was on his deathbed, called all his children round him and said: "Now, in my lifetime I have searched most carefully through all the traditions I could find of our family, and I never could discover that there was a dishonest man among our forefathers. If, therefore, any of you, or any of your children should take to dishonest ways, it will not be because it runs in our blood; it does not belong to you. I leave this precept with you: Be honest."

David's grandfather, in order to support his family, removed to the neighbourhood of the Clyde, near Glasgow, where his sons were received as clerks in the cotton manufactory of Monteith and Co. He acquired a reputation for unflinching honesty, and was employed by the proprietors of the works to convey large sums of money to and from Glasgow; and when he had grown old in their service he was pensioned off, so that his declining years were passed in comfort.

David's uncle, during the French war, entered the army and navy; his father, however, remained at home engaged in the not very important duties of a small tea dealer. His kindliness of manner and excellence of disposition caused him to be loved and respected by his children. His example to his offspring was such as that which is so beautifully and truthfully depicted in Scotland's great poem—"The Cottar's Saturday Night." He died when Livingstone was on his travels, expecting some day to return and have the pleasure of sitting by the cottage fire to relate his adventures.

David was born at the village of Blantyre, Scotland, in or about the year 1817, and when he was ten years of age, he says: "I was put into the factory as a 'piercer,' to aid by my earnings in lessening my mother's anxiety. With a part of my first week's wages I purchased Ruddiman's 'Rudiments of Latin,' and pursued the study of the language for many years afterwards, with unabated ardour, at an evening school which met between the hours of eight and ten. The dictionary part of my labours was followed up till twelve o'clock or later, if my mother did not interfere by jumping up and snatching the book out of my hands. I had to be back in the factory by six in the morning, and continue my work, with intervals for breakfast and dinner, until eight o'clock in the evening. I read in this way many of the classical authors, and knew Virgil and Horace better at sixteen than I do now. Our schoolmaster, happily still alive, was supported in part by the company; he was attentive and kind, and so moderate in his charges, that all who wished for education might have obtained it. Many availed themselves of the privilege; and some of my school-fellows now rank in position far above what they ever appeared likely to come to when in the village school."

Everything in the shape of good books—that is, books of travel and treatises upon scientific subjects, he read with avidity; and, from his subsequent life, there can be no doubt that what he read he remembered—no mere time-killing, but earnest, anxious, thoughtful reading, in order that he might *know* and *learn*. While he was at his work, even, he managed to turn to good account the stray moments which his employment afforded him.

"In recognising the plants pointed out in my first medical book," he writes, "that extraordinary old work on astrological medicine, 'Culpeppers's Herbal,' I had the guidance of a book on the plants of Lanarkshire, by Patrick. Limited as my time was, I found opportunities to scour the whole country side, 'collecting simples.' Deep and anxious were my studies on the still deeper and more perplexing profundities of astrology, and I believe I got as far into that abyss of fantasies as my author said he dared to lead me. It seemed perilous ground to tread on farther, for the dark hint seemed to my youthful mind to loom towards 'selling soul and body to the devil,' as the price of the unfathomable knowledge of the stars. These excursions, often in company with brothers, one now in Canada, the other a clergyman in the United States, gratified my intense love of nature; and though we generally returned so unmercifully hungry and fatigued that the embryo parson shed tears, yet we discovered so many, to us, new and interesting things, that he was always as eager to join us next time as he was the last.

"On one of these exploring tours we entered a limestone quarry—long before geology was so popular as it is now. It is impossibe to describe the delight and wonder with which I began to collect the shells found in the carboniferous limestone which crops out in High Blantyre and Cambuslang. A quarryman seeing a little boy so engaged, looked with that pitying eye which the benevolent assume when viewing the insane. Addressing him with, 'How ever did these shells come into these rocks?' 'When God made the rocks, he made the shells in them,' was the damping reply. What would Hugh Miller have thought of this Scotchman?

"My reading while at work," he further says, "was carried on by placing the book on a portion of the spinning-jenny, so that I could catch sentence after sentence as I passed at my work; I thus kept up a pretty constant study, undisturbed by the roar of the machinery. To this part of my education I owe my present power of so completely abstracting the mind from surrounding noises, as to read and write with perfect comfort amidst the play of children or the dancing and songs of savages. The toil of cotton-spinning, to which I was promoted in my nineteenth year, was excessively severe on a slim, loose-jointed lad, but it was well paid for; and it enabled me to support myself while attending medical and Greek classes in winter, also the divinity lectures of Dr. Wardlaw, by working with my hands in summer. I never received a farthing of aid from any one, and should have accomplished my project of going to China as a medical missionary, in the course of time, by my own efforts, had not some of my friends advised my joining the London Missionary Society; but it was not without a pang that I offered myself, for it was not quite agreeable to one accustomed to work his own way to become in a measure dependent on others; and I would not have been much put about though my offer had been rejected."

Livingstone does not regret that his first years were devoted to intense labour; on the contrary, he rejoices that they were so spent. He says: "Looking back now on that life of toil I cannot but feel thankful that it formed such a material part of my early education; and, were it possible, I should like to begin life over again in the same lowly style, and to pass through the same hardy training."

These sentiments are alike creditable to his head and heart. What eminence is there in the world which can equal that which has been won from indigence and obscurity? To be born to riches and rank is certainly no disgrace; but riches and rank do not of themselves entitle to honour and esteem. We respect men for their personal merits, for their efforts to acquire knowledge, and to diffuse to others the results of their attainments. These things constitute the true *nobleman*. If, therefore, we had no other reason to esteem Livingstone, this confession of his, of not only coming from the ranks of the factory workers, but glorying in the fact, secures the admiration of good men, and presents an example for all coming time to every youth and earnest man.

An observation may be made here, in opposition to the opinion generally entertained, that greatness or eminence is the result of some accident, or peculiarity of situation, or class of mind born or inherited. It was the opinion of Sir Joshua Reynolds that "the superiority attainable in any pursuit whatever does not originate in an innate propensity of the mind for that pursuit in particular, but depends on the general strength of the intellect, and on the intense and constant application of that strength to a specific purpose." And in confirmation reference need only be made to the habits of any really great man, who will tell you that the secret of his success has been—application, constant and ever enduring work. David Livingstone, as we have seen, is no exception to this rule. By dint of hard work he finished his medical course of study, and was admitted a Licentiate of the

Faculty of Physicians and Surgeons. His delight on this consummation arose from the fact that he was now better fitted for works of practical benevolence.

Owing to the China war, it was not deemed advisable that he should proceed to that country. Hearing the celebrated Robert Moffatt preach, upon his return from Africa, he determined, and, acting upon his determination, offered himself to the London Missionary Society to go out to that country. He was, to his great satisfaction, accepted, and returned with Moffatt to the Kuruman station. While there, he learned many things which were afterwards of great service to him; made himself acquainted with the language, and learned to ride upon oxen. After leaving Kuruman he proceeded to Kolobeng, about two hundred miles to the north, where he built mission premises—chapel, school-house, dwelling-house, &c. Desirous of ascertaining the truth of the statement made by the people at the station that about a month's journey there was a large river and inland sea, he set out on an exploring expedition. Great difficulties were encountered in crossing the Sahara desert, but finally the noble river Zouga was reached. Here, impatient for further discoveries, Livingstone got a rude canoe constructed, and committed himself to the mercy of the waters of the newly discovered river. His object was, if possible, to arrive at the lake Ngami. On the 4th of July, 1849, David reached the broad part of the lake, "when, for the first time, this fine-looking sheet of water was beheld by Europeans." Having ascertained beyond all doubt the existence of this great river and lake, Livingstone planned a further journey across the Zouga, with the intention of seeing what country lay beyond. In this second journey he ascertained that the lake was seventy miles in length, about twenty-five miles in breadth, and that it was nearly 3000 feet above the level of the sea. In the December of 1851 he commenced his third journey. This time he packed up all his property, and with his wife and three children started for the interior of Africa. His intention was, if possible, to reach Linyanté—a town said to be in existence, and where a friendly chief was said to reside named Sebitome. After crossing the Zouga and travelling 200 miles north, he arrived at a dried-up salt lake, or inland sea, about 100 miles in length and fifty in breath; it was encrusted with pure white salt. Diverging in a north-westerly direction he made the discovery of the splendid river Chobe, which is larger, and surrounded with finer scenery than the Zouga. After crossing the Chobe, he soon reacked Linyanté, where he was most hospitably received. He remained here some considerable time, occupied in taking observations and noting the manners and customs of the natives. Finding, however, that the place was unfavourable for a missionary station, on account of its inundations, he returned to

Kuruman, and wrote to the Directors of the London Missionary Society that he had only half done his work; but, having had his arm broken by a lion—though that was nothing—and his throat being diseased, he should be compelled to go to the Cape to recruit. Whilst at Cape Down, where he embarked his wife and family for England, he placed himself under the instruction of Mr. Maclear, the astronomer royal, so that in his journeys he might be able to take solar and lunar observations. He was subsequently enabled to take 146 latitudes and longitudes, and about 190 observations; so that now, any person, by using the map made by Livingstone, may go straight to any part of Africa he traversed.

Livingstone left Kuruman on his fourth journey in June, 1852. He crossed the river Zouga, and the dried salt lake, going in his former westerly direction. On this journey the weather was so bad that his oxen and waggon stuck in the mud, so that he had to go forward almost alone. Making use of a small boat he had brought with him, he cut his way for three days and nights down the river for twenty miles, by which means he arrived at Linyantè a second time. The young chief, when he saw Livingstone, lifted up his hands with astonishment, and said, "Well, we did not think any one could reach Linyante in the rainy season, and we intrenched ourselves here that wemight never be invaded. You Englishmen must have dropped from the skies on the back of a hippopotamus." After resting awhile, he again started to reach the western coast, being accompanied by forty-seven of the natives. The chief lent him his canoe, which was twenty inches wide and thirty-four feet long. He and his party reached St. Paul de Loando, on the western coast, having endured on the journey a variety of perils. When the natives saw the sea, their astonishment exceeded all bounds. They said, "Our fathers told us the world had no end; they deceived us; we have come to the place where the world does end, and the world says, 'I'm done, and there is no more of me, but all the rest is water.'" Now that the natives have seen the sea, they attribute all the wonders they cannot understand to it. When they are asked where the cotton goods come from, they always reply, "From the sea." Hence they have a belief that Englishmen live in the sea. All the natives of North Africa have no other idea. Livingstone, when he passed through the villages, was shown as the man living in the sea. As confirmation, the natives pointed to his hair, and said that it was all scaled out with water; and when he was accompanied by his friends from Linyanté, the inhabitants as they passed through the settlements tried to persuade them not to go, "For," said they, "You will be taken down into the sea and eaten." When the party arrived at the coast, Livingstone invited the poor people to go on board some of the ships; but they were still afraid there was some truth in the statement. However, when they were told they could go or not as they liked, they consented. After this visit Livingstone was treated with great respect. The marvels of the ships had made an immense impression upon them.

In 1854, Livingstone commenced his last trip, prior to visiting his father-land. It was his intention to reach the other side of the continent of Africa. On this journey, which was full of difficulty and peril, he discovered that the language into which the Scriptures had been translated by Moffat and Hamilton, was the language spoken throughout Africa. He soon found, also, that which had been the anxious object of his search for six years—a high table land, in every respect well suited for a mission station. On this spot Livingstone founded a mission establishment; and then only did he return for a brief period to old England. He was anxious to bring over one of the natives, who had served him as a faithful servant, but such an effect was produced upon him by the steam-engines and the other novelties of the vessel, that he jumped over-board in a fit of delirium and was drowned.

Livingstone during his sojourn in Africa had many narrow escapes from death. One of his hair-breadth adventures he thus narrates:—

"Returning towards Kuruman, I selected the beautiful valley of Mabotsa as the site of a mission.

ary station; and thither I removed in 1843. Here an occurrence took place, concerning which I have frequently been questioned in England, and which, but for the importunities of friends, I meant to have kept in store to tell my children when in my dotage. The Bakátla of the village Mabotsa were much troubled by lions, which leaped into the cattle-pens by night and destroyed their cows. They even attacked the herds in open day. This was so unusual an occurrence, that the people believed that they were bewitched—'given,' as they said, 'into the power of the lions by a neighbouring tribe.' They went once to attack the animals, but, being rather a cowardly people compared to Bechuanas in general on such occasions, they returned without killing any.

"It is well known that if one in a troop of lions is killed, the others take the hint and leave that part of the country. So the next time the herds were attacked, I went with the people, in order to encourage them to rid themselves of the annoyance by destroying one of the marauders. We found the lions on a small hill, about a quarter of a mile in length, and covered with trees. A circle of men was formed round it, and they gradually closed up, ascending pretty near to each other. Being down below on the plain with a native schoolmaster, named Mebálwe, a most excellent man, I saw one of the lions sitting on a piece of rock within the now closed circle of men. Mebálwe fired at him before I could, and the ball struck the rock on which the animal was sitting. He bit at the spot struck, as a dog does at a stick or stone thrown at him; then leaping away, broke through the opening circle and escaped unhurt, The men were afraid to attack him, perhaps on account of their belief in witchcraft. When the circle was re-formed, we saw two other lions in it; but we were afraid to fire, lest we should strike the men, and they allowed the beasts to burst through also. If the Bakátla had acted according to the custom of the country, they would have speared the lions in their attempt to get out. Seeing we could not get them to kill one of the lions, we bent our footsteps towards the village; in going round the end of the hill, however, I saw one of the beasts sitting on a piece of rock as before, but this time he had a little bush in front. Being about thirty yards off, I took a good aim at his body through the bush, and fired both barrels into it. The men then called out, 'He is shot, he is shot!' Others cried, 'He has been shot by another man, too; let us go to him!' I did not see any one else shoot at him, but I saw the lions tail erected in anger behind the bush, and, turning to the people, said, 'Stop a little till I load again! When in the act of ramming down the bullets I heard a shout.

"Starting and looking half round I saw the lion just in the act of springing upon me. I was upon a little height; he caught my shoulder as he sprang, and we both came to the ground below together. Growling horribly close to my ear, he shook me as a terrier dog does a rat. This shock produced a stupor similar to that which seems to be felt by a mouse after the first shake of the cat. It caused a sort of dreaminess, in which there was no sense of pain, nor feeling of terror, though quite conscious of all that was happening. It was like what patients partially under the influence of chloroform describe, who see all the operation, but feel not the knife. This singular condition was not the result of any mental process. The shake annihilated fear, and allowed no sense of horror in looking round at the beast. This peculiar state is probably produced in all animals killed by the carnivora; and, if so, is a merciful provision by our benevolent Creator for lessening the pain of death. Turning round to relieve myself of the weight, as he had one paw on the back of my head, I saw his eyes directed towards Mebálwe, who was trying to shoot him at a distance of ten or fifteen yards. His gun, a flint one, missed fire in both barrels; the lion immediately left me, and attacking Mebálwe, bit his thigh. Another man, whose life I had saved before, after he had been tossed by a buffalo, attempted to spear the lion while he was biting Mebálwe. He left Mebálwe and caught this man by the shoulders, but at this moment the bullets he had received took effect, and he fell down dead. The whole was the work of a few minutes, and must have been his paroxysm of dying rage. In order to take out the charm from him, the Bakátla on the following day made a huge bonfire over the carcase, which was declared to be that of the largest lion they had ever seen. Besides crunching the bone into splinters, he left eleven teeth wounds on the upper part of my arm. A wound from this animal's tooth resembles a gun-shot wound; it is generally followed by a great deal of sloughing and discharge, and pains are felt periodically ever afterwards. I had on a tartan jacket on the occasion, and I believe that it wiped off all the virus from the teeth that pierced the flesh, for my two companions in this affray have both suffered from the peculiar pains, while I have escaped with only the inconvenience of a false joint in the limb. The man whose shoulder was wounded showed me his wound actually burst forth afresh on the same month of the following year. This curious point deserves the attention of inquirers."

On several other occasions Livingstone was in imminent danger, at times by hunger and thirst, and then his life was in peril by the hands of savages, and the repeated attacks of fever, while exposure to drought and rains, to heat and cold, make it almost a miracle that he should have been preserved. After braving these dangers he returned to his dearly loved country but for a brief season—scarcely sufficient to render to his countrymen an account of his wanderings, and then returned to the scene of his usefulness;

this time, as an explorer, bearing a government commission, and accompanied by companions suited for observing the various features of a newly opened up country.

So recently as June last Sir George Grey received a letter from the distinguished traveller, containing a sketch of some important geographical discoveries.

"River Shire, June 1, 1859.

"MY DEAR SIR GEORGE,—We have lately discovered a very fine lake by going up this river in the steam launch above 100 miles, and then marching some fifty more on foot. It is called Shirwa, and Lake N'gami is a mere pond in comparison. It is, however, particularly interesting from the fact reported by the natives on its shores, that it is separated by a strip of land of only five or six miles in width from Nyanja, or Lake N'yinyesi—the stars—which Burton has gone to explore. We could hear nothing of his party at Shirwa, and having got no European news since you kindly sent some copies of the 'Times' last year, we are quite in the dark as to whether he has succeeded or not. Lake Shirwa has no outlet, and its waters are bitter, but drinkable. It abounds in fishes, leeches, alligators, and hippopotami. We discovered also by examining, partly a branch of the Shire, called Ruo, that one portion of the Shirwa is not more than thirty miles distant from a point that may easily be reached by this launch, which by newspaper measurement draws thirteen inches, and actually thirty-one. The Lake Shirwa is very grand. It is surrounded on all sides by lofty green mountains. Dzomba, or, as people nearest it say, Zomba, is over 6,000 feet high, of same shape as Table Mountain, but inhabited on the top; others are equally high, but inaccessible. It is a high land region—the lake itself being about 2,000 feet above the sea. It is twenty or thirty miles wide, and fifty or sixty long. On going some way up a hill, we saw in the far distance two mountain tops, rising like little islands on a watery horizon. An inhabited mountain island stands near where we first came to it. From the size of the waves it is supposed to be deep. Mr. Maclear will show you the map. Dr. Kirk and I, with fifteen Makololo, formed the land party. The country is well peopled, and very much like Londa in the middle of the country, many streams rising out of bogs—the vegetation nearly identical also. Never saw so much cotton grown as among the Manganga of the Shire and Shirwa Valleys—all spin and weave it. These are the latitudes which I have always pointed out as the cotton and sugar lands; they are pre-eminently so, but such is the disinterestedness of some people, that labour is exported to Bourbon, instead of being employed here. The only trade the people have is that of slaves; and the only symptoms of impudence we met were from a party of Bajana slave traders; but they changed their deportment instantly on hearing that we were English, and not Portuguese. There are no Maravi at or near Shirwa; they are all west of the Shire, so this lake can scarcely be called Lake Maravi; the Portuguese know nothing of it; but the minister who claimed (blue book for 1857) the honour of first traversing the African continent for two black men with Portuguese names, must explain why they did not cross Shirwa. It lies some forty or fifty miles on each side of the latitude of Mozambique. They came to Tete only, and lacked at least 400 miles of Mozambique. We go back to Shirwa in July, and may make a push for N'yinyesi.

(Signed) DAVID LIVINGSTONE."

No doubt the wonders of Africa are only just entered upon; and that, if the life of Livingstone is spared, his labours will not only result in incalculable blessings to the natives, but be the source of material advantages to his own countrymen. This imperfect sketch of Dr. Livingstone may be fittingly closed by the estimate of his character, given at a great meeting held at the Senate House at Cambridge, by the eloquent and learned Chancellor of the Exchequer, Mr. Gladstone. Upon that occasion he said:—

"Dr. Livingstone is such a man as raises our idea of the age in which we live. That simplicity inseparable from true grandeur, that breadth and force, that superiority to all wordly calls and enjoyments, that rapid and keen intelligence, that power of governing men, and that delight in governing them for their own good—he has every sign upon him of a great man, and his qualities are precisely those which commend themselves with resistless power to the young by whom we see this building crowded. For when I stand in this noble structure, I cannot stay for a moment to admire its magnificent proportions. It is not the gold, but the temple that sanctifieth the gold; it is not the Senate House of Cambridge, beautiful as it is, but it is the minds and hearts of those by whom it is filled that alone can draw attention for a moment. Let us render to Dr. Livingstone the full tribute of what we feel. Dr. Livingstone is a Christian, a missionary, a great traveller; he corresponds in every particular to that great name which the admiration of all ages has consecrated—he is a hero. Your own great poet—the great poet of this age—Alfred Tennyson—in his 'Idylls of the King,' a work which has taken its place in the deathless literature of the world, has carried us back to a period of heroic manners, heroic deeds, and heroic characters; but if the power which he possesses could have gone beyond what it has effected, could have gone beyond the almost living men whom it has portrayed, and could actually have evoked them from the tomb, not one among them, though the ideal of human nature, would have failed to recognise Dr. Livingstone as a brother, and to acknowledge him as his most worthy companion."

Since these words were spoken, the following very interesting communication has been received by Mr. William Logan, of Glasgow, from Dr. Livingstone's brother, Mr. Charles Livingstone:—

"Kongone, mouth of the Zambesi, Dec. 1, 1859.

"My Dear Friend,—We have explored the river Shiré to its source in the great lake Nyassa. This river is about 200 miles long, and has a deep channel for 112 miles from its mouth. A series of rapids then commence, extending about 30 miles, after which there is no other impediment to navigation to Lake Nyassa; and how far that extends to the north, we are as yet unable to say; natives informed us that it took three months to reach the head of the lake.

"The Shiré flows through an exceedingly fertile valley, which is bounded by two ranges of lofty hills, and is from 10 to 12 miles wide at the lake, and from 20 to 30 below the cataracts. East of the cataracts are the highlands—a magnificent country, well watered, and wooded, with a rich soil, and pretty numerous population. From the large number of old grey-headed people we met, it would appear to be a fine healthy country, well adapted for European constitutions. The men are all armed with bows and arrows, or spears, yet they do not seem to be blood-thirsty. As a general thing, they treated us with civility. As was natural, they were at first somewhat suspicious, but as soon as we told them what our object was, their suspicions vanished. One chief, however, said that parties had come to them before with as fine a story as we had, and after a few days, jumped up, seized a number of his people, and carried them off as slaves. We suspected that he himself engaged in this business. The country is well adapted for cattle and sheep, yet the inhabitants possess only a few goats, and still fewer sheep. Besides various kinds of provisions, &c., they grow cotton largely. In the highlands and lowlands, through two and a half degrees of latitude, we met with cotton everywhere, and it may be as fine a cotton country for several degrees farther to the north than we were. We went no farther than the foot of Lake Nyassa. Some cotton patches covered three acres, though for the most part they did not exceed half an acre. Each family seems to have its own cotton plantation, which is carefully cultivated. They could raise almost any amount if they had a market for it. The cotton is of two kinds—the foreign and the native. The former is of good staple and quality; the latter is short in the staple, and feels more like wool than cotton. The foreign is perennial, and requires planting only once in three years. It is burned down before the rains, and soon springs up of its own accord. The native has to be planted every year in the highlands. The people prefer it, because, they say, it makes the stronger cloth. In well nigh every village, we saw men spinning cotton, while others were weaving it into strong cloth, in looms of very simple construction. Both spinning and weaving are a very tedious process.

"They are all anxious to trade. The women were often up all night grinding their corn to sell to us. One village we passed without halting. The inhabitants followed us, calling upon our guide to return with them to trade. As a last argument, they shouted 'Are we to have it said that white people came to our country and we did not see them?'

"They are by no means teetotalers. Large quantities of beer are manufactured by them, and they are as fond of it as our countrymen are of whisky. The chief of a village almost always presented us with a large pot of beer. We passed a village one day, and saw a large party of men sitting smoking in the public square, who did not seem at all communicative. After resting a little under a tree, a short distance from them, they sent us a calabash of beer, to see if we were friends, which was to be manifested by our partaking of it. We saw many partially intoxicated people, tipsy chiefs, and even members of the learned professions get 'a little elevated at times.' A native doctor, with his cupping-horn hanging round his neck, who had evidently been making some deep potations, came out and scolded us severely: 'Is this the way to enter a man's village, without sending him word that you were coming?' Entering a hut, he came out staggering under a large pot of beer, which he presented to us. Perhaps his patients only pay him with beer. I wish we had a few hundred good, industrious Scotch families on these fertile highlands. Instead of, as at home, toiling for a bare subsistence, here they could cultivate largely sugar and cotton, &c., benefit the natives by their example, and furnish materials for our manufacturers at home. We have a healthy country, and, with the exception of thirty miles, over which a road can be constructed, water communication all the way to England. The natives are industrious, and somewhat ingenious. They have better houses and implements than any on the Zambesi. They would not, I think, molest emigrants. With good missionaries, the most happy results might be anticipated.—Yours, with much esteem.

"CHARLES LIVINGSTONE."

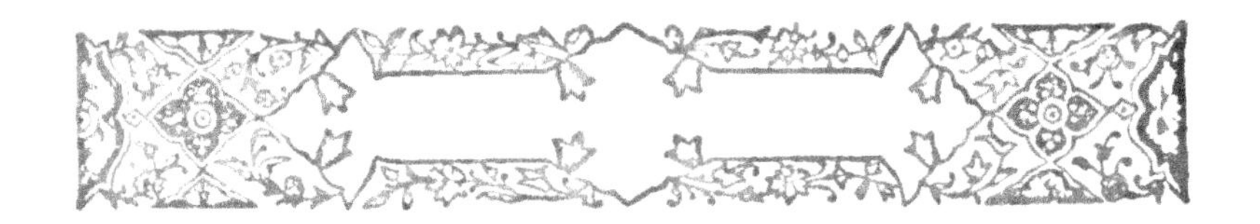

JAMES MORRISON:

STABLE BOY, MERCHANT, MEMBER OF PARLIAMENT, AND MILLIONAIRE.

WHEN the Right Hon. B. Disraeli, M.P., addressed the associated members of the mechanics' institutes of Lancashire and Cheshire, in the Manchester Free Trade Hall, he gave birth to a number of truisms which it would be well should find a resting-place in the mind of every youth and young man that has his way to make in the world. On that occasion he said:—"I do not think there is any greater fallacy than that which holds up England as a country in which it is difficult to advance, for those who have intelligence and integrity. Take this as an incontrovertible principle, accept this as a moral dogma of your life, 'every man has his opportunity.' It may be a long time coming, but, depend upon it, it is sure to arrive; and what you have got to do in the interval is, to prepare yourselves for that opportunity. Life is not a lottery. Life is a science, and certain qualities and certain talents, properly handled and properly managed, must lead to certain results."

In confirmation of this opinion, no better illustration could be adduced than that furnished in the life of James Morrison, who rose from the utmost obscurity to the possession of immense wealth. His parents, like the parents of many great men, were in indigent circumstances and unknown, save to the poor neighbours by whom their humble dwelling was surrounded. James first saw the light in 1780, the county of Hants being his birthplace. His first years were passed in the midst of the difficulties which labourers in the agricultural counties have specially to contend with. But so soon as he became conscious of his position—aware of the actual circumstances by which he was surrounded—he determined, with much strength of mind and will, to make an effort to advance himself in life. His desire was to obtain a situation in some large thriving town, where, as he thought, opportunities would constantly occur by which a boy could "get on." His poverty, however, prevented this consummation of his wishes; he did therefore the next best thing: he engaged himself as a stable-boy on Wallop Common, near Salisbury Plain, where the mail coach for the West of England to the metropolis changed horses.

The novelty and interest of this new and quick mode of travelling was not calculated to still the longing desire which had taken possession of young Morrison, to see something of the great world beyond the confines of his limited sphere. After long brooding and considering the matter, he formed a resolution not to allow the mail to make many journeys to London without being one of the passengers. Consulting a friend on the desirability of the venture, he was strongly urged to take the journey, and an offer was made of a loan of two guineas, to enable him to live in London for a little time, without absolute want, until a situation was obtained. After this needful provision was made, James was not long before he found himself on the outside of the mail on his way to the great world of London. No doubt, like many other adventurers, his anticipations and the first realization were not exactly one and the same thing. Whatever was ultimately realized, James found London streets *not* paved with gold. For a length of time he wandered about in great despondency, quite unsuccessful in obtaining work of any description, and finally was so much reduced as to be compelled again to appeal to his friend, who had assisted him on starting, for a further advance of thirty shillings. When this needed assistance came to to hand, James took fresh courage, nerving himself for another battle with the difficulties of his position. We can scarcely conceive of a state more lonely and disheartening. Here he was in the city of all others where sympathy and friendly aid were least to be expected. He had no introductions, he was a perfect stranger, his previous situation was not likely to be a passport to one in London, and, withal, he was ignorant of the simplest elements of common education. Notwithstanding these serious sources of discouragement, he persevered with almost unexampled diligence, which at length resulted in his obtaining a situation as a porter in a small drapery establishment on Fish Street Hill. Here he was not fated long to remain. His inward craving for progress prevented his being satisfied with his laborious and comparatively ill-paid situation. He was fortunate, however, to meet with employment and advanced wages in the firm of Messrs. Todd, East Cheap. Here he had ample opportunity to bring into activity his commercial spirit, his wonderful perseverance, and exemplary attention to business. As his tact and ability were recognized by the head of the firm, he was advanced to a position of considerable trust and responsibility, until ultimately he became chief salesman in the wholesale department. His new position emboldened him to sue for the hand of Miss Todd; whom he subsequently led to the altar, amid the congratulations of friends, and with the prospect of much domestic happiness. The relation in which he now stood to the head of the firm, made it desirable that he should have a closer connection with the business, and he was at once taken into partnership. Ultimately, at the death of Todd, the entire concern fell into his hands. Then it was, when he could command the needful capital, that his clear-sighted commercial spirit manifested itself. He was not satisfied with the progress made by his own concern, but with the keenness of a speculator he bought up, from time to time, tea, sugar, silk, &c. His capital enabling him to hold these goods over until the price advanced, he was by this means enabled to derive considerable profits, and ultimately amass immense wealth. He did not consider it neeful to sell in the dearest markets, if he bought in the cheapest. He was, in this respect, a trade reformer—selling at a less rate of profit than any other firm.

But commercial success by no means satisfied him. He had gone through the entire routine of business-life—he had experienced its anxieties, and had reaped its golden rewards. But there was yet another step to which his ambition pointed—he desired the honour of being a member of the British Parliament; ultimately he attained his wish by being returned for the borough of St. Ives; and when the new parliament was convened, after the passing of the Reform Bill, he was elected member for Ipswich. Subsequently he represented in the House of Commons the district of Inverness Burghs, for which he sat until his health failed.

His political principles were those known as "advanced liberal." In the early days of his political life he had avowed himself in favour of a fixed duty on corn, but afterwards joined the great Anti-corn-law League, and most magnificently contributed towards its funds. When the landed interest interposed by every means the attainment of the object of the "League," Morrison proposed that a mammoth subscription should be raised that should at once set the question of funds at rest. He proposed to head the subscription with a donation of one *hundred thousand pounds!* The concession on the part of Sir Robert Peel, and the subsequent repeal of the truly obnoxious impost, rendered this princely donation unnecessary.

We have thus traced the progress of Morrison from indigence to affluence. His closing career furnishes another and very striking illustration of the mutation of all sublunary things, and of the great evil of setting our affections too completely upon objects of time and sense. The possession of wealth, as shown in the case of Morrison, was, in one respect, a good thing, because it enabled him to do good and to communicate, and to give practical effect to the promptings of his benevolent disposition; but it ultimately, in a moral sense, proved to his disadvantage. He had made business and the process of accumulation an object of too absorbing interest, regardless of the oft-felt experience, that the mind centred upon one object merely, is apt to become unsettled by the perpetual and unnatural strain upon it. It proved so in the instance of Morrison. The great law of compensation, which enjoins that mortals shall reap that which they sow, was no more abrogated in his case than in any other. He had abused his mental constitution by too great an absorption in the prosecution of one idea, and the evil recoiled upon him by inducing a certain mental hallucination, under which he was affected by a constant and most harassing fear of impending poverty. Of course, with a man who could count his resources by hundreds of thousands of pounds—one rich beyond the dreams of avarice—such fear was not only unnecessary, but peurile; so complete a hold, however, had it obtained upon his mind, that he could only be appeased by a nominal payment to him of twenty shillings per week, in the shape of wages, and his morbid condition was such, that in his declining days his chief satisfaction consisted in poring over and counting this paltry pittance. Hereon a homily might be written upon the vanity of all earthly possessions; certain it is, that our desire to compass the good things of this life should be controlled by reason, to receive the blessing of Providence, or the approval of conscience.

ALDERMAN THOMAS KELLY:

FARMER'S BOY, AFTERWARDS LORD MAYOR OF LONDON.

"FROM little causes great effects arise." Thus runs the "old saw," and certainly numberless "modern instances" go to prove the verity of the asseveration. The late Alderman Kelly was at one time a very poor boy on a very poor farm, engaged in the merest drudgery of the roughest agricultural labour; whose educational opportunities were of the most meagre description, who entered the (to him) wilderness of the great metropolis, penniless and friendless, at the age of fourteen years, and after having by his own unassisted efforts passed through a protracted and not very agreeable period of servitude, succeeded in amassing a large fortune, and was ultimately raised by the spontaneous suffrages of his fellow citizens to the highest honours it was in their power to bestow.

Thomas Kelly was the oldest son of John and Ann Kelly. He was born at Chevening, in the county of Kent, about the 7th of January, 1772. His father was only an ordinary shepherd at the period of his marriage; with which, however, he occasionally combined the occupation of cattle dealing, and by dint of great industry and carefulness he contrived to save as much as two hundred pounds. The abandonment of his original calling, and the taking of an inn in his native village, entailed the loss of the whole of his savings, and ultimately led to his resumption of agricultural occupation. Kelly, the elder's, farm was a very poor one, consisting of about thirty acres of cold, wet land; it has been said that its utmost worth at the present day would not have been more than five shillings an acre, as an annual rental. While the husband was employed in the out-door occupations of such a farm, his wife appears, by the concurrent testimony of all who knew her, to have been a perfect model of industry and frugality, and was not less active and assiduous in the various employments that fell to her lot. To his latest day the subject of this notice was apt to speak in terms the most affectionate and respectful of the many obligations he owed to his parents; ascribing much of the prosperity which had attended his subsequent years, to the salutary impression produced upon his mind by the example of their integrity and uprightness.

At the age of six years Kelly was sent to school to a female named Humphrey. Here he remained two or three years, receiving his first scanty instruction. He was afterwards sent to the school of a neighbouring hamlet, kept by one Phillips. At school Kelly was a quiet, docile, tractable boy; the hours which were allowed for play were spent, not in association with his noisy companions, but in the voluntary seclusion of the deserted schoolroom; where, gladly taking advantage of the quiet that reigned, he endeavoured to perfect himself in his various studies. When he was but twelve years old, he was taken from school, and was obliged to assist his father in the labour and hard work of the farm. "Handling the plough" he never could achieve, however, and he had a special distaste for the care and cleaning of horses.

He retained to the end of life a vivid recollection of having accompanied his father on foot to Weyhill Fair—a distance, there and back, of at least 150 miles—and of having assisted him to bring home some thousands of lambs, which the latter had been commissioned to purchase for the neighbouring farmers and gentry. The terrible fatigue of the first day's walk to Farnham—not less than forty miles—their passage across Salisbury Plain, while in Wilts, and on their way home, the apparently indefinite length of the row of lambs, when confined within some of the narrow lanes through which they had to pass, were among the features of the journey which appear to have made a most striking impression on the mind of the younger Kelly. On these occasions he followed in the rear of the flock with his sagacious dog, while his father, who went first as pioneer, was frequently, owing to the number of lambs between them, completely out of his sight, and so far in advance of himself as to impress him, when passing through some of the more secluded spots, not only with a sense of loneliness, but at times, with something allied even to a fear for his personal safety. His growing dislike of this pastoral mode of life began at length to express itself, not in murmurings or complaints, but in the desire for some other employment more in accordance with his taste. This indeed may be inferred from the vague and indeterminate reflection, "Surely I must be born for something better than this," which he remembered frequently to have crossed his mind when pondering on his condition. In this state of feeling, a circumstance occurred which gave a more decided impulse to his aspirations. A son of his old schoolmaster, Phillips, who was established, as it was supposed, prosperously as a wine-merchant in Idol Lane, Tower Street, London, paid a visit to Kelly's parents. Here, the youth thought, was an opportunity which ought not to be lost sight of, and he accordingly pressed his mother to use her influence with young Phillips, to obtain for him, if possible, some situation in the metropolis. Whether a promise was given by Phillips, or if given, whether it was remembered, it were useless to inquire. Nothing more was heard of it, and poor Kelly again sank into despondency.

These repeated disappointments, however, began to

tell seriously upon his health, and so disturbed was he in mind, that he began to be addicted to somnambulism, or sleep walking. At length Kelly's parents became alive to the necessity of procuring him a situation away from home; inquiries were set on foot in the neighbourhood, which resulted in his engagement to be apprenticed to a tallow-chandler at Oxtead. A day was fixed for young Kelly's entering on his new duties; and it was arranged that his father should accompany him to the place of his destination—a village about five miles off. They had scarcely proceeded half a mile when the boy was overcome by his feelings and burst into tears. His father seeing this, and rightly interpreting the cause, said, in a tone of affectionate remonstrance, "Why, Tom, you're crying; I see you don't want to go, and you shan't go." The engagement was abandoned; they returned home, to the infinite surprise of the mother. It is worthy of being put on record, that on this occasion, on taking leave of the family of a poor neighbour, on the eve of his departure, he presented each of the little children with a penny. Sixty-four years rolled away, and the donor and one of the recipients again met. The associations of childhood were reverted to; and the less fortunate candidate for this world's favours, acknowledging the gift of the parting token, became again, in his declining years, the object of his playfellow's bounty. How different the destiny of these two men! Brought up in close proximity to each other, and under circumstances not materially dissimilar, to one was assigned a life of unmitigated toil and labour, with an old age of penury and want; while, in the ordinary course of things, little else could have been expected of the other, though in the end he rose to honour and wealth, and the highest civic dignity.

At length, through the medium of a friend, a situation in London was found for Kelly, and was at once accepted by him. It was as assistant in the office of a brewery at Lambeth. Preparations were accordingly made by his mother for his removal to London. In anticipation of his leaving home, she had found time to make for him half-a-dozen shirts, and as many pairs of stockings. She had also purchased for him some other necessary articles of wearing apparel. Putting together these, which constituted his whole wardrobe, and were no more than he was able easily to carry himself, and at the same time giving him a few shillings, she bade him farewell. When alluding afterwards to the incidents of this parting, he described them as unspeakably touching. To add to the sorrowful feelings produced by a separation from his parents, the day was a gloomy one. A thick fog prevailed, from the effects of which he was soon nearly wet through. It was under these circumstances, and with many melancholy forebodings, that he set out, on foot, in the year 1786, and when only fourteen years old, for that great City, over which, in the revolution of exactly half a century, he was destined to preside as its chief magistrate.

On arriving in London he entered upon the duties of his situation at Lambeth, which, however, after the lapse of two or three years, was brought to an abrupt termination by the bankruptcy of the concern; but his employer interesting himself in his behalf, succeeded in obtaining for him the situation of shopman in a bookseller's establishment in Paternoster Row. These were the circumstances which introduced him to the ward, of which, in due time, he became the alderman. The terms on which he accepted the engagement were those of the ordinary domestic servant. He was to board and lodge on the premises, and to have ten pounds a-year. Though he had accepted the situation in Paternoster Row, a day's trial was to be allowed, that he might have the opportunity of seeing how far he should like the situation, or be qualified for its duties. In no respect discouraged by the issue of the day's experiment, at the close of it he announced to the housekeeper of his master his intention of returning to Lambeth to sleep, and of being back on the following morning in time for commencing business; his object in going being to take leave of his friends, and bring back with him the few clothes he possessed.

His master, on being made acquainted with the fact of Kelly's absence, at once concluded that it was a mere excuse for leaving altogether, and exclaimed in a tone of irony:—"Depend on it you'll see no more of him; he's had enough of it already." The sequel proved that he was mistaken in the character of the youth he had to deal with.

True to his promise, Kelly repaired to the City, with his bundle under his arm, long before the time appointed. Finding the shutters of his master's shop still closed, he spent a solitary hour in pacing up and down the Row; until at length, observing the impediments to his admission withdrawn, he placed his foot within the threshold of those premises, "where," adverting to the event sixty years afterwards, he remarked, "I have been ever since."

The establishment in question was kept by Alexander Hogg, and was confined to No. 16, Paternoster Row. The business was even then considerable. Kelly's duty, as the shopman, was to make up parcels for the retail booksellers; to write out invoices; to assist in keeping the books; and, generally, to meet the calls of casual customers. When these duties of the day were over, he applied himself with diligence to his own studies, endeavouring especially to improve himself in grammar, in which he had previously had no instruction, and also in history, geography, &c. Conceiving that a knowledge of French would be serviceable to him he contrived, without any instruction from a master, so far to perfect himself in the rudiments of the language, as to be able to read some of the most popular French works with ease and fluency. The pronunciation, in which he was unusually accurate, he made himself master of by attending the Sunday evening service in the French Protestant Church, then in Threadneedle Street, where he took and paid for a sitting expressly for the purpose.

We may not exclude from this summary of Kelly's duties and occupations while in the service of Mr. Hogg all reference to the spot where he was condemned to pass his nights. It was thought necessary for the security of the premises that some one should sleep in the shop, and this duty fell upon Kelly; the very counter on which he transacted business during the day, formed his canopy and resting place at night. A state of things more calculated to have a depressing influence on mind and body, it is scarcely possible to conceive; but that inflexible perseverance, which appears never to have forsaken him, carried him hopefully through all his difficulties. When after the lapse of years he could place in favourable juxtaposition with these early struggles, the accumulated blessings of a long life, he endeavoured to extract from the contrast subjects for meditation and thankfulness. In his master's aged housekeeper, Mrs. Best, he found, from the first, a kind and faithful friend. It was with this humble woman, who appears to have been the only society the place afforded him, that he took his daily meals, and spent most of his leisure hours. As an instance of consideration it should be observed, that she never once exercised the power she possessed of compelling him to do anything menial. But Kelly's steady and consistent behaviour was already beginning to excite the jealousy of an out-door servant, who for some reason evidently wished for, and tried to procure, his removal from the establishment. The following conversation between this man and his master, overheard by Mrs. Best, and by her repeated to Kelly, demonstrates clearly the weight which the youth's docile conduct was giving him in the estimation of his master. "Well," inquired Mr. Hogg, "how is the new lad getting on?" "Oh!" replied the other, "I don't think he'll do for us at all; he's so slow." "I like him," remarked Mr. Hogg, emphatically; "he's a biddable boy."

The sequel to the story, as respects this man, may be briefly disposed of here.

Some little time after the above occurrence, Kelly discovered him stealing his master's property, and he at length divulged the secret. The man was accordingly watched. Soon repeating the offence, he was detected in the act of taking from the premises a number of books concealed under his clothes. The unoffending object of his dislike had been made the instrument of his detection. He was dismissed from the establishment.

One day, on passing a cheesemonger's on business Kelly saw in the window some loose printed sheets, which he instantly recognised as forming part of his master's works. On entering the shop for the purpose of making inquiry, he was astonished to find the shelves at the further end piled with an enormous quantity of similarly printed paper. This, it seems, had been purchased of a woman, on representing it as a portion of the misprints and damaged paper of a printer who was clearing his shop, and had authorized her to dispose of it. The fact, however, was, that it consisted of sheets of some of Mr. Hogg's new periodicals, which had been sent direct from the printer's to a certain house, for the purpose of being folded and stitched, and been clandestinely conveyed from thence. Kelly immediately acquainted his master with the discovery, and the result was, that the woman was tried at the Old Bailey, convicted, and sentenced to an imprisonment of seven months. Reverting to this occurrence, in a letter written at an advanced period of his life, he thus comments upon it:—"This being my first appearance as a witness in a court of justice, I felt (more than words can express) an extreme fear lest I should state a single word incorrectly, being fully impressed with the sacred obligation of an oath, ever remembering the Third Commandment of God's Law, and always desirous to possess a conscience void of offence towards God and towards all men. Little did I then think, when humbly trembling in the witness-box, that, at a future day, I was destined to be raised to the dignity of Her Majesty's First Commissioner of the Central Criminal Court of England; and with the sword of Justice suspended over my head, and the mace of authority placed at my feet, should myself occupy the very judgment seat at which I then glanced with such awful emotion! Oh! how often, during my experience as a magistrate, has the verification of the sacred aphorism, 'the humble shall be exalted,' and the contrary, 'the proud shall be abased,' occurred to my mind:—sorry to have seen many men of high station in the world fallen; subjecting themselves to be placed at the bar of the Old Bailey, tried and condemned for having madly violated the laws of God and man, and become the victims of their own folly and inordinate desires. True it is, honesty is the best policy."

In Mr. Hogg's situation, Thomas Kelly continued for twenty years; during the first fifteen of which he never had a day's holiday.

Two things are clearly memorable during that long period of servitude. When the youth's wages were only ten pounds a year, he gave nearly half to help his parents. As his salary slowly increased, he increased his aid in proportion. He wanted to help his father to stock his farm better, and to improve his crops—and he especially wanted to lighten his poor mother's toils. There were some griefs he could not ward off: sickness came often to his parents dwelling; five of his younger brothers and sisters died, the expense of their funerals, and partly of their illness, being defrayed by Thomas.

When Thomas Kelly was thirty-nine years of age, he began business for himself. He had only a very small capital, and no connections who could help him.

For two years he contented himself with dealing in miscellaneous books and publications; at the end of that time he ventured to launch into a new and important branch of business, that of undertaking the printing and publishing of some important standard books, and circulating them in numbers, employing agents and travellers to sell them.

From this period, the usual casualties incident to commercial life excepted, his course was one of almost uninterrupted and brilliant success; his trade transactions were estimated by hundreds of thousands of pounds, and his advance towards the goal of fortune was certain and rapid.

His career as a citizen of London is easily traced. Early in his residence, he became a freemen of the Plasterers' Company, and was elected Common Councillor of the Ward of Farringdon-within, in 1823; served the office of Sheriff in 1825; was removed to the Court of Alderman in 1830; and was chosen Lord Mayor in November, 1836.

Full of days and honours, all his prospects brightening to the last, he closed his valuable life at Margate, in August, 1855, at the advanced age of eighty-four.

One affecting incident will close our record of this

truly good man. He made an annual visit to the grave of his parents, generally accompanied by his beloved and only sister. This visit led to his friendship with the clergyman of the parish, who became his biographer, and whose first admiration for the character of Alderman Kelly was called forth by the filial piety that annual memorial-visit displayed.

JOSEPH STURGE:

WHO WENT ABOUT DOING GOOD.

"Of many public characters," writes a journalist, "we hear men speak as 'the great,' 'the illustrious,' 'the learned,' 'the gallant;' but with Joseph Sturge's name will ever stand connected the appellative by which his friends loved best to designate him, and which was at once the most expressive of his character and most honourable to his name. Good Joseph Sturge was his familiar title, and the only one which distinctively marked him as a public man." A second journalist writes:—

"In every land that love could penetrate, and sympathy find an object to succour or befriend, Joseph Sturge had a constituency who knew his name, and will deplore his loss. Down the sable cheeks of many an aged negro, once furrowed by slavery, will flow the tears of loving and reverential sorrow. In many a home of toiling industry there will be the choking utterance and the stifled sob, as the bereaved poor talk together of the friend who is lost to them. In the palace where imperial splendour reigns, and in the distant Finlander's cheerless hut, his name will be remembered and his memory blest."

The editor of the "Birmingham Gazette," in his notice of the death of his eminent townsman, said:—

"Although Mr. Sturge held strongly pronounced opinions, at variance with those of the majority of his countrymen, it would be difficult to say whether he was more respected by his opponents or his friends. The perfect simplicity of his character, his high honour, his sterling honesty in every relation of public and private life, and his readiness to concede to others the same freedom of action and the same purity of motive that he claimed for himself, all contributed to ensure him the respect and regard of every person who knew him. The sentiment of regard his generous beneficence deepened into attachment. His ear was never deaf nor his hand closed against any tale of distress; but not a tithe of his benefactions is known to the world, for, like all good men, he was much given in his charities to observe the Scriptural precept, 'Let not thy left hand know what thy right hand doeth.'"

Joseph Sturge was born at Elberton, in Gloucestershire, on the 2nd of August, 1793. He was the second son of a repectable farmer, who bore the same name as himself, and who could trace his descent through a line of "Friends," going back almost to the origin of the society. Not having much liking for his father's occupation, as soon as he was of age he commenced business as a corn merchant at Bewdley, where he was joined by his brother Charles, and where they laid the foundation of that fine commercial fabric, which by their united industry, energy, and high integrity, grew to be one of the foremost in the kingdom both in extent and in honourable estimation. In 1822 he removed to Birmingham, as affording ampler scope for mercantile enterprise. In 1834 he married the only daughter of that excellent man and eminent philanthropist, James Cropper, Esq., of Liverpool, but, after the brief happiness of little more than a year, was doomed to follow her and her infant to an early grave. In 1846 he married Hannah, the daughter of Barnard Dickenson, Esq., of Coalbrookdale, in whom he found a "true yoke-fellow," sympathising with and aiding him in all his projects of benevolence and public usefulness.

Mr. Sturge became early and deeply interested in the Anti-Slavery cause. He had for some years borne a conspicuous part in that long and arduous agitation, which preceded and produced the Act for the abolition of slavery in our West India Colonies, by the government of Earl Grey, in 1833. He was always strongly opposed to the interval of compulsory apprenticeship, which was one of the serious blemishes in that great measure of tardy justice. Determined to examine for himself into the operation of this scheme, he visited the West Indies at his own expense, in 1836, and spent many months in traversing the various islands, and collecting evidence as to the state of the negroes under the system of apprenticeship. He was accompanied on this journey by Mr. Thomas Harvey, of Leeds, a gentleman singularly qualified to be his associate in such an enterprise, and by his able and accomplished pen to present the results of their united labours in an impressive form to the public. The use which Mr. Sturge made on his return to England of the information he gathered during his West India tour, was to go through the country denouncing the iniquities he had witnessed. For several days he stood a rigid examination before a Committee of the House of Commons, where his evidence could not be impugned. He convened a conference of the friends of the slave in London, and, in fine, awakened an agitation, which, in spite of a powerful opposing interest, the dead-weight of a reluctant Government, and the lukewarmness, if not the positive hostility, of a portion of the old Anti-Slavery party itself, swept the apprenticeship system clean away before it, caused the negro's heart to leap for joy at the tidings of unconditional freedom, and cleared the character of England for ever of all complicity in the master abomination of slavery. In 1841, he visited the United States, mainly under the same impulse of sympathy for the oppressed, though he combined with that a variety of other philanthropic objects, especially the question of international peace, and the treatment of prisoners. On his return from America he threw himself, with all the ardour of his brave and generous nature, into the movement in favour of free-trade, which was then beginning to stir the country, and after a brief interval, took up, with a view to direct it into the right channel, the agitation in favour of extending the suffrage, which at that period was a topic of such absorbing interest with the working classes.

On these passages in his career we are not called upon here to dwell. But we have the strongest conviction that, though his connection, especially with the latter movement, exposed him to great obloquy, and to no little coolness and suspicion from some of his own friends, there is no portion of his history that, when the facts are properly known and appreciated, will more redound to the honour of his character. The bold part which, at the time in question, he took in the political discussions of the day, turned the attention of many constituencies to him, as a fitting man for a place in Parliament. He stood three unsuccessful contests for a seat in the House of Commons—the first at Nottingham, the second at Birmingham, and the last at Leeds. He was wont in the latter years of his life to express his deep satisfaction that he had not succeeded; and it may, indeed, be greatly doubted whether that assembly, which is the scene of so much party conflict and personal intrigue, would ever have proved a congenial atmosphere for one of such transparent simplicity of motive and purpose as he was. His manifold labours and benefactions in the cause of education, of temperance, of the health and recreation of the working classes, of reformatory schools, of prison discipline, and other forms of philanthropy which his active mind and large heart comprehended, who can fully describe? His innumerable private charities were performed in a manner so quiet and unostentatious, that their course could be traced, like that of some tranquil and noiseless stream, only by the verdure and beauty which they spread around.

He had imbibed early and earnestly the principles of the society in which he was born on the subject of war. This is strikingly proved by an incident which happened to him when quite a young man, before he had attained his majority. He was engaged in his experimental probation as a farmer, to which it is understood his father wished him to devote himself, when he was balloted for the militia. As he could not serve himself, he did not choose to evade the responsibility by procuring a substitute to do that which his conscience forbade him to do in person. He therefore took joyfully the spoiling of his goods, and saw several of his sheep and lambs seized to pay the penalty he had incurred by his refusal. By this act of youthful decision and sacrifice, he committed himself to the line of conduct from which he never afterwards swerved by a hair's-breadth. He associated himself with the labours of the Peace Society soon after its formation in 1816. During the last tour he took in the service of this cause, only two months before his death, he was pleasantly reminded by his old friend, Mr. Thomas Pumphrey, of Ackworth school, how they had been united, some forty-one years ago, in forming an Auxiliary Peace Society at Worcester, Mr. Sturge being the chairman, and Mr. Pumphrey the secretary, at the first meeting. Referring to that meeting, Mr. Pumphrey says: "I only recollect that he was the chief agent in originating it, and in carrying it on for the first three or four years; that he used to come from Bewdley, fourteen miles, to attend the committees; and that, as a youth of only sixteen, I was deeply impressed with his earnestness and devotion." In 1827 he took part in the formation of an Auxiliary Peace Society at Birmingham. But the first time that he came conspicuously before the public in connection with this question, was on the outbreak of the war with China in 1839. The occasion and the object of that unrighteous conflict—to protect the interests of opium smugglers—deeply moved his indignation; and in April, 1840, he addressed a letter "To the Christian Public of Great Britain," earnestly calling upon them to protest, in the name of religion and patriotism, against proceedings which were so deeply dishonourable to both. At his instigation, principally, an important public meeting was held at the Freemasons'

Tavern, in London, presided over by Earl Stanhope, at which resolutions were passed, "deeply lamenting that the moral and religious feeling of this country should be outraged, the character of Christianity disgraced in the eyes of the world, and this kingdom involved in war with upwards of 350.00 ,000 of people, in consequence of British subjects introducing opium into China, in direct and known violation of the laws of that empire." In 1841 he renewed his appeal to the Christian public on this subject, in a second letter, in which he adjured them to send petitions and memorials to the new Government which had then come into power, "strongly suggesting a reference of the existing differences with China to commissioners mutually appointed, who shall be authorised to adjust them, and also to determine on the best means of suppressing the guilty traffic in opium."

The first general Peace Convention was held in London at the suggestion of Mr. Sturge. In the preface of the volume he published on his return from the United States, he says that, in visiting that country, "the objects which proffered the chief claim to his attention were *the universal abolition of Slavery and the promotion of permanent international peace.*" In pursuance, accordingly, of the second of these objects, a special meeting of the American Friends of Peace was held at Boston on the 29th of July, 1841. In the minute of proceedings drawn up by the gentlemen who officiated as secretary on that occasion, it is stated that "the meeting was called for the purpose of meeting Mr. Joseph Sturge, from England, and there were present most of the active members of the American Peace Society. Amasa Walker, Esq., was chosen chairman, and Mr. J. P. Blanchard secretary. Mr. Sturge addressed the meeting, and suggested the expediency of calling, at some future time, a convention of the friends of peace, of different nations, to deliberate upon the best method of adjusting international disputes." Ultimately the meeting unanimously adopted a resolution approving the proposal, and suggested that the Convention should be held in London at the earliest practicable opportunity. On his return to England, he submitted this and other resolutions passed by the same meeting, to the committee of the London Peace Society, by whom they were warmly taken up, and the Convention was accordingly held at Freemasons' Hall, on the 22nd, 23rd, and 24th of June, 1843. Mr. Sturge was one of the vice-presidents of this meeting, and contributed largely, by his zeal and energy, to the success of the demonstration.

When the project, which originated with Elihu Burritt, was first conceived of holding something like a congress of nations on the Continent, to discuss the subject of international peace, Mr. Sturge was one of the earliest to give it his warm support; and in connection with the whole of that remarkable movement, which issued in the Peace Conferences that were held at Brussels, Paris, Frankfort, London, Manchester, and Edinburgh, and which led, moreover, to the motions brought forward in Parliament by Mr. Cobden, in favour of international arbitration and mutual disarmament, it is little to say he was one of its most ardent promoters. He was, in fact, the soul of the entire movement, encouraging the timid into decision, kindling the lukewarm into zeal, provoking others to love and good works by the fervour of his own spirit, and the contagion of his noble and generous example. In consequence of the eloquent appeal made by Dr. Boderistedt, of Berlin, at Frankfort, Mr. Sturge, in conjunction with Mr. Burritt and Mr. Frederick Wheeler, undertook the task of mediating between the two hostile States of Denmark and the Duchies of Schleswig Holstein. Chevalier Bunsen, who was then Prussian Ambassador to this country, expressed his belief that there was a stronger hope of a satisfactory adjustment of the matter in dispute from that pacific embassy, than from all that had been done before by the professional diplomatists of Europe.

In the winter of 1854, in conjunction with Mr. Henry Pease and Mr. Robert Charlton, Mr. Sturge undertook a journey to St. Petersburg, to make one last effort to stay the outbreak of hostilities. Nothing is more certain than that the Emperor of Russia was stirred with deep and genuine emotion by the simple but fervid appeal which fell in accents all tremulous with Christian tenderness and zeal, from the lips of Joseph Sturge. How profoundly he was affected with wonder, indignation, and distress, at the deplorable manner in which the professedly Christian people of this country abandoned themselves to the evil spirit of war, during these two melancholy years; how earnestly he laboured to allay that spirit by all efforts within his power, and how eagerly he watched every opportunity to promote the restoration of peace, those can best testify who were in close and constant communication with him during that painful episode in our national history. But whoever faltered in opposition to the war, whoever yielded to the torrent of popular excitement and unreason—and, alas! their name was legion—he stood firm as a rock, ready to brave any amount of obloquy rather than violate the integrity of his Christian conscience by a cowardly deference to the demands of a spurious patriotism. He lived long enough to reap the reward of his resolute constancy to principle, by seeing the general conviction spreading through the minds of his countrymen, that the opponents of the war were, after all, in the right—that that bloody and desolating strife, while prolific of many and lasting evils, had proved utterly barren of all appreciable good. When the war was over, Mr. Sturge joined very heartily in the effort made by the peace party in this country to obtain from the representatives of the Great Powers sitting in conference at Paris, a recognition of the principle of arbitration as a substitute for war. For this purpose he accompanied Mr. Charles Hindley and Mr. Richard as a deputation to Paris, to lay the matter before the Plenipotentiaries, and had the satisfaction of finding, when the Protocols of the Congress were published, that the question had been earnestly discussed, and that a resolution had been adopted, which though unhappily not containing the clause *binding* the parties to abide by the decision of the arbitrators, to which the deputation attached most importance, yet "giving for the first time," as Mr. Gladstone afterwards said, "at least a qualified disapproval to a resort to war, and asserting the supremacy of reason, of justice, of humanity, and religion."

In the course of the year 1856, distressing accounts reached this country of the sufferings that were being endured by the people of Finland, occasioned in a main degree by the ravages committed on their coasts by the English fleet during the war. The heart of Mr. Sturge was deeply touched by these reports, and he determined to repair in person to the scene, and investigate the case for himself. Accompanied by Mr. Thomas Harvey, his old associate in the West Indies, he accordingly visited the southern parts of Finland. They found not only a good deal of distress, which became greatly aggravated shortly afterwards by the failure of the harvest in the northern districts of the same country, but "that the good feeling previously existing among the population towards England was changed into one of bitter animosity." After they had formed a committee of relief on the spot, Mr. Sturge authorised the gentlemen so acting to draw at once to a large amount, for immediate use, upon the firm of which he was a member. On their return to England an appeal for help was issued, and a fund amounting to about £9000 was raised, principally among the Society of Friends, of which Mr. Sturge and his brother Charles —a true brother in all noble and generous deeds— contributed no less a sum than £1000.

When the mutiny—or, to speak more accurately, the rebellion—broke forth in India in 1857, Mr. Sturge, convinced that there were deeper causes for that terrible disaster than those so confidently assigned in this country, became exceedingly anxious to ascertain, if possible, from the natives themselves, the story of their grievances. He was prepared to expend a large sum to send out an agent for that purpose, if a suitable person could be found. But as none such appeared, Mr. Sturge, with that wonderful self-devotion which was so characteristic of him when the interests of humanity were concerned, had at one time made up his mind to go to India himself. On consultation, however, with gentlemen intimately conversant with India, it was felt that the disturbed state of the country, and especially the extreme terror and suspicion which had taken hold of the native mind, would have rendered it impossible at that time to conduct such an inquiry as Mr. Sturge contemplated with any satisfactory results.

We can only touch on some of the salient points in his long course of service to the cause of Peace, leaving untouched his constant, habitual efforts, year by year, month by month, we might almost add day by day, by journeys, conferences, correspondence, circulation of tracts, organization of public meetings, and unbounded liberality in the use of his means. In all these exertions he was admirably seconded and sustained by the generous co-operation of his brothers, and by the earnest sympathy, executive skill, and vigorous eloquence of his fellow-townsman the Rev. Arthur O'Neil. At the anniversary of the Peace Society for 1858, he was elected President of that institution. Never was there an appointment the fitness of which was more instantly and unanimously recognised. It was obvious to those in close intercourse with him, that, strenuous as had been his labours in that cause for many years, he felt that this new position in which he was placed entailed upon him additional obligations, which he was prepared to take up with the thoroughness which was characteristic of his nature. His mind had for some time been much occupied with the wish to press the claims of peace upon the young, especially among the members of his own Society. In pursuance of this object he had been engaged during the year in attending a series of meetings in the north, in conjunction with Mr. Smith of Sheffield, and Mr. Richard. None who heard him on those occasions can ever forget the earnestness, the humility, the pleading and pathetic tenderness which marked his addresses. They were listened to by many then with throbbing hearts and tearful eyes; but, oh! if we had known that he was standing so near the threshold of heaven when he spoke to us, how we should have caught and treasured every word that fell from his lips! None but those who have some practical acquaintance with the large amount of anxiety and toil involved in the conduct of such a cause can adequately appreciate the value of a co-worker like Joseph Sturge, whose faith never faltered, whose energy was unwearied, whose generosity was as inexhaustible as it was unostentatious. His character was to them as a host. His presence was a solace and an inspiration in the darkest moments. The very consciousness of his existence was a tower of strength.

The foundation of Mr. Sturge's character must be sought in his deep and devout religious earnestness. He was not a ma to make any display of his religious emotions. But those who were admitted into his intimacy were at no loss to discover the secret source whence he derived his strength for his long and strenuous labours in the service of mankind. It was because he held habitual communication with the eternal Fountain of life and power, that his own soul was replenished with a divine might which enabled him to stand unmoved amid the flowing and ebbing tide of circumstance and opinion. The structure of his intellect, also, simple and practical as it was, did not interfere to prevent his enjoying the full advantage of this blessed privilege. Having taken firm hold upon a few vital Christian truths, he reposed upon them with absolute and unquestioning trust, and never could have had occasion to use the language which one of our poets has put in the lips of a man of subtle and speculative intellect:—

> "Spirit of speculation, rest, oh rest!
> And push not from her place the spirit of prayer."

His faith was strong, and simple as a child's.

He possessed naturally what we should call a singularly healthy mind. There was nothing in the slightest degree moody, morbid, or capricious about him. There are men, and very good men too, with whom it is difficult and painful to co-operate, from deficiencies of temper. You have to study their moods, to humour their eccentricities of thought or feeling, to beware how you touch their too vigilant self-esteem, to watch your opportunity before you can get them to act, for while sometimes ardent and enthusiastic, they are at other times gloomy and irresolute. But not so with Joseph Sturge. He was blest with a most fresh, free, vigorous nature. You were sure of always finding him the same, always cheerful as the day, always firm of purpose, always generous and ready. Never was there a man more thoroughly reliable. You could count upon him as you could upon the ordinances of nature that are fixed by a divine law. He had, moreover, wonderful force of will. This indeed was the secret of what we may call his *intellectual* strength. He did not affect the possession of any faculty that was either brilliant or profound. His understanding was plain and practical, and he had little or no imagination. But he was a man of most resolute determination. He wanted only to be clear on the question of principle, to have his conscience satisfied in regard to any course, and then no labour could daunt him, no obstacle suffice to turn him from his path. His firmness was, however, tempered by a most gentle and generous disposition. It was quite a study to watch how these two qualities acted and re-acted upon each other, and were sometimes brought into conflict. But when, as was generally the case with him, his benevolent feelings ran in the same line with his resolute will, the junction of the two imparted to him that force and fervour of character by which he was so distinguished. He had a remarkable power not only of working himself, but of getting others to work. As one of his dearest friends said, "It was impossible to refuse Joseph Sturge anything." And hence it was that, in all the public enterprises in which he was engaged, he drew around him, with the utmost ease, those who could supply what may have been lacking in his own qualifications. Every one who came near him felt it a pride and a privilege to serve him.

As Mr. Charlton remarked at the peace meeting, his conduct was marked by an utter absence of self-seeking. Ceaseless as were his charities, abundant as were his labours in so many departments of Christian philanthropy, important as were the results he had achieved in more than one direction, and honourably conspicuous as his name had become for many years, no man was ever so little self-conscious of his own goodness or greatness. There was no assumption of authority, no jealousy for his own reputation. He was willing to the last to render the humblest service to any cause he loved, content to bear the heat and burden of the day, let whosoever list take the praise.

It pleased Providence to place him in circumstances eminently favourable to the development of a character so beautiful. His home was the very abode of peace and love. He was surrounded from the early part of his career, and so it continued to the close, with members of his own family, who, loving him with a devoted affection, animated by a kindred spirit with his own, and sympathising with him cordially in his benevolent aspirations, did everything to help and nothing to hinder him in following the impulses of his own generous nature. To know such a man was to think better of the whole human race. When wearied with unsuccessful labour, when cast down by disappointment or hope deferred, when in danger of being soured by the selfishness of some, and the lukewarmness of others with whom we may be brought into contact, the memory of him, his strong faith, his Christian gentleness, his high courage, his unselfish dedication to the service of God and man, may well come to us with healing on its wings, soothe our irritation, and, by his example, nerve our hearts to a patient continuance in well-doing, irrespective of the world's smiles or frowns.

Can we more fittingly close these sketches, then, in reference to the character, the industry, the perseverence, and the high aims of Joseph Sturge, say to the reader: "Go thou and do likewise?"

BOY'S HANDY BOOK OF SPORTS, PASTIMES, AND GAMES.

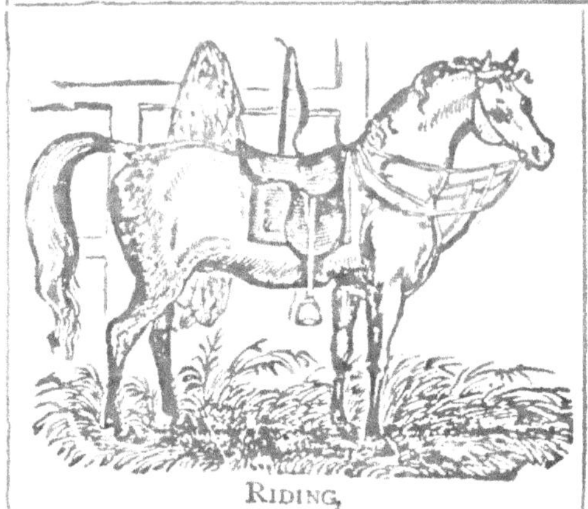

RIDING.

THE CROSS-BOW.

WHIP TOP.

BUCK, BUCK.

FOLLOWING LEADER.

RUNNING.

Milton Keynes UK
Ingram Content Group UK Ltd.
UKHW040139160224
437928UK00003B/30